THE LAST ALCHEMIST

ROBERT MCPARLAND

Apeiron Publishing

2023

THE LAST ALCHEMIST

This notebook, stained and cryptic, is a deadly secret in my hands. The street-lights outside are a blur. A man stands below the window: a silhouette on the dimmest edge of the lamplight, his presence signaled only by puffs of air from his nostrils and mouth. There is frost on the windowsill, but the apartment is warm. I hear Alessandra's footsteps in the hallway. There is an unmistakable attraction between us: something invisible, filling body and breath, like the heat from the radiator on this cold night. For the past several months we have been watched from across the street. That shadow there may be one of Schneider's people. He wears a coat to keep off the sleet. His eyes remain fixed on the window. That man outside knows more than he should about the alchemist. Yet, he has not seen this volume I hold here at my desk: the alchemist's notebook.

The writing in the notebook appears in dark lines, like sweeping clouds, enigmatic symbols. The past lives in these words: the breath of time gone by. I sit on the window seat, listening to the sounds beyond the window. Ali looks in, wearing her bathrobe. "Jake, is he still there?" I nod, as she joins me by the window. I smell vanilla scented body lotion, Johnson's baby shampoo. She is braiding her thick auburn hair for the tenth time. Every few minutes, the man below looks up. He knows of the Lebensborn. He knows of the story of Jan Sorenson, imprisoned for years in an asylum. He knows of Freyda Tikven, a woman who was for years blind to her father's Nazi past and to her mother's role in a dark experiment.

The phone rings. Alessandra stares down at the phone before picking it up. I hear her sigh: nervous relief. Her mother, Sharon, is on the line. Ali vanishes into the next room and I am left with the alchemist's notebook.

For months, I have been puzzling through the notebook, seeking the pieces of a man's life. His story lies scattered across more than fifty years of a life lived in secrecy. He was a man scathed by war, healed by love, and chased to his end, although he saved more lives than he destroyed. He called himself an alchemist – and perhaps he was the last of his kind. The last alchemist was a source of hope and a source of danger. His life was engaged in a fearful legacy. It is why I must write this.

Looking back now, I can see that as soon as we first met the nightmare was taking shape. It took me deep into the shadow world of the neo-Nazi. I sought to create a documentary and found my focus in the lebensborn, who have sometimes been called 'Hitler's children.' The work has brought trouble. Mostly, the trouble has come from the legacy of this most peculiar man who came to the rescue of the lebensborn children. I have traveled across distances, into the peculiar myths and twisted logic that supports the neo-Nazi notions of a master race. Time has passed and it seems as if I have been caught in a dissolve where the film segues from one scene to the next.

RED CAT FARM, OCTOBER 1985

The day that I first met the man, I was jogging. It was shortly after dawn and the chill air stung my lungs. Up the road, as I ran toward the pink rim of the sky, I first saw him as he rounded the black iron fence which circles Veteran's Park. A gray shawl billowed from his shoulders. He wore a hat, and his head was lowered, inspecting a scribble on the wall. I stopped for breath on the path next to the man. Over his shoulders, I looked to the wall at the figures etched there: lines twisted, black and jagged.

"There is trouble," the man said.

His face was lined deep, his eyes burning behind dark glasses.

"I have some paint back at the farm," I said. "I could get rid of that."

"You can erase it from the wall. Not from the mind," the man said. "You are a painter?"

"I paint houses," I said. "We're painting one at that farm up the hill. The Red Cat Farm they used to call it."

"Yes, it is time it was painted," the man said, and all the color seemed to go out of his face. For a moment there were no other words between us. A scattering of leaves took off into the air, settling along the edge of the woods nearby.

"I'm Jake Kincaid," I said. "And you?"

The man's lips quivered for a moment.

"My name is Ezra," he said.

"Good to meet you, Ezra," I said. "I'll go up and get some paint. That will be gone from that wall before you know it."

"You are the one who is painting at the farm? You paint like Michelangelo - but houses, not chapel ceilings. So, is that is what you do all the year around?"

"It's what I do when I'm not in school."

"You are in school. Do you study painting there?"

"No. I'm going to college this year for media arts. I want to major in movie making. That's what I'm most interested in."

"Enchanting," he said. "You wish to be making the movies. You are young, Jacob. When we are young, we study many things. Young people are like pliable wooden boards. Your mind moves freely. It bends more flexibly. Me- I am hard like old wooden desks. So then, that is your dream? It is movies you wish to be in?"

"I'd like to make them. Of course, my dad says I should be more realistic. Jake, that's not the real world, he says. I tell him that movie making is creative and there are some real interesting movies coming out these days. The people who make them are creating lots of great special effects. Do you like movies, Ezra?"

"I would not know much about the movies these days, Jacob" Ezra said. "My life, it has rarely come into contact with the company of young people like you. No, not for many years. I am an old man, Jacob, an old man who has seen too much."

I resumed my jog, waving back at the man as I rounded the park. The man watched me for a moment. Then the billowing gray shawl turned back to the wall. I took one last look back at him, held there like a statue amid the newly fallen leaves.

There was a movement in the forest. I heard footsteps crackling on the leaves. Someone came forward from behind the trees. The man was tall; his face, a long and indistinguishable shadow under a wide-brimmed hat, looked hard and determined. He was following me. Hurrying from that spot, I went back to the farm. I went quickly, never glancing back. I pretended I hadn't noticed the man. Yet I could sense him there, always behind me: someone following, someone watching me.

Jogging, I passed the white fences around the hills of the Red Cat Farm. As I turned in the front gate, I noticed that the strange figure was gone. Yet, still I felt his presence, as if the stranger might be lurking about somewhere.

My friend, Tom Sheffield, had already set up the ladders along the farmhouse. Taking one look at me coming up the driveway, he could tell that something was wrong.

"Someone is following me," I said.

"I don't see anybody, Jake."

We looked together back down the long driveway. No one was there. A single figure dominated the hills: a bulky milk cow swatting its tail at flies. Sunlight played along the hills and the farm seemed as peaceful and remote from the world as when we had first seen it.

"Maybe it was some kind of mistake," Tom said.

"It was no mistake, Tom. Somebody followed me from the park. It was right after I met an old man. He was just standing there, looking at a couple of swastikas that were scribbled on the wall there. It was like he was looking at a ghost. So, I said hello. Then, as I was leaving, I saw somebody in the woods behind me.

"Strange," Tom said. "You said swastikas? Like the Nazis?"

Atop the ladder, Tom looked like a bird on the heights. He finished a broad stroke of paint above the first-floor window and stepped down to refill his paint can.

"So, you think it has something to do with the old man?"

"It must," I said. "It happened right after I spoke with him."

"Who is he, the old man?"

"I don't know," I said. "Just some old guy named Ezra."

"Okay. So, you talk with this guy Ezra and then all of a sudden there's somebody following you?"

"That's just it, Tom. Everything has been a little bit strange ever since we got to this farm."

"Like those stories about the German baron, you mean? Yeah, I guess they'd give anybody the creeps."

I felt my stomach tighten. Being followed was bad enough. But those strange stories about the German baron – now that was odd!

"He must have been nuts, huh?" Tom said. "I mean, to kill himself and his wife like that."

Tom went back up the ladder. Swish – his brush raced across another beam. He swung it back down and the bristles emerged wet from the paint can, white, reflecting sunlight. "Or maybe she killed him and then took the poison. It was poison, wasn't it?"

"Therese didn't say. She doesn't like to talk about it."

"Sure. What if the old baron's ghost is around here somewhere listening – huh?"

With a long dash of paint, I finished a board. I felt the muscles in my wrist tighten. The paint assaulted my nostrils. I curved my fingers lightly around the brush, the way that Tom had taught me.

"Do you think Therese will like the yellow border?" Tom laughed. He gazed out across the farm for a moment and then reached for a spot far above his head. "That German guy who owned this place must have been loaded. I wonder what this farm cost him."

"His life," I said. "At least that's the story."

"The story Therese didn't want to tell," Tom said. "You know what I think the story behind this farm is? The story is that he probably had some land in Germany and then he bought this farm here. And then he gave away this land to a religious charity to save his soul."

The aluminum ladder creaked as Tom climbed another step. His paint can was swinging from his hand.

"Yeah, that's what I think."

Sunlight caught in his hair and I could swear he was looking up at Mount Olympus, like a golden boy reaching for the sun. The ladder shook as he went up. I could see that Tom was favoring his right leg again. He'd been doing that ever since the football injury in high school.

It all came back to me again: Tom's blue football jersey, number 32 running up the high school field. I watched him shake one tackle and another. Then there was a popping sound. A linebacker had done it, quickly, from behind. Like a knife. Tom snapped like a branch and fell. His knees were buckling up in the dust. He rolled onto his side. Then he just lay there. I could see players leaning over him, people rushing across the field with a red blanket, a stretcher rolled out from an ambulance. I pushed the memory away.

"You're trying for the peak today?" I said.

"Later on," Tom said. "We'll get it."

"What do you mean we?"

To me the peak of the house, a skewed triangle forty feet up, did look like Mount Olympus. Moving up toward it, Tom looked so at ease, like a hang glider, a bird on the heights. I hesitated from making such a climb. If you ask me – I'd rather stay with both feet close to the ground. I wasn't about to do any climbing. All this business about a German baron and a double suicide on the farm was making me feel a little dizzy.

Tom paused in mid-flight, leaning out from the ladder, reaching for a difficult spot. That's when I heard the sound of a car coming up the driveway. For a moment I felt my stomach tighten. I thought of the man who I'd seen following me. I looked out at the bulky milk cows, big blotches of black and white on the hill, their tails chasing away flies. From behind them came a car, an old station wagon, gravel crackling under its tires. There past the silo and the hay cart, coming past the red barn, the car turned into the farmhouse's driveway.

Therese, who ran the farm, had also heard the car. In the farmhouse window, I could see her: a woman in a green sweatshirt, gray hair pulled back, leaning her head out. A collie burst from the porch door and began to chase the car, its sharp barks cracking into the air. It was followed by another dog, a thin, brown terrier. Leaping from its business behind a tree, it came running down the hill, tearing at the earth. Circling the car, the dogs formed a greeting party, a barking chorus. I could see a girl in the car laughing. She leaned out to pet the dogs and waved to Therese.

"Hi!" Therese called. "You made it! I'm Therese. And you must be Laura."

"That's right."

The collie was climbing on the car seat. Laura was laughing, petting the dog.

"They certainly are affectionate," Laura said.

"Yes, they are," I heard Therese say. "Welcome to God's little acre, Canaan Farm."

I'd only heard that name once or twice before. Usually, I'd heard this place called by its original name: The Red Cat Farm. I watched as Laura stepped out of her car. I could see her more clearly now. She was young, about eighteen or so, a thin girl with finely spun hair and sharp features. Her dress was simple; she wore a jeans skirt and a light-yellow blouse.

"You've brought some of your paintings for the arts and crafts fair," Therese said.

"They're in the back of the car," Laura said. "My father let me take the station wagon."

"Great!" Therese said, rubbing her hands together. "I think you'll like it here, Laura. The farm needs a little tidying up. I'll be the first to admit it. It's a lot of work. But it's good, healthy work. In fact, we've got a couple of good workers right here today, Jake and Tom. They're painting the farmhouse. Getting everything ready for the fair. It's going to be a big success. We're going to do it, Laura. I think we're going to do it."

They began walking toward us, toward the farmhouse. I guessed that Therese would soon be talking about organic farming, the new age, or the earth, or any one of her favorite topics. Then I heard her say:

"Won't you come in and make yourself feel at home? Do you like herbal tea? We've got lots of herbal teas. We've got Apple Cinnamon and Gentle Chamomile and Apricot Delight and Lemon Zinger! Watch out for that one!"

At the raised pitch in Therese's voice, the small brown collie began yipping.

"And we've got something for you too, Mulch, you tiny terror," Therese said.

The other dog chimed in and Therese leaned down to pet it.

"And you too, Tomberry," she said.

The dogs, tails wagging, followed Therese and Laura up the steps to the farmhouse.

I was too distracted by now to keep painting. So, I just listened to what they were saying. Laura stopped on the cobble stones which lead to the farmhouse door. There she saw a design on the shed which leans on the edge of the farmhouse. It was the image of a red cat. Beneath it, in a semi-circle, was some black lettering: "Red Cat Farm – 1954."

"Red Cat Farm," said Therese, pausing on the path next to Laura. "That's what this farm used to be known as before we … received it. Now we call it Canaan Farm. That was the land flowing with milk and honey. Would you like to taste some of the honey? It's very good in tea."

Therese stopped suddenly. I saw her frown. She was looking at the tool shed where a hinge was hanging loose. The door there was swinging open.

"That's strange," I heard her say. "We never leave the shed like that."

She pushed the door closed. "I must ask Hans about this," she said.

"Hans?" Laura asked.

"Hans is our gardener," Therese said. "He never leaves the shed open."

That's when I stepped off the ladder and made my grand entrance. I walked over to them and touched my cap in a salute.

"Hello, Jacob," Therese said. "The house looks good."

"Thanks, Therese."

"Laura, I'd like you to meet someone. This is one of our finest house painters, Jake Kincaid. He and his friend Tom Sheffield come highly recommended. Jake, this is Laura. Jake is brightening up the house for the arts and crafts fair. It looks wonderful, Jake."

"Thanks. Pleased to meet you, Laura," I said.

Therese pointed up toward Tom. Laura's eyes followed the rungs of the ladder up to the bottom of Tom's sneakers. Then Tom's feet started down.

"Well, hello," he said, his voice booming.

"So how is life up in heaven, Tom?" Therese asked.

"Oh, it's fine. We have Bingo up there on Wednesday nights," Tom said.

I think I saw Tom take a step back when he saw Laura. When their eyes met it was like the sparkle when the sun strikes the sea.

"Laura, this is Tom Sheffield," Therese said. "He is the also a fine house painter. And he's the boss, I think."

"Hi, Tom."

"Hello. You've just arrived?" Tom asked her.

"Yes. With my paintings. Yes, I just got here."

"So, I see you paint too."

"They're for the arts fair. I wanted to help out the farm."

"That's good. I hope we're doing that too," Tom said. "We just got here last night. Let me take your bag."

Tom took her bag to the porch. I wondered why I didn't think of that – to take her bag.

"Oh, thank you very much," Laura was saying. Tom took the bag and I picked up a paint can.

"Yes, Laura's a painter too," Therese said. "She'll be exhibiting her work here at our arts and crafts fair. I'm sure you'll be seeing a lot of each other over the next few days. You'll be staying here how long, Laura?"

"About three days. They want me to start at the camp this weekend."

"The Starlight Day Camp."

"Yes. It's for physically and mentally challenged kids. I always wanted to study special education. I'm going to work on art projects with them."

"That's wonderful. I used to teach art too, you know. As a matter of fact, that's how I found out about you, Laura. From our sisters at the high school. I'm told you're very good."

"Well, I do work at it. I like painting."

There was a bounce in her voice now, a bounce in her step, as she and Therese walked up the stairs to the house.

"The bees here are very good workers too," Therese said. "They practice a natural art, making wonderful honey. It's very good in tea. Come inside. I'll put some on."

As I walked behind them Tom's voice skipped down the stairs toward me.

"She's going to be here for three days. Did you hear that, Jake?"

Later that evening, as we carried our painting supplies to the storage barn, there was smoke in the air - Hans burning leaves - and Laura was seated on a wooden chair by the barn. She was carefully fitting one of her paintings, an ocean scene, onto an easel. Walking up behind her, Tom rattled the paint cans. The sound startled her and she looked up at us.

"Hi, Laura. It looks like we might be getting some rain," Tom said. "We ought to get these paintings inside."

Laura looked from the paintings to the darkening sky.

"I guess you're right," she said. "I was setting them up here to see how they'll look for the arts and crafts fair."

Behind her was the ocean scene: a sandy beach, blue waves coming in on a dark shore.

"They look really good," I said, carrying the paint cans into the barn.

From the doorway I could see Tom leaning near to the painting, admiring it, admiring Laura. Her hair was long, a trace of red running through it. Her face was intent, like one of those Flemish portraits, with a soft mouth and expressive green eyes. Laura looked like she had emerged from one of her own paintings. Or else she had come from a sad romantic novel set in some gentle place and time.

"Do you do any painting, Tom?" Laura asked.

"Just houses," Tom said.

"Well, I can see that. I'm glad that I don't have to go up on ladders to do this. I'm afraid of heights."

"Oh, it's not so bad," Tom said.

I looked back at the farmhouse. Its border now was yellow, like the diminishing sun which had begun to surrender to the clouds overhead. Laura dipped her head down and examined a corner of her painting.

"Do you think it could use a little more blue here?"

"More blue? No, it looks fine."

Laura straightened up, took a step back, and looked at the painting again.

"Some people are pretty critical about my paintings," she said. "Everybody has an opinion. Like my boyfriend Norman. Make that former boyfriend. What does he know? That doesn't look very marketable, he says. He's a hot shot assistant manager at the Quick Check. Who does he think he is? The art critic for the *New York Times*?"

I stepped out from alongside the barn as Tom lifted the other paint cans and started toward the door. Together we put the ladders inside. Tom pointed at the design there.

"Red cat. Did you ever see a red cat before?"

"I'm not sure," Laura said.

"Well, there's one for you."

Suddenly, we were all at the door of the barn, looking at the design of the cat. Inside the barn the ceiling was high, dark, and made of wooden beams and rafters. There were smells of grass and hay. Lawn mowers, hedge clippers, rakes and hoes surrounded us, stacked on gray metal shelving or hung on steel rungs. Other tools lay in the corners of the barn: some new, others rusted with age or disuse. The floor beneath us was concrete - a long, cold slab of gray - as if someone had poured a bucket of cement one day and left it to harden and dry.

Tom put the drop cloths, smelling of paint, into a pile. As he stepped back, he looked across the arch of the ceiling at the low wooden beams. I saw a puzzled look cross his face.

"Did you forget something?" Laura asked.

"No. I don't think so," Tom said absently.

Tom continued to scan the ceiling. He looked up at the posts, the long wooden crossbeams.

"Is something up there, Tom?" I asked.

He sensed it. He sensed that something was there, but he said nothing. It was Laura who spoke.

"Jake, Tom, maybe you guys could help me to take my things to the farmhouse."

"Sure. We can do that," I said.

"We can leave the paintings here," Laura said.

Tom seemed to be thinking about that and he kept looking up at the rafters.

Stepping out, we felt the cool, damp air which suggested the approach of a storm. I felt the first drops of rain. I saw Tom look back at the barn. He looked back with the look of someone with a hunch, a fleeting intuition. Later, Tom would tell me that he suspected all along that there was something - or someone - in that barn.

3.

The farmhouse was warm on that October day, and I could smell apple pie baking. I flopped down onto a chair and sat with my sneakers off, still thinking of the man who had followed me from the dark. Why had he been there at just that moment? Back in high school no one had paid much attention to Jake Kincaid. Find our class picture. That's me in the back row. I sat in the back of the classroom. At football games, I sat quietly in the stands scribbling notes for the local newspapers while Tom was the hero on the field. Now suddenly I was the center of attention. It didn't make any sense. Unless you were to consider the dog. I guess that for Mulch, the collie, it was because I had a plate of food on my lap. Mulch started sniffing at my feet and eyeing the food.

Tom and Laura were in the kitchen washing cucumbers, tomatoes, carrots, lettuce - anything that they could find to make a salad. For me, it was time to take a break. Let them put dinner on. I was going to watch some T.V. and tease a little dog with a biscuit. I waved to Therese as she passed by, a feisty little woman in a freshly pressed green sweatshirt carrying a dish of casserole to the oven.

"We'll let that heat at 450 degrees for about twenty-five minutes or so," I heard her say to them. "Could you look in on it from time to time? I have some calls to make."

"Sure, Therese," Laura said.

The short gray hair and green sweatshirt disappeared out the door and the collie followed her.

"She really is something," Laura said. "It's amazing how she runs this whole farm. What a lively lady!"

"I'll bet she roots for Notre Dame," I said, finishing my soda. I tossed the bottle into the garbage.

"Oh, no!" Laura said. "That's for compost!"

She pointed to an orange crate on the counter. "Bottles are recyclable," she said.

"Sorry," was all I could manage to say.

I frowned and picked the bottle out from the can, kind of like a man removing a dead skunk from a rosebush. Some carrot shreds stuck to the bottle. I brushed them off and placed the bottle into the orange crate marked "Glass." Next to it was a small apple basket marked "Metal."

"Food scraps are organic," Laura said. "They make good fertilizer. They go in the compost over there."

"Sorry," I said again, and I dropped the carrot shreds into a separate container. I took a piece of Land of Lakes American cheese from the refrigerator and ate it as I left the room.

They must have heard the wooden steps creak as I started to go upstairs, but I stayed in the living room. They must have thought I'd gone because they started talking about me and I heard every word. Of course, I'll never tell…

"Jake's okay," Tom said. I could hear the knife banging down on the cutting board as they cut vegetables. "He works pretty hard. And he's not your typical guy."

"He seems nice too."

"He fooled you too, huh?" Tom said. "No, he is nice. Jake's real good company. He's a good friend. He's a real decent and kind-hearted guy. He talks a little over my head sometimes though."

"Well, he's taller than you are."

"Yeah. Maybe that's it. Jake's real smart. He knows a lot of things."

Tom had by now won me over with his flattery. So now I was waiting for the other stuff. Bang. Slice, slice, slice went the knife chopping the celery, or whatever it was. I figured he'd be cutting me up pretty soon.

"How long have you been painting together?" Laura asked him.

"Since Jake decided he needed the money."

Uh-oh, I thought. Yeah. Now here it comes.

"That was about a year ago. After his job as a mail sorter. Or maybe it was his job at the supermarket, cutting cold cuts in the deli. I can't remember. He used to deliver flowers for a florist for a while. That was about a year after he got his driver's license."

"He sounds versatile. How is he as a house painter?"

"Jake's good. He's very careful. Sometimes I wish he'd work a little quicker though. Jake likes to daydream a lot. I think he wishes he were in Hollywood."

"He wants to be a movie actor?"

"A movie director, I think. Jake's addicted to movies. He's always going around with his camera. I think he's been in a couple of things as an extra.

Student films, I think. But mostly he just dreams about it. I tell him he'd be out there doing it if he was serious. He says he wants to go to college first. I just tell him, follow your heart, Jake. I think he could do something with it. Jake's pretty talented. And so are you, by the way. Those paintings were pretty good. Whatever made you decided you wanted to paint?"

"It was a feeling, I guess. I just started doing it. Making sketches at the shore. Drawing the family car. And flowers. I liked to paint flowers. I guess I like beautiful things. Whatever started you painting houses?"

"My cousin Larry is a house painter. So, I tried it out one summer during high school. It was good money. It was something I could work at on my own. I guess I'm independent in that way. I like to be my own boss. And I've always been good with my hands."

"Well, you're a great salad maker."

"Thanks. I used to make heroes a long time ago. Sandwiches, I mean. I worked at a sandwich shop."

"Lots of oil and vinegar."

"Lots of bread. I used to take some home to my mom and dad and my brother Sammy. After work, Sammy and I hung out with the guys by the milk machine near Capalbo's Deli. We used to stuff a case of beer into it on Fridays. We watched one little old lady who went to get a pint of milk one day. You should have seen her face!"

"I hear that you played football," Laura said.

"Did Jake tell you that?"

Tom must have been looking out the window into the rain, remembering, because I didn't hear him speak for almost another minute.

"I played halfback," he said finally. "Until my knee went out. That was right before I was supposed to start college this year. I had a football scholarship. The injury blew that to hell."

Laura, I think, could see that football was not a happy subject for Tom. I heard the oven door open and close. Checking the casserole.

"This looks like it's done," Laura said. "Shall we call the others?"

"Therese is in her office. I think Jake is upstairs."

"I'm right here," I said, stepping into the kitchen.

They stood blinking at me.

"Mmmm…Ah…" was all I said. "Ah! Vegetarian!"

I love to eat. What can I tell you? I helped myself to the casserole, the zucchini, the bean sprouts, the French bread. This was all an improvement on lunch.

Lunch had been bologna sandwiches on wheat bread. It was Tom's idea. Tom is an everyday food kind of guy. Hamburgers and stews. Nothing fancy. He's very down to earth, Tom. Even if he does spend most of his day on a ladder.

"So how about this arts fair!" said Therese. "We're gonna knock 'em dead, right?"

Like I've told you, she's like a Notre Dame cheerleader. I reached for the casserole and the bean sprouts. It's a good thing I go out jogging every morning.

"Do you expect a lot of people, Therese?" Tom asked.

"More than last year, we hope," Therese said. "Last year it was pretty good. This year we've had more items donated. That should mean a little more money. God knows we could use that."

Therese took a bit of the casserole and then continued.

"It was all donated by a very... how shall I put it? A very peculiar sort of German man who says he is in the antiques business."

I swallowed hard.

"He's a German man, Therese?"

Tom and I looked at each other.

"Yes, I think he said that he was German. He told me that he would be glad to read my chart. He claims to be an astrologer, among other things. Oh, and an alchemist too."

"An alchemist? What is that?" Laura asked.

"It's an ancient practice which predates chemistry," Therese said. "It was believed that the alchemist could find the philosopher's stone, the basis of life. He hoped that he could one day find ways to turn basic things like coal and mercury and copper into gold."

"He sounds like an unusual man," Laura said.

"Well, I do know that he bought a number of pieces from the farm at our auction a couple of years ago," Therese said. "He bought furniture mostly. He seems to have a great interest in that. He purchased a table or two and an old desk that the Baron owned that was made by a master German craftsman. It was handmade, I believe."

"For the Baron," Tom said.

"That's right."

"Was he here long before he died?"

Therese balked at Tom's question. I could see she didn't enjoy this topic.

"For a few years he lived here. Maybe a dozen years or so."

"He died in the barn. Didn't he?"

"I don't know," Therese said. "They never found the body."

Laura's fork fell. It dropped from the table and hit the floor.

"Excuse me," she said.

"It scares me too, Laura," Therese said. "It gets very quiet under the stars here at night. And when you're alone... You know what they say about people who have died tragically."

"Restless spirits," I said.

"The Germans have a word for them: poltergeists," Therese said. "It is said that they linger because they are searching for something."

"His wife's killer maybe," Tom said.

"What'?"

I heard Laura breathe in sharply.

"His wife died also," Therese said. "It was a very tragic thing. We did get the farm though. So maybe some good come in somewhere to heal the sorrow of it all."

Therese took a small sip of wine. Laura looked like she had lost her appetite, but I was making up for it. I had another helping of casserole.

"So, you inherited the farm somehow," I said.

"Funny how that happened," Therese said. "The baron had no relatives... No relatives we knew of. So his lawyer was entrusted with the estate. He was given instructions in the baron's will to give the property to a religious group."

"So that is how you ended up on this farm?"

"Well, there's more. The religious group could have been anybody. But the baron's lawyer had a daughter who attended a school where our sisters teach. That was good enough to satisfy the term "religious group." So, we got the farm."

"But how about you, Therese?"

"How did a little old person like me get here, you mean? That's a good question. I'm a little crazy, I guess. And I like preserving things of beauty. I've got a bit of a green thumb too and I don't mind getting my hands dirty. I'm no farmer really. But you know what Emerson said: Cultivate your garden. I guess I take that literally."

Therese traced her finger around the rim of the wineglass as she spoke.

"Maybe I look at the farm as a symbol. When I look at what we're doing to our earth these days, I feel we're not just burning a rainforest, we're violating something sacred. We're blindly stepping on the cord of life. So, personally, I believe this is critical work we're doing here on this farm. It may be something very little. What we do here is not healing the ozone layer. But by doing this, by bringing one small speck of land back to life again, I'm involved in the process, you see. And we're teaching people here how to live in ecological sanity. We're saying that the earth is alive and gives us life. That's what we're trying to say. I guess that sounds like my sermon for the day."

She laughed and finished the food on her plate.

"I wonder why the Baron wanted to give this farm to a religious group," Laura said.

"Maybe to save his soul," Tom said.

Therese just looked at him.

"Do you have much help here?" Laura asked, seeing the paleness that had come to Therese's face.

"We have some staff," Therese said. "There are many volunteers. People do all sorts of good things for us. We're not fully operational, of course. But we do sell berries and some vegetables. And we make honey. Would you like some tea?"

She went to the stove and returned with hot water from a kettle.

"Hans is a wonderful gardener," she said. "I tell him he has been working magic for the past eighteen months. Magic begins in the earth, he says. I only bring it forth. I honestly don't know how he does it."

"Hans is German, isn't he?" Tom asked.

"Yes, he was born in Germany. He learned much there about organic farming. He's very reliable. We might soon need more workers than Hans. This farm is a big piece of property," Therese said. "We may be adding to it soon. That is if we can find the land deed."

"What's that?" Laura asked.

"A deed to part of the farm. We haven't cultivated it yet because we don't know who it belongs to."

"Don't they usually keep records of that?" Tom asked.

"At the county offices, yes," Therese said. "The deed to the farm is there. We even brought a surveyor in to look at the land and research old maps. But the other 100 acres is still open to question."

"Where is that 100 acres?" I asked.

"It's over the hill behind the barn," Therese said. "The land is good there. There is also another house there. I'm not quite sure what to do with it."

"Has it been painted recently?" I asked. Might as well drum up some business.

"Actually, no. Not for a long time. You know I was thinking of asking you two fellows if you'd have a go of it."

"We'll look at it," Tom said. "Would after dinner be okay?"

Therese turned a napkin over in her hands. Her eyes looked across the table.

"Maybe you'd better wait until morning," she said." It's raining."

She looked pensive, I thought. Not a good place to go after dark, Therese?

"I've been thinking of making a social service center out of it," she said. "Or maybe a special school for challenged kids."

"That's a great idea," said Laura. "Maybe I could talk to the people at the Starlight Day Camp."

"That's a good idea, Laura. Of course, the Baron didn't specify anything in his will about his house."

"His house?"

"Yes. The house that Tom and Jake will be looking at. That's where the Baron and his wife lived."

"And it's empty now?"

"Oh, yes. Almost all the furniture has been sold. The electricity works. But the house is very empty."

"Then you should try to rent it," Laura said.

"Well, I don't know," Therese said. "You see, it belongs to the order. The whole farm does. I supervise it but I don't make all the decisions around here, believe it or not. The property may be ours. But that 100 acres, or part of it, may belong to the horse farm next door, or to someone else. That land deed, if it were to be found, would let us know for sure."

"Do you think it might be in that house?" I asked.

"It may be. If it is, it is hidden like a speck of gold in a valley. I sure haven't been able to find it."

"We'll find it," I said. "I'll bet on it. If it's there, we'll find it."

"Well, I wish you luck, Jake. But there is another little problem we are facing," Therese said. "Actually, it's a very big problem. There is a real estate developer in this area, a man named Curt Casey. Mr. Casey tells me there has been some interest in the property. A man says he has a claim to this farm and the 100 acres."

"Does that mean you could lose the farm?" Laura asked.

Therese nodded. "It could be a problem for us. I've heard that the interested party claims to be related to the Baron. If that is true, we may be on some very shaky ground."

It was after dinner, when all the dishes were put away, that we put on our raincoats and went out to see the old house on the other side of the farm.

"Wouldn't you rather go in the morning?" Laura asked as we stepped out of the house.

"Now is as good a time as any," Tom said.

The wind stirring across the path seemed to catch Laura's voice and lift it into a swirl of wet leaves.

"You're sure there are lights in this house?" I asked.

"That's what Therese said."

"What if a storm knocked out the electricity?"

Tom beamed the flashlight into Laura's face. She shielded her eyes as a halo of light spilled around her.

"That's what this is for," Tom said.

The path smelled of damp, fresh leaves. The pine trees and evergreens hung dripping around us.

"It's up there," Tom said. "Beyond that ridge."

Ahead of us the path was muddy. Leaves lay wet, stuck to the earth, stuck in the shrubs, stuck to the bark of tree trunks. We paused to look at a maple sapling which had fallen.

"That was some wicked storm," I said. "It's a good thing we got the paintings into the barn."

Laura had become very quiet. The soggy ground sunk into footprints as we moved on. We could hear the horses now. Five of them were swinging their heads, their long manes. Laura pointed to them - five shadows beyond a long fence.

"Aren't they beautiful, Tom? Horses are such incredible animals."

Behind the fence the horses moved in darkness. Tom held his light low to avoid attracting their attention. One of the horses moved up along the fence. It sent up a whinnying that brought the other horses running.

Laura gasped. A high-pitched whine reached our ears. The horses had awakened the stallion and they began running in circles through the mud. The black stallion galloped behind a fence across the road. Muscularly, it cut a sharp path across the grass. It raced back and forth, cropping its hooves into the earth. Back and forth, snorting, it summoned the other horses and they came racing, crying into the night air.

Laura lifted her flashlight to see the stallion. Tom touched her arm.

"Don't let it see you. Come on."

He took her arm. We hurried across the hill.

"There it is!" said Tom, pointing down the hill.

The abandoned farmhouse rested like a dark animal beside a long road. Its windows were dark eyes. The front awning looked like a low frown.

"Well, what do you say? Let's go have a look!" Tom said.

We hurried down the hill to look more closely at the house. The house stood empty. It rose above us: sixteen rooms that echoed and welcomed our muddy feet on wooden floors. Old walls that reproduced every footfall, every shiver. Windows the wind sneaked through, whistling as it traveled through those sixteen empty rooms.

"Do you think it happened here, Tom?" Laura asked.

"What's that?"

"That thing with the German baron. Do you think it happened here?"

Laura whispered it but the walls echoed her words.

"They found the wife in the kitchen, I think."

"They never found him. Did they?"

"'No.'"

"How do they know he's dead?"

"They don't."

Tom lifted his flashlight and looked along the wall for a light switch. He found it but the light didn't work.

"Let's try another room," he said.

The next room we walked into was completely empty.

"They've taken pretty good care of the interior here. Beautiful woodwork," Tom said.

Laura stopped at a closed door. I should say she hesitated. I think she felt like running. Tom pushed open the door.

We were in the kitchen, standing on a linoleum floor. Wooden cabinets came into view. A cupboard. A sink. The overhead light worked. It shined across a drain, a table, washcloths, utensils. Laura picked up a fork.

"Someone has been in here," she whispered.

Tom nodded and showed me the fork. There was food on it. Tom began opening cabinets. He found soup cans, a blender, a box of raisins, a half-empty Corn Flakes box.

"Do you think maybe Hans has been in here?"

"We should ask Therese," Tom said. "Want to try upstairs?"

"Do you?"

"Yeah. Of course, I do. I have to get a good look at this place to do an estimate. Right?"

We were all quiet for a moment. The house seemed almost too quiet. It was Laura who broke the silence.

"You've got the light," she said.

The stairway was dark and it creaked. I could see our shadows on the wall as we went up.

"Tom, what if there's someone, somebody crazy in those rooms?"

"Shh... Come on."

At the top step was a narrow hallway. We entered a room which had two windows and two closets. In the first there was nothing. Tom ran his hand along a shelf and his fingers came out dusty.

The second closet, like the first, had a white door, a brass doorknob. Tom turned it and the door swung slowly open. Inside were two black overcoats and a pair of brown gloves.

"Wasn't much of a dresser. Was he?" Tom said. He closed the closet door. "Well, I guess I give up on that land deed for now," he said.

Laura touched his arm.

"Wait," she said.

She leaned against him and her hands came to his shoulders. In the dark they seemed to find each other.

There was no light in the next room. As I swung up my flashlight, I could see dark fingerprints on the door. Like a burglar cracking a safe, we pushed ever so slowly at the door and heard it creak, wood on a rusty hinge. As it opened, Tom swung his light in a high arch along the wall.

"Tom!" Laura gasped. "Tom!"

Faces. Thick, cold faces. Dark eyes were staring back at us. Laura slammed the door and hurried out. Down the stairs, Laura ran. We ran after her. "Laura! Laura!" She began tugging on Tom's shirt, holding on for dear life, going down the steps, stumbling out to the muddy yard. Running.

We stopped under the dripping leaves and Tom held her.

"It's okay," he said.

"It's them."

"It's okay, Laura."

"Tom, that was him. It was him and his wife."

"They were paintings, Laura. Oil paintings."

The damp trees loomed over us, dripping. Then the sound of the horses startled us.

"Tom, the horses!" He tightened his grip on her hand.

"Come on!"

There was a thrashing of hooves. The bray of the horses rose up. We ran. Shoes, mud, grass, water and breath, we ran down the hill. In the dark, our flashlights made crazy patterns across the lawn. We heard a shriek and it stopped us.

"Tom!" Laura yelled. "Look!"

Quick, tiny things ran past us, shrieking. Dark frightened shadows. Cats. One climbed the wood fence. It sat there and began to wail. Tom raised his light to see it and it opened its mouth in a shriek. It clung to the fence: its fur soaked by the rain. It looked more like a spider monkey than a cat.

"Tom, it's red."

We heard footsteps then. Someone was hurrying up the hill. The horses raced along the fence. Then a scream shook us. A scream from below the hill.

"Look! The barn!" Tom yelled. "The barn is burning!"

There was a red glow at the top of the barn. Smoke was already rising over the trees. We moved then in a chaos of sound - of horses' hooves and running feet, twigs and branches cracking. The horses were racing, the cats screeching. We looked up at the flames, red circling, rising along the wood, catching along the high weeds around the barn.

"Therese," Tom said. "Therese was going to the barn after dinner."

"Hurry up!"

There were voices, people hurrying toward the barn. Therese, among them, was waving her arms. Across the hill came a siren. A tail of light traced across the road, moving toward the farm.

"The paintings! They're in the barn!" Laura yelled.

Tom pushed open the heavy doors and dark smoke blew out toward him

"Tom! You can't!" I yelled.

"The paintings. Tom, save them!" Laura said.

"Get back. Go back, Laura," Tom called to her.

I began tossing water on the fire, spraying it from a garden hose. I saw a scorched piece of wood drop near Tom.

"Will you get out of there!" I yelled.

Laura muffled a scream.

"It's them. Tom, it's them!"

In the blaze the ceiling had broken free. Two large paintings had swung down from the rafters: the Baron and his wife swinging from ropes. Oil paintings of them. The hose water rushed through the door. Tom pulled Laura's paintings out. But then he could do no more. He stepped back. A red light spun, filling the dark driveway. Sirens screamed across the hill. Tom was pushing, prodding the door to close. His shirt soot dark, he backed away from the door and coughing miserably, he fell into Laura's arms.

4.

We wanted to forget about the fire in the barn. Yet the acrid smell of charred wood and smoke stayed in the air reminding us of that night. The fire inspector and the police agreed that the fire in the barn had been a case of arson. Who had done it, no one was sure. On the inside of the barn door black spray paint had left a revealing mark: a jagged swastika. We were told that the farm had suffered another fire- some ten years before. It too had appeared deliberate.

This caused some alarm in us but we were determined to go ahead with the arts and crafts fair. Therese insisted that the bright hope would not go out of Canaan Farm. So, we finished painting the farmhouse several days before the festival date. We did what we could to repair the barn. We painted over that marking there and I went to the park and painted over that jagged swastika on the wall.

"You can erase it from the wall but not from the mind."

Ezra's words came back to me forcefully. The scribble I covered with paint on the wall in Veteran's Park would not be the last of those signs of hatred. It would take a lot more than paint to make them go away.

Again, I saw Ezra look at that terrible figure; like a jack turned sideways, a snake turned backwards, letters fierce. Dusk was settling and there was a bird convention in the trees. I raised my video camera, panning across the upstairs windows of the old house. The branches of the maples cast shadows on the house. In one window, the light of the evening sun was a red ball of fire.

In that evening light, Laura first told me of her friend Ali. She was home for the weekend from college. Her given name was Alessandra Stanley. She was a biology major, but she wanted to go to the Fashion Institute of Technology. It sounded like an odd combination. But later I found out that Ali was a remarkable girl: one who brings together all kinds of things that might seem very different on the surface. I suggested that we all go to a movie, to help us to forget about the fire in the barn. Laura said she would invite Ali to join us.

We ate sandwiches for dinner and then, about an hour before Ali came into my life, I remember I took a walk. I soon reached a creek and across the creek was a meadow. I walked through it, listening to the crickets. Back in high school, I learned about light and gravity and motion but I knew little about the creatures of the fields. Now I know a mockingbird by its songs, its attenuated beak, the slate gray of its feathers. I know it by the white on its wings and its tail. Sometimes it sings, when I am there to hear it. My favorite places are the ones that have never been developed: the scrubby woods, the thick undergrowth where the forest meets the stream. Years ago, while my brother played Little League, I went to catch frogs. Winters while he skated and hit hockey pucks on the pond, I walked there collecting specimens for my science projects. I waited for the world of life to come out from under the snow and for the meadow to renew itself in the spring. Once I found a turtle. It slopped up from the algae on the water's surface and crawled onto the muddy banks. I kept him in an aquarium, in an environment of water and grass and twigs.

It felt natural to be painting at the farm. I ran along the hills nearby and with each day the place became more familiar. I jogged each morning before we began painting. Usually, I ate a bowl of oatmeal and I went out through the yard, jarred awake by a bird call that filtered through the trees with a steady stream of light. Jogging is good. The hills are there. You can toss your breath out toward all those hills as you run. The road makes a loop and I like to go east. Into the morning sunshine where it hits the stream, lighting the sides of the trees. I always pass the wooden fences of the farms. I look up at clouds pulling through the sky like yarn. There are dozens of random events in the fields that eyes can barely see: the bees settle, the dragonfly lands, those butterflies float there. I am like an arrow that flies out from the farm. I streak out on sneakers, over the road, lungs seeking air. I am a speck of life moving 10 miles per hour on an earth moving 64,800 miles an hour through space, my face to the sky. Nature is a video: the vertical drop of the flight of a bird, the little dog barking excitedly behind a fence, shuttling back and forth, back and forth.

When I run on the path, I am one with the wind. I smell the fields and feel the sun, and with the soaring birds, the broad forests, and the clouds that sweep over the hills, I am alive, and their wonder is in me. Sometimes I think nature is a peculiar friend. In August it is hot. In January, it's too cold. Nature is cruel. The wolf is spared, but it howls. The coyote runs its predatory paths. The deer appears in the headlights of a car.

Life turns like that sometimes- and that is how life turned when we were young at the Red Cat Farm. It turned like a hiker who drifts down one of those unexpected paths in the woods. No longer were we in the sure world of the house painter. The ladder had grown rickety and uncertain. We needed some escape from it all. So, I had suggested the movie and Laura suggested Ali. It was the best suggestion of my life.

Ali appeared like a break of sunshine: wide brown eyes, a playful laugh, and those long auburn braids. She and Laura met, exchanging a hug on the driveway at the farmhouse. I stood spellbound on the stairs. I thought she looked a little like Vivien Leigh from *Gone with the Wind* and almost as impish.

The movie was called *Back to the Future*, I told them. A crazy scientist creates an invention that brings a guy, young like us, back to the past. "Well, you're the movie expert," said Tom, and the four of us packed into Laura's dad's station wagon. Jammed in next to Laura's painting supplies, I felt a little like an astronaut on the space shuttle.

A week ago, there had been paintings in the back of the car - boards, oils, sketches, brushes, everything but the family cat. Now it was just me in the back seat, knees to my chin, sitting next to painting supplies and a styrofoam wall pushing me in like a butterfly mounted for a science exhibit.

"So, I hear you're into fashion," I said to Ali.

"I'd like to be a designer," she said. "It's colorful. It's creative. Do you have an interest in fashion, Jake?"

"Oh, I don't get much past baseball caps and sweatshirts and jeans. I guess it'd be a little weird to be painting houses in a tailored suit."

She laughed at that and I looked out at the night, at the small lights drifting by along the hills. I started to hum a tune.

"My mom used to sing," Laura said. "She played the piano too."

"Laura plays a little," Ali said. "Don't you, Laura?"

"My mother taught me. I was never very good at playing the piano. My dad used to try not to listen. He'd prop his feet up on a cushion right in front of Dan Rather on the news. He'd be puffing on a cigarette, blowing smoke up Dan Rather's nose and I'd be saying, "hey, smoking is hazardous to your health, dad." "And so is Norman to your health, young lady," he'd say. "Aren't there any nice guys in that high school you go to?" You know, I'd try to ignore him. Just like he tried to ignore our piano playing. But, of course, I heard him. And, of course, he heard it. And you know what? We sometimes sit there now and we really wish we could hear mom playing that piano again."

"I didn't know your mother played the piano," Tom said.

"Not very well. She had a nice voice though. It used to nudge me awake every morning. I still feel her arms sometimes, like around a Teddy bear, you know? Like when I won my first art awards. Or when I broke up with Norman. She was always there for me. Even when she got sick, she tried to be there. Dad still talks to her sometimes. It's a in a whisper behind the bedroom door. But I can hear it once in a while. As if she was still with him."

"Maybe she still is, Laura. In some way," I said. "I mean, Ezra says he feels like his wife is still with him."

"I think about how she got sick and all that," Laura said. "He seems to miss her a lot. Don't you think so?"

"I think so," Tom said.

"Who is Ezra?" Ali asked.

"He's a man who lives near the farm," Laura said. "Jake met him while he was jogging in the park."

"Did he go jogging with you?"

"No. He's in his eighties, Ali. And he walks with a cane."

We parked down the block from Holstein's. That was the ice cream place where the road curves near the park. As we returned, a police car went by. Some headlights beamed from another passing car. Lamplights illumined the road around us but only moonlight crossed the iron fence into Greenlawn Cemetery. We had just parked the car when we heard a sound that came from behind the trees.

"What was that?" Laura asked.

"It sounded like an owl," Tom said.

There it was again - a high shrill pitched sound like a pipe moaning on the wind.

"That's an owl?" Ali asked.

But it wasn't. It was a person, someone moving. He was pulling something heavy up across the fence. A sheet. A pile of sheets sagged in his arms.

We got into the car. Keeping the headlights off, we watched. It was a young man lifting that bundle of blankets to his car. Then he was turning, looking toward us.

"Get down…" Tom whispered to us. "Don't let him see you."

Now we inched up, peeking past the steering wheel. We heard a car motor. A car lurched forward; it then sped away. Laura spoke to Tom as we watched it go.

"It was nothing, right? Somebody doing his laundry."

"In a cemetery?"

"Maybe it was the groundskeeper taking out the garbage."

"Hopping over the fence? What is he doing, trying out for the groundskeeper Olympics?"

"Tom, tell me that wasn't a body. Tell me he wasn't taking a body out of there."

"There are others," Tom said. "Get down!"

Tom and Laura went under the dashboard. Ali bent down next to the painting tarps. I pushed against the paint supplies and tried to lie flat across the back seat.

Up we saw another figure go. His face turned back toward us as he gripped the fence. There was fear in his eyes. There was something haunted in them as he reached up the cemetery wall. Moonlight played on his back and the trees bending over him looked as if they were fingers that might snatch him up. But then he reached the top of the wall and was up over it, falling somewhere on the other side.

Suddenly, another figure followed him: a jacket stitched with emblems, moving quickly. Up he went, hands pulling, feet sliding over, falling down to the muddy earth.

"What are they doing?" Ali whispered.

"I don't know," Tom said. "I'd say they were in a big hurry."

"Maybe they're late for a seance," I said.

"Guys, this may sound crazy," Laura said. "But did it look to you like they were wearing uniforms?"

We all looked at each other then. We were silent in the car, under the darkness of the trees. We probably should have reported what we had seen to the police. Instead, feeling more than a little uneasy, we got out of the car and hurried together up the block to the movie theater.

Back to the Future was funnier and more dramatic than I thought it would be. But it wasn't nearly as weird as what we'd just seen: three guys in gray uniforms climbing over a cemetery fence with what might have been a body. I bought a Super Combo jumbo popcorn and a coke. The popcorn was good. After a while the hands stopped reaching for it. That's when I got the sense that Tom and Laura were paying more attention to each other than to the movie. Ali was looking my way, as if she had something similar in mind. As if things weren't already strange enough.

5

Perhaps, the only sure thing was the stability of the farm itself and the morning sun coming up over the lawn. The farmhouse was nearly ready. On the morning before the arts and crafts fair we were sure our work of painting it would soon be finished. With another day of painting around the window ledges we would put the finishing touches to the new centerpiece of Canaan Farm. That, at least, made us feel hopeful.

Before we began work that morning, I went for my usual jog. Mostly I was thinking about Ali and still hearing her laughter. I drove the station wagon to a spot just inside Veteran's Park. Then I got out and started up the hill, recalling how that laughter had dissolved into something like genuine fear. Fixed in my mind was an image of Ali peering anxiously over the car seat at the figures that stole from the cemetery. Her eyes were wide and her mouth betrayed more than a slight tremble. I could hear the commuter train clacking in the distance as I jogged. The hill that rose to the west of the park, past the Greenlawn Cemetery, was steep. I took my time, climbing step by step, hearing the train whistling somewhere beyond the trees. As I came to the crest of the hill, I saw police cars, their tops flashing red circles that played on the fence and across the cemetery grounds. A dozen or more people had assembled near the gate. A man, hat in hand, was talking to a young policeman there.

"I came to visit my wife's grave," he said.

"I'm sorry, sir. This area is closed to the public. We are not allowing anyone in here today."

"Is there some kind of a problem?"

"We are full of problems here today. We've been asked to close off the cemetery."

"Was it those kids again?"

"We don't know who it was, sir. It appears that someone has been up to some mischief with some spray paint."

"Have they painted the gravestones? I have to go there!"

"I'm sorry, I can't let you do that. That's County Sheriff's orders."

"I came to visit my wife. Her memorial. I'll just be a minute."

"My orders are: no one. This is a crime scene, sir. We expect to open the gate later this afternoon, after the investigative team has finished its work."

The man lowered his head. He turned away and stepped back into his car. He gazed over the fence into the cemetery, across the wide green lawn. Along the hills, among the grave markers, several police detectives, in suits and ties, were pacing. One was taking photographs. There was a reporter nearby taking pictures from alongside the fence. A young mother with a baby carriage paused to look in at the men who were walking along the hills. The man who had come to visit his wife's grave sat quietly in his car, a dejected look on his face.

I heard a voice behind me say, "I don't know what they get out of it. Tearing up a cemetery. Putting strange swastikas and drawings on the trees. What is with these kids?"

I turned to see a large man, with a receding hairline and a sweaty, jowly face frowning at me. He reminded me of a bulldog that wants its dinner.

"Well, young man," he said. "Do you see what young people are doing these days? Don't they have any respect anymore?"

I was about to ask him how he knew this was the work of 'young people' when he thrust a newspaper into my hands. There was an article by a man named Matthew Alan Rockoff in the morning paper. The man jabbed his index finger at it.

"See what this says there? They say it was probably teenagers. 'Heavy metal enthusiasts' it says. This cemetery is hallowed ground, young man. There are people's memories in there."

I looked at the paper, thinking of what we had seen the previous night.

"It's the schools," the man went on. "They should teach young people the value of life. Don't they get any values at home anymore? Somebody ought to teach them respect. They can't just desecrate a cemetery. It's not right. This isn't just a bunch of stones for them to write on. This cemetery is hallowed ground, young man. Hallowed ground."

The woman with the baby carriage next to him was nodding. She was probably hoping that his speech wouldn't wake up the baby. I nodded, shrugged, thanked him for the newspaper and stepped away, resuming my jog down the hill and around the park. I tucked the paper under my arm as I jogged. The article in it said that black, jagged marks had been spray painted on more than two dozen headstones. Slogans of racial hate and swastikas defiled the graves of the Jewish community, the article said. The mayor, the police chief and the Jewish

Defamation League had all spoken out against it. There was speculation about who had done this. But so far there was no hard evidence. It was 'under investigation.' Apparently, the police thought it was the act of vandalism by teenagers. But I had a hunch that it was something more malicious than this.

County Prosecutor Abe Rockleigh has called for a computer surveillance police team to investigate last night's vandalism at the Greenlawn Cemetery. According to Mr. Rockleigh, the desecration of tombs may be the work of juveniles who are fans of heavy-metal music.

"Such youths are known to gather near a sewer pipe in Veteran's Park and other locations near the cemetery," said the County Prosecutor. A police team has been assigned to watch closely for youths reported to frequent these areas.

Mr. Peter Foreman, a lawyer for the Civil Liberties Union, called Mr. Rockleigh's strategy "an outlandish example of stereotyping." The attorney stated that he grew up with rock music.

"Rock has always been regarded as a music of rebellion, but it has been absorbed. In and of itself, heavy metal rock music poses no threat to society, as Mr. Rockleigh would have us believe. This is a matter of theater and fantasy."

Mr. Foreman went on to say that there is no conclusive evidence that heavy metal music promotes anti-social behavior. "Maybe Mr. Rockleigh should get more in touch with where young people are at these days," he said.

Abe Rockleigh replied that the issue is not to blame music fans or to censor rock music song lyrics. "The memories of people are at stake here," Mr. Rockleigh has commented. "It is a matter of respect that we are dealing with."

After reading the news article, I flopped down onto the couch and tossed my sneakers into the corner. What was that band of light under the door? Was someone there? The door was edging open, the band of light expanding. I heard footsteps. There was a shadow in the doorway. A face in the light. It was Therese.

"Oh, Jake, I didn't hear you come in."

"Therese, I thought you were someone else."

"Someone else?"

"Sorry, Therese. I'm just a little on edge, I guess."

"We all are, Jake," she said. "We all are."

To calm my nerves, I sat down in the dining room and wrote a letter to the editor of the local newspaper. The incident at Greenlawn Cemetery was still on my mind. It had been on my mind all day: The swastikas on the gravestones. The police roaming across the hills. The man at the gate wanting to visit his wife's grave. The reporter who said it had to do with "heavy metal music and disaffected youth." The man by the fence who blamed it all on 'young people.' It bothered me. So, I wrote a letter.

Dear Editor:

There is something misleading about equating the enthusiasm of teenagers for heavy metal music with the recent events at Greenlawn Cemetery and Veteran's Park. In response to Matthew Alan Rockoff's recent article in your paper, I believe that his association of hate crimes with heavy metal music is entirely wrong. It is wrong to blame this on what he calls "disaffected teenagers." The recent desecration of the Greenlawn Cemetery may instead suggest that there is a neo-Nazi movement in this area. We have witnessed similar markings at local farms and Veteran's Park. Law enforcement is the appropriate response. Not news articles aimed with further venom against groups of young people. Yes, there are heavy metal groups who associate with "skinheads". But to blame this kind of activity on kids listening to heavy metal music lyrics is absurd. As Mr. Foreman has said, this music is based on fantasy.

Yesterday morning, an elderly couple outside the police bar-ricade at Greenlawn Cemetery said to me that this incident had to do with "young people" in general. I believe this is wrong. What is important for people to recognize is that "young people," including those of us who listen to heavy metal music, are a diverse group. We too have values and we too have relatives whose memories we wish to preserve and honor. The ignoble acts of a few do not represent the attitudes of a whole generation. Also, it should be noted that there are disrespectful people of every age. The Nazi's of the 1930s and the early 1940s were certainly disrespectful, as these present neo-Nazis are. Overall, today's "young people" are just as concerned about respecting the memories of those who have gone before us as anyone else. Old or young, we should all speak out about this disrespectful gesture at the cemetery and in the park to uphold the lasting memories of those who have lived here in our communities.

Jacob Kincaid

I placed it in the mailbox, thinking about Ezra. My letter was in the newspaper two days later, in two columns across the editorial page. There was a call from my father, who had seen the morning edition. So had other people, he said.

"Jake, this letter in the paper. Your mom and I have been getting calls. What's this about a neo-Nazi organization?"

"I think there is one around here, dad. All the signs point to it. People have to know."

"Is it your job to let them know in a letter signed with your name? Jake, it's one thing to say that the memories of people should be respected. But Jake, I've got people calling me thinking that you know something more about this than you're telling. So, one question: Do you?"

"No. It's just what I've seen, dad. It adds up."

"So do headaches, son. Your mom and I really don't need any more. No more letters to the newspaper, okay? And I don't know what you're up to at that farm but stay out of trouble. Jake, someone has been here. He's been asking a lot of questions."

"People are bothering you, dad?"

"Somebody has been – yes. Now I don't know what this is all about, Jake. Have you gotten involved with something I should know about?"

"No, dad. I was just talking with some old man in the park. He says he's an alchemist."

"A what?"

"We saw some markings on the walls at the park. Then we saw them at the farm. So, after they were found in the cemetery, I figured there must be a neo-Nazi group around here somewhere."

"And you're not involved."

"With them? No, dad. I'm wondering who they are and why they're doing this."

"Listen, Jake. If you have the time to write letters to newspapers, you have time to attend classes at the college."

"But dad, there's a lot going on here. Stuff that is unbelievable. I was thinking of starting classes in January."

"In January? Jake, you need to get started now or you'll fall behind."

"I want to work to pay for it."

"That's commendable, Jake. But college can be expensive. I want to help you get started."

"Tom and I made a deal, dad. The deal was that we were going to paint houses and earn our tuition money for school."

"Well, that may be alright for Tom Sheffield. I realize that that football scholarship fell through for him, with his knee and all that. But Jake, you have the means to go."

"Dad, if Tom can't afford it, how come I can? We're in this together. We started this business and it's going to pay our way."

"Well, we'll see about that. I appreciate the ambition, Jake. But your mom and I are here to help." I heard him clear his throat and his voice softened slightly, as he sought to change the subject. "So, you've got an event happening there today, so I've heard."

"It's the farm's annual fundraiser," I said.

"Does that mean that you are done with the painting job there?"

My father wasn't sure what to make of my staying overnight at a farm to complete a painting job. I heard the uneasiness in his voice.

"Actually, dad, we have another house to do. It's over on the other side of the farm."

"Okay, you finish that painting job. But just make sure you go to school, Jake. You've got an opportunity here. Don't blow it."

He was right about that, of course. I couldn't study film unless I went back to school. But who was I kidding? I liked film. I didn't like school. And to say I was waiting for Tom, that was just an excuse. Tom wasn't going to any college any day soon. He had a painting business and he would always have a painting business. So, what was I doing?

Tom and I had decided that, with a painting business, we could make some money for college. The community college wouldn't cost as much as the university and we'd try to keep the business going for a while. Painting at the farm was a big job. It was a lucky break for us, and I just couldn't see not doing it and going to school. Not yet anyway. My parents weren't too happy about that. Especially when I told them we'd be living at the farm until we got the job done. "I thought you and Tom were getting an apartment," my mother said. "We are," I told her. "Once we're done with the job at the farm."

Dad was incredulous. "You're living in a tent on a farm? What is this, my son the circus performer?"

Even though my father wanted me to start classes, I agreed with Tom. Now was no time to pack up and leave the Red Cat Farm. With every day the problems around the farm became more curious. Someone had placed bids on the land. A realtor was calling Therese and Hans had seen some strangers on the property again at night. When Tom and I finished painting the farmhouse, we decided that we would stay around to help with other tasks. We would begin painting the house on the other side of the farm. We had a lot of reasons to stay: We liked being around Laura and I hoped I might see Ali again. We wanted to find that land deed to the other hundred acres. But mostly, it was because we were curious.

Someone, it seemed, was curious about us too. Every day, we found ourselves looking back over our shoulders and we wondered: Was someone lurking about watching us? As I looked out the window of the farmhouse, I couldn't stop thinking of the man I had seen following me from the park. Bald and lean, that man seemed to be moving toward me in his long coat like a sleek animal after its prey. We were sure that he was connected with the neo-Nazis in the old dairy facility. We wanted to know what they were doing. So, Tom and I made a plan. We would find a way to go down there, under the abandoned building.

6.

The old dairy facility was an eyesore: an abandoned building in a weed-knotted field. We went there on a night that an ominous moon shone over the farm. We stole from our beds shortly after midnight, sneaking quietly down the stairs, out the screen door to the yard. Tom held a lantern aloft and we walked to the truck. He started it up and drove a quarter of a mile down the road, parking the truck in the high shrubbery alongside the reservoir. The moonlight shone upon a stream, as if wrestling with the shadows that fell across the desolate area into which we walked.

There I could see a hulking figure in the distance. The abandoned building rose like a megalith, a vast gray temple surrounded by smaller buildings. Its drab exterior ran diagonally across the scraped-out space of dirt, the narrow slats of its windows hazed with dirt, barely letting in any of the light of the moon. We walked up to metal doors as forbidding as those in front of any fortress. Yet one of those doors was open, a gap as between earth and hell, inviting us in.

Tom extinguished the lantern. Turning on our flashlights, we moved into that cavernous space. We stepped across the oil-stained concrete. The pattern of turns seemed to force us to a space at the end of the building. The air was dense, like smoke and oil from a truck in the rain. On the walls our flashlights played into faint shadows like ancient hieroglyphics.

"There's no one here," I said.

"There is," Tom said. He pointed down. "Underneath the floor. I feel as if there is something down there."

We were looking for a basement, a trap door, anything that led downward. It was behind the building that we found it. Ahead of us, there seemed to be an empty elevator shaft and a narrow stairway leading down. Placing our hands on a cold iron rail, we followed the stairs, descending into the darkness. There the walls grew wider apart. We shone our flashlights up and saw that we had entered a cave. We were underground in caverns formed by the natural processes of centuries under the countryside.

We brought the flashlights down but still the beam played on the walls. Before us was a wide hallway leading past a series of rooms. My voice echoed again in the chill air. Shadows tumbled before us, like wild birds in a city stricken by war. Walls rose around us. I felt I was in a vault, trapped here, claustrophobic. Seeking balance, I stood with my legs wide, my feet firmly planted on the concrete floor. Yet, the room swirled, as in a shadow show and we descended further into that cold vault.

"It's been stripped bare," Tom said. "No pipes, no wall sockets, no trace of anything. They've gotten rid of everything here. But there might be another level below this."

From our flashlights, faint, changing lights played on the walls, across concrete walls and floors; they were swallowed in the darkness. In the air was the scent of lime, or gas - what if there was carbon monoxide, or some odorless gas, I wondered. We wouldn't last long. Our flashlights shimmered against the walls, beamed through the concrete bunker, spiraled along the walls as we pushed ahead. Every surface absorbed the light, as we followed the hallway past a series of rooms, each one sterile, cold, clear of any visible sign of life. But as we turned a corner, ahead of us we saw someone. In the rim of the glow around a lantern the figure appeared. He was young. The face above the gray uniform weaved in a soup of light from the lantern. In the next moment, Tom and I looked at each other.

"Can we take him?"

"Jake, are you crazy? What if he has a gun?"

"We jump him and drag him outside."

"You watch too many movies, Jake."

"Let's distract him then."

That's when Tom picked up the rock. Finger to his lips, he nodded toward the light. He hurled the big rock high toward the stalactites. The rock hit and fell, popping in the distance. Startled, the young man turned toward the sound. Then with a second rock Tom aimed at the lantern. Crack, it struck, shattering the glass.

"Good one," I whispered.

We were in darkness. We crouched lower and started swiftly back to the mouth of the cave where we had come in.

"He might come out now," Tom said. "If he can find his way."

Past the concrete building, we took a position behind the fence. Across the ground Tom pulled a long hose which had been left there. He gestured to the paint cans along the fence. Weapons. If we needed them.

The man appeared in the evening light outside the mouth of the cave. He was alone. He moved along the edge of the warehouse, looking out across the patch of dirt that circled the building. Seeing no one, he took a few steps back and disappeared again within the walls of the cave.

"So, what's down there?" Tom asked me.

"Three guesses. One, it's a meeting hall, two, a computer station, three, it's their private pathway to hell."

"That isn't the guy who was following you. Is it?"

"No."

"So, what do you think we should do next?"

"I want to go back down there and find out what they're doing."

"Me too. But we can't go back in right now. Should we let the police know about these guys?"

"Know what? That some crazy guy in a gray uniform is walking through the abandoned caves under an old dairy warehouse? That we think these are the guys who followed me? We still don't have any idea why. We need to go back in there and get some evidence."

"Okay, Jake. I'm with you. So, when are we going back?"

"In a couple of nights. We'll bring the flashlights again. Then we'll see what's really going on down there!"

7.

Veterans Park appeared golden in the morning light: a peaceful place, an oasis set apart from the world. I had by now met Ezra there several times. He seemed curious about me, curious about the farm and the fire. Yet, the park now also seemed an uncertain place. Returning there, I tossed a newspaper into Laura's father's station wagon and reached for the colored flyers in a box in the back seat. I had brought with me dozens of bright orange flyers to advertise the arts and crafts fair. Taking them from the car, I rounded the park on foot, placing flyers on every metal stand but the flagpole.

He came up the path quietly, as he always did, his hat pulled low over his eyes, carrying a cup of coffee and a bagel in his hands. He sat down at one of the tables and motioned to me to sit down with him.

"Do you remember me, Ezra?"

"Yes, I remember," he said.

"I painted over those markings on the wall," I said.

"Thank you," he said. His moustache moved up and down like a little gray broom. "But have you not heard? There are others."

"I know," I said.

"Who has done this?"

He stared for a time into the still waters of the pond. At last, he spoke again.

"You should come to the farm, Ezra. We're having an arts and crafts fair. You could meet my friend Tom. He's a painter too. And there's a girl named Laura. She's a real painter. She paints portraits and landscapes. And she has a friend named Alessandra. And you could meet Therese. She's not young but she acts it."

I handed him one of the rumpled orange flyers. I was keeping them in my jacket pocket, and they were a bit creased. He took it in his hand, looked at it and nodded.

"Very well," he said. He thanked me and he began to walk slowly away.

When Ezra had gone, I stood by the stream watching it tumble over the rocks. For a moment, I was entranced by the rippling surface. But then from behind me I heard the crackle of footsteps on the fallen leaves. I looked back into the woods. There stood a balding man in a long black coat, gazing at me. His face was young, harsh and vibrant. I walked quickly away from him across the fallen leaves. Picking up my pace, I crossed the park to a pay phone by the rest rooms.

"Tom, someone is definitely watching me," I said into the phone. "I'm in Veterans Park. I was talking with Ezra. Then this guy comes up behind me. I think that he was watching us."

"Okay, Jake. Get back to the farm as fast as you can," Tom said. "Make sure if he follows you that he's right behind you. I'm going to take the truck and follow this guy."

"Got you."

So, I did that.

Stepping from the phone booth, I turned quickly around the building and began to jog down the road toward the car. The man was right behind me.

I got into the car and pulled out on the road. The man got into a dark blue Ford pickup truck and pulled out behind me. Quickly I drove, pushing back the nightmare I was feeling. I turned off the highway and I drove once more back through the park. It was full of winding turns and I took them swiftly. I glanced back again. He was still behind me.

The sun was bearing down on the windshield. The tires snapped over the loose stones. I turned up the narrow road to the farm and raced through the gate. Tom's truck raced by me, kicking up dust. I looked back. The blue pickup truck was no longer there.

I pulled the station wagon into a space behind the farmhouse and stepped out. Laura and the two dogs were hurrying toward me across the lawn.

"I think he's gone," I said.

"Who's gone?" Laura asked. "Tom?"

"No. I was followed."

"Why?"

"I don't know. It sure isn't because I'm a house painter."

"Tom left in his truck," Laura said. "He said he had an errand to do."

"He's going after him."

"After who?"

"I don't know. But he's been watching every move I make."

Mulch raced from the driveway to greet us. I reached down to pet the dog, a shaking fur ball at my feet.

"Jake, what's going on?"

"Someone has been following me, Laura. Like I told Tom, it's been happening ever since I went to the park and met the old man."

"Somebody's following you because you met an old man?"

"I think so. I took the usual route again this morning, up the hill, around the fence. I put up some flyers for the crafts fair. Then I stopped by the pond and talked with Ezra. Laura, I think it all has something to do with him."

"You mean the fire too? Everything?"

"I think so. There was somebody else there in the park. When I finished talking with Ezra some guy was there just looking at me. I felt I was being followed so I went to the pay phone by the rest rooms and called Tom."

"And now Tom's following him?"

"That's the idea. He won't recognize Tom's truck."

"But isn't that dangerous? You don't know who this guy is. Did you get a look at him?"

"Just a passing glance. His head is shaven and he's wearing eyeglasses."

"An old man?"

"No. Someone younger. Much younger. He's handsome, like a movie actor. Somebody is suspicious about my talking with Ezra. That's for sure."

"Jake, we've got to find out what's going on."

"When Tom gets back maybe we'll see what's up."

"He shouldn't have gone after him, Jake. What if this guy figures out that he is being followed? He won't hurt Tom, will he?"

"We've got to sit tight, Laura. We'll hear from Tom soon."

Minutes later the phone rang. It was Tom on the line.

"I followed him as far as I could," he said. "Then he turned his truck into one of the other farms. He's almost right next door, Jake. He's down the road from us. It's the strangest thing. I looked back beyond the gate there. I could swear I saw a guy in a uniform."

"It's a military base?"

"Well, if it is, it's like nothing I've ever seen before. There are no signs or anything. Just a guy in a uniform. It was a gray uniform, I think."

"A gray uniform? Since when do they wear gray?"

"Something's up, Jake. I'm coming back to the farm."

I clicked off the phone. Laura turned to me.

"Jake, why are they following you?"

"I don't know. Maybe it has something to do with the old man."

"Who is he?"

"Just some old guy named Ezra. He walks in the park by himself. I don't think he has anybody. Any wife or friends, I mean."

"That's so sad."

"The question is why is someone watching him? Why is he watching me? Is somebody around here watching us?"

"That's so paranoid."

"But what if someone is watching?"

"Then maybe it has something to do with the old man," Laura said. "Jake, you've got to see him again. You've got to find out who he is. Hey, I've got an idea. Why don't we all go and talk with him? Do you know where he lives?"

"No. I just met him when I was out jogging in the park."

"But you could find out where he lives. Couldn't you? Why don't you ask him?"

"I already did. He wouldn't tell me."

"There are other ways to find out."

"What do you expect me to do, follow him like those other people are doing?"

"That's an idea."

"All right, we'll talk about it with Tom when he gets back. And maybe we'll go and pay a visit to Ezra. But don't be surprised if you see someone following you, Laura, because somebody is definitely following him."

"I don't get it," Laura said. "Why would anybody be following around some simple old man?"

Minutes later, Tom pulled his truck, dust rising from its tires, into the driveway. He stepped out and walked with me to the farmhouse.

"So?" I asked.

"So, we've got something weird on our hands. He was a tough looking guy: tall, head shaven, just like you said. I followed him to an abandoned property back behind one of the farms. The place is empty. Just a big patch of dirt and weeds. But it looks like it might have been a dairy once."

"But it's not that anymore."

"No. It couldn't be. The fence there has been torn away and there's a big, vacant building with dirty windows just standing there like some kind of prehistoric monster."

"And he went in there?"

"I think so."

"You said you saw a guy in a gray uniform. Do you think it might be a military base?"

"No, Jake. It didn't look like any military base I've ever seen before. Mostly it just looked like a dump. But I'd say it's a dump that deserves a closer look. We should go back there."

"You think we'd find something to help us figure out why they've been following me?"

"Maybe. It could be they think you know something."

"Maybe. The problem is - I don't."

"Well, I'll tell you, I'd like to know something. I'd like to know what that place is all about and why that guy went in there."

"Then it's time we went and found out what's going on. Why don't we go there tonight?"

"It'll have to be late. Sometime after midnight. We're going to be busy this evening. Tonight, we've got a guest."

I stood squinting into the sunlight.

"Your friend Ezra Foote is coming to visit," Tom said.

"He's coming here to the farm? Why?"

"You gave him one of your flyers, Jake. He told Therese that he wants to make a donation."

As we reached the door of the farmhouse, we heard the phone in the kitchen ringing. Laura picked it up, heard a man's voice asking for Jacob Kincaid and handed the phone to me.

"Do I have Jacob Kincaid?" said a voice on the other end of the line.

"Yes. That's me," I said.

"Mr. Kincaid, you are involved with something you ought not to be. I am calling to inform you - you must not. You must back off."

There was a click. A dial-tone. And that was all.

Laura and Tom looked at me curiously as I turned toward them.

"It was him," I said. "I'm sure of it."

Of course, Laura asked the expected questions and I couldn't answer any of them. What was I involved in? I had no idea.

The man followed me in my dreams. I saw him stepping from the woods, circling the pond. He followed me into town, where I brought groceries. He watched me in the glare of the storefront windows. My gaze swept like a camera across the street: up an alley, past the dim streetlight, across the trees along the curb. I felt panic, the urge to get home. It was happening again. I fumbled with the house keys, under a moon that seemed like a mocking smile out of the sky.

The rain began to fall, but the storm passed quickly and before long the evening sun rinsed its bright light over the hills. The light was good and I got out my video camera and tried to cheer everyone by making a home movie. I followed everyone around as they stepped over puddles, setting up shelves and tables for the arts and crafts fair. I followed the cows with my camera. I focused in on Laura's paintings, beginning with the eyes of a portrait, then pulling back to reveal each painted face. I did the same shots of Hans and the cows. Up on a ladder, Tom was waving. I took a close up of Mulch after putting a hat on the dog.

Ezra arrived at about six o'clock and I went to greet him. As he stood on the driveway, leaning on his cane, I asked to film him. No, no, he said. He wished to remain anonymous. But I filmed him anyway. From the second-floor windows of the farmhouse, I aimed the camera out toward the driveway as he walked toward the farmhouse door.

Laura answered the door in response to Ezra's knock. In the doorway, gazing back at her, a look of surprise came to his face. Tom helped him take off his coat and led him through the wide living room. He stood for a moment staring at the room as if he were seeing it for the first time. For a moment it seemed to me as if he were still in his own book lined study, beside his fireplace, puffing his pipe.

"I'm so glad you could make it, Mr. Foote," Therese said.

"It's my pleasure to be here. Thank you. This is lovely. You've done a fine job with this house."

"You must be hungry, Ezra. Come, sit down. Dinner is ready."

The dinner we had with him began with French onion soup and went on to roast beef. Afterward, we sat with our eyes on the candles on the table before us. They created a dreamlike quality- a glow in front of the curtain- darkened windows.

"Ezra has come to help us with the farm," Therese said. "He has made a rather generous donation. Of course, we can't know for sure what the lawyers for the developers will be doing next. But we have a big crafts fair coming up. Right?"

Ezra cleared his throat. It looked as if he was about to speak. But for a moment he just looked across the table at us. Silently, we all looked back.

"This farm will survive," he said at last. "There are those troubles that hang over us like smoke above our head for a time," he said. "They flicker up with their disasters like the tip of a pipe, like a blazing light. But after a time, it burns itself out and the quiet and the peace return after all in the end."

He was quiet then for a time, his eloquence fading like the afterglow from the candles. If his life were a movie, I thought, this would be the part where the room fades into darkness and into the sound of cellos and a single stream of light beams upon an isolated figure in his armchair. But this was not a movie. Ezra was here with us and he was not alone. We were drawn for moment into his solitude.

Yet, how animated Ezra was at other moments! He asked us to take him on a tour of the farm. Even as night fell and we returned from the other farmhouse and passed by the burned-out barn he seemed to want to know more about the place. We talked of the arts fair. Laura talked to him again of his wife. I think she reminded him of her. He looked into those friendly green eyes of hers and felt the press of her hand that spoke of friendship.

"Enchanting," he said. It was a favorite word of his.

When we returned from our walk across the farm, Ezra went with Therese off to another part of the house to talk about his donations. It sounded like he was concerned that a developer was trying to purchase the land. When they were gone, Laura and Tom and I washed the dishes in the kitchen. We talked about Ezra. I made sure this time to separate the recyclables from the compost and the garbage.

"Wasn't it special of Ezra to come by tonight?" Laura said.

"It's good that he finally got to see the farm," I said, finding the buckets marked "Recycled."

"He's already seen this farm, Jake. You know that," Tom said.

We stood looking at each other for a moment, neither of us speaking.

"I've known that ever since I met him that first day in the park," I said, finally. "I knew it from the look he gave me when I said we were painting the old farmhouse."

"He seems so lonely," Laura said.

"You hardly know him. How can you say that?"

"I can just tell. There are a lot of elderly people who are lonely. Their children are busy, or their families are gone. They are forgotten by the world."

"I get the feeling that Ezra likes it that way."

"How could anybody like that? What does he do all day? Does he have a family?"

"I think he said that he's a scholar. He's an alchemist. I think that's what he said."

"An alchemist. What is that?"

"It has something to do with turning metals into gold. It's a search for the philosopher's stone," I said.

"Whatever that is."

"Ezra told me that Isaac Newton used to be interested in alchemy."

"That was a long time ago," Tom said.

"Well, I think he must be lonely," Laura said. "He came here to the farm. I think we should go visit him."

"Maybe he doesn't want us to visit him, Laura."

"He said he had some more old furniture. Didn't he? Maybe he would donate something else."

"There is something strange about him, I think," Tom said. "Doesn't it strike you as odd that when we showed him the farm he asked if there was any more to it? 'Is that all?' he said. It was as if he expected there to be more."

"Or knew there was?"

"Exactly. He knows this farm."

"He mentioned the barn too," I said. "He asked me if we were painting the barn. The next day it was destroyed by a fire."

"That's strange."

"And when we showed him the old farmhouse, the one we were in a few nights ago, he said he felt a chill in the kitchen. Something there was making him uncomfortable."

"But there was no one there. Just us."

"As far as we know there was no one else there."

"You think he was there? The bald guy?"

"I don't know. It seems like he's everywhere."

"Ezra knew that house like the back of his hand," Tom said. "Do you remember when we went to the basement? It was as if he led us down there. It was as if he knew the way already. Then he led us to that old oak desk."

"He really liked that desk. Didn't he?"

"He was fascinated by it. He wanted us to sell it to him. He said he would pay a good price for it. A very high price."

"Why would anybody pay such a high price for an old desk? It's just an old desk."

"Maybe he really wants to help out the farm. Maybe it's his way of making another donation."

"No, there's something about that desk."

We heard footsteps, voices, and our conversation soon ended. We heard Ezra and Therese returning. They stood outside the doorway and I heard Therese say,

"We just wanted to thank you for all that you have done for this farm, Ezra."

"Oh, you are welcome, then," Ezra said. "You have all been gracious to me."

He stood for a moment gazing past us at the rooms of the farmhouse. For him the spell had broken. It was time for him to go home again.

The morning came brightly. We hadn't slept much, and we rolled wearily out of our beds and out to the yard. Tom and I began pulling tables from a truck that had arrived with the sun. We decorated the yard area in colors with signs and streamers. The craft displayers brought their tables. The town provided the port-a-johns. Before long, people began to arrive in cars from all over the state. They brought their children, their friends, and that bright human energy and enthusiasm that the farm would soon become famous for. They climbed the grass and hay scented hills of the farm. They walked through its pastures and gardens. The children played. Therese led a meditation under the elm that she called the grandfather tree. By evening, four of Laura's paintings had been bought by visitors. She was so excited that she called her friend Ali and then passed the phone along to me. I felt a chill up my spine as I heard her voice. I said something like "Oh, hi, Ali. The arts and crafts fair was great! How's school? You're coming back home for the Thanksgiving break?" I don't remember anything else we said. Everything else is a happy blur. Our newly painted farmhouse caught the sunshine in its windows and life was good and hopeful that day on Canaan Farm.

Therese held a thank you dinner that evening after the arts and crafts fair. It was her way of celebrating hope. Her friend Margaret brought along some food. She also brought along a neighbor named Ida. I guessed that Ida must have been well past eighty.

"Curt Casey called," Therese told them. "There is a lawyer who is representing a German man. He says he shares some interest in the farm from years ago with the original owner."

"They'll have to go through legal channels," Therese added. "But so will we. We might lose more than just the barn by the time this is over. We might lose the whole farm. If that happens, there goes a year of hard work and a lot of dreams."

After that mournful note, it was time to cheer things up, I decided. I took out the videotape and put it into the VCR while everyone was having dessert.

Then the eyes came at them from Laura's paintings and from the cows. We could hear the voices and movement around the craft display tables. We saw wooden benches, jars of honey, knitted shawls. Everyone laughed at the floppy hat on the dog Mulch and at the cow with a sign on its tail that said, "Crafts Fair This Way." I wanted to put another sign on the cow that said, "Get in the Gate, Dummy." Margaret smiled to see her handcrafts booth featured for a moment. She nudged Ida and Ida giggled at seeing herself on the screen.

Then we heard her gasp. Ida put down her teacup and stared.

"Are you all right, Ida?"

"Who is that man?"

"He is a donor. He has been very generous," Therese said. "His name is Ezra. Do you know him, Ida?"

The woman was speechless and nodded. Then she finally found words.

"Yes, I knew him," she said. "He was my neighbor. But I thought he was dead."

Therese motioned to me to rewind the video. I played it back again, returning to the scene in which I observed Ezra on the driveway from the upstairs window. We looked from the screen back at Ida. She seemed to have gone pale.

"Where have you seen him before, Ida?"

"Why, right here on the Red Cat Farm," she said. "I went to his funeral. That is Jonas von Klaus!"

8

THE ALCHEMIST'S NOTEBOOK

The past rose up today, as from a grave, to meet me. A wall was stained with the insignia of the Nazi Party. Things like this come abruptly, like a stranger. They are the unexpected end of innocence. A young stranger has come today, as unexpectedly as Schneider arrived on that winter day long ago. The young man said that he would wash that symbol from the wall; he would cover it over with a coat of paint. His name is Jacob. Some turn of fortune has brought him to the farm. He would say that he is painting a farmhouse. Yet, to hear him speak about his interest in film reminds me of the youthful fascination I once had with science. I believe that I may have found in young Jacob one who can chronicle the past, one who can bring dark secrets to light. For, much has been hidden from view and the world must know. The images that are seared into my memory still burn me with their pain. The philosopher once said that he who does not know the past is condemned to repeat it. I write to remember, to set it down. I write to make my reckoning with what once was, to transform the lead mass of past sorrow into remembrance.

In the winter of 1940, when the snows came to the frozen northland, a solemn darkness had fallen upon the continent and the entire known world was ensnared in war. Outside a small lodge in the woodlands, far from those killing fields, we three grown men like schoolboys tossed balls of snow at one another. My heavy coat powdered white with snow, I rolled on my side, aiming high toward Wilhelm and pummeled him with ice and snow. Steffan and I dragged him inside the cabin, his chapped lips, the wet ringlets in his hair drying in the smoke and warmth of the fireplace.

Outside the door, where the snow fell, a deer hung upon a tree. Evidence of our hunt, it hung like a talisman. I looked curiously at the deer, remembering how it left its blood upon the snow. I called it an omen and they all laughed at that. I turned toward the fire and warmed my hands.

We were three young men alone in a cabin in the woods: medical students on leave from our studies. We were certain that we would soon be drafted into the army and we had thought to make a holiday of it, a hunt in nature after the Yule season. But the snow had kept us there and it dashed against the windows and bound us in.

That evening we heard sounds from the forest. There was a cracking branch, a dog's bark. I went to the window and looked out. Across the snow, a man was approaching. He was a vague, spectral figure in the airy drifts of white. He was dragging two canvas bags across the snow. The snow trailed through the tree limbs above him in a white dance around the cabin.

When the man yelled for his dog his voice broke like a whip across the silence. The dog barked back and the man cursed it. The winter stillness was then filled with a harsh sound that reminded me of violence.

I went to the door. The man came in toward us, hat down over his wild eyes, dragging the bags on the snow. The dog paused with him, taking a long look at the deer hanging by the door. The man's head came up, showing a bearded face and wild blue eyes. He greeted us in our native tongue as he slapped the snow from his feet.

"Ah," I heard Wilhelm say. "It is Schneider."

For weeks Schneider had been missing from the troops. We believed him to have been on a raid. Now he had appeared in the backwoods, steps cracking the ice, a shadow beaten back by the snow. Standing at the door, he reeked of smoke. The snow hung from his cloak as if from a tree. There was ice in his blue eyes.

"Have you room for a stranger?" he asked us. "I have some important news."

I recall how Schneider's arrival at the cabin had ended our holiday, our reward for courage under fire in Poland months before. We believed that we would be sent back to the front, to the new war in Poland. During the previous summer, tension had increased over Danzig, a largely German speaking region. We had been sent before September to the Polish border as medical support for our military's first, decisive strategic move. Poland is a broad plain- flat and open, a place of forests and farmland. The Carpathian Mountains lay in the South, where our military came through at the Jablunka Pass. In the low fog at 4:30 in the morning of September 1, the army began to strike along the Polish frontier. Forty-four German divisions blasted into Poland, attacking from both North and South. We were med-ical support behind the lines.

On the first of September, in gray dawn, the artillery began penetrating a weak and indefensible border. The Vistula and Narew rivers carried supplies and we crossed with heavy motor vehicles. The Polish army was encircled. Stoic faces, men of determination, horsemen against powerful tanks; they were no match against the iron machines of the Wehrmacht. The Luftwaffe began flying low, grazing fields with sharp wings, bombing anyone who was on the roads. Men surged through curtains of smoke. Shattered, the land was laid open, like a body cut by incisions. There were bullets for horses and bullets for women and children, stinging the life from them. Prisoners in Polish uniforms drifted down the road toward us like skeletal ghosts, led into the clouds. In the city of Warsaw there was panic. People huddled in shelters, hiding under the buildings in ruins.

That anguished humanity held on to life, resisting. Yet, toward the end of September, at last the city succumbed. Black crosses, swastikas, red flags now moved in the wind before the massive old church where the Poles honored the saints and the Virgin. I saw how the cross lay shattered beneath the cracked rectory wall. A crying girl was clinging to the leg of a man who had fallen in the street. I heard Polish words, repeated over and over. In the countryside, where we set up a medical camp for our wounded, the eerie quiet was broken only by the sound of Stukas flying, shooting across a farmer's field at anything on the road.

Poland had been divided many times, taken apart like a puzzle by the Russians and by Prussia. Germany set its sights on the land from East Prussia in the North to the Oder Neisse Line, where many of the people were more German than Polish. The Wehrmacht had come to claim the land- lebensraum was the cry. The nightmare had begun.

In January, we young physicians were to be moved back to Berlin for special training. To my thinking, there was little doubt that the man who had been sent to us with this message was SS. The plan to enlist us in a new project was a subtle one. It spoke like a devil's whisper to our deepest desires. It appealed to our honor. Yet, it was so secret that not even we knew what the research would involve.

It was then that we became a secret society, a brotherhood. We thought of ourselves as a Faust society of young romantics. Dealing with medicine and with natural healing, we would live like otherworldly miners in underworld secrecy. We were transported by train to Mecklenburg, where the winter mornings were cold and bright. I recall how the church bells sounded across the rooftops when I visited Alt-Rehse. It was a place of beauty along Lake Tollense. We were brought to a school in a small village. There we learned about natural healing and genetics. In the small classrooms where we sat at wooden desks, often I heard the word "organic." We were instructed there to treat the whole person and to be whole persons ourselves. We were to be athletic and healthy, so in the yard outside we played ping-pong and soccer. To show our connection with the workers we ran with shovels over our shoulders. It was part of our exercise. A physician must be healthy, we were told. A physician must be a leader of the Volk. We learned that health was related to genetics and racial care. For six weeks we did that. Interns, doctors, and nurses. Then we moved on.

Next, we were enrolled in a course at the Eglfing-Haar mental hospital. There a thin doctor in a starched shirt raised a pointer to a motion picture screen and in proud tones he declaimed: "Young gentlemen, these are films of regressed patients. They are unworthy of life, for they are defective. Thus, if allowed to live, they will damage the gene pool. We have classified them T4. Now see here. Note that this Jewish mental patient has dangerous genes. One cannot permit this tendency toward insanity to be transmitted to future generations. In this frame you will see several images of the crippled. It is your duty – I repeat, it is your duty in such a case to provide the Gandentod, the mercy death for the crippled and the insane. You must always consider the social consequences of hereditary impairments." By these lectures, I was led to believe in the promise of science, the promise of the nation.

When I was young, I believed in many things. I believed in the myths of the dawning of a new society. I believed that a new age would rise from the ashes and losses of war. We were young and proud. With the new party's program, the people had been given work again. They told us that we would build our nation on its traditions and return it to its rightful place in the world.

As a child I saw the political rallies of the party and the state. It is as if I see them again as I lift this candle. Night torches. Storm troopers. The man with the hypnotic eyes, the simple brown uniform, the Iron Cross pinned to his left pocket. I hear his voice rising shrilly over clenched hands: "We are strong! Let none interfere with the sovereign rights of this people. We are a strong people!" I hear the loudspeaker crackling. The voices are drifting. Distant voices calling me by name. "Jonas... Jonas..." I went too far. Too far in my experiments in the well-lit room. Too far in esoteric experiments, biological mysteries, chemical marvels. It was the sublime practice of alchemy.

My father's voice comes back to me. The round, cheeky face fades into a blur, like the clouds in the pond at the park. I hear the voices of father and his friend Professor Gruden. So long ago, I hear them. "This scientist you speak of. Who was he then?" "Paracelsus was a Swiss, a brilliant and curious man in search of the deepest secrets of the universe. The deepest." Yes, again I hear them speaking. "Paracelsus worked in the mining districts of Tyrol and Sweden," the professor is explaining to my father. "Then he wandered across Europe in search of the mysteries of the science of healing. He was a surgeon in the armies of great kings. He mixed with gypsies and conjurers, astrologers, and grave robbers. He was an alchemist, Jonas. He was one of those with the peculiar dream of finding out the secret of life.

One who had the desire to turn common metals into gold. He was an alchemist."
And father would say, "Do you think that my son should study the works of this
man?" "Yes" was the professor's answer. To know medicine as a truly healing art, I
knew that I too must follow the path of the great Paracelsus.

You see, I wondered at times about this genetic current that flows from generation to generation within a race. The genetic doctor was one who would care
for the future of the race. In my father's time they first talked about racial hygiene.
If the gene pool were to gather any defects it would, across generations, become
weaker. We learned this Rassenhygiene in school. "You have an inheritance," we
were told. "Your inheritance is always stronger than any environmental influence.
The future is in our race; it is in our blood. You will learn this through applied biology and racial science. Racial hygiene is your task."

"How will you keep the race pure? You must observe closely, with a clinical
eye. Look at the fingernails, the half moon at their base. Open and look into the
mouth, at the shape of the teeth and the tongue. Yes, and look at the nose; look at
the forehead to determine racial ancestry. The inferior must be selected out. The
weak must be eliminated."

Back then it was known that the war would mask the program. In the midst
of such fighting and drama, no one would see how they were eliminating the mentally ill, the disabled, the lives they called not worth living." If the healthy soldier
would risk his life in the war, should not the sickly do the same? It was a strange
notion. How did these mentally ill persons threaten the society? Who was to say
they were mentally ill?

I have heard that at first children were starved rather than making use of
infections. Those small faces, wide-eyed, were led down corridors to their doom.
Muller did not hide the fact that among them were children who were not mentally
ill. There were those with cerebral polio. The doctors would give them sedatives to
help them to sleep. That is how it began. Luminal tablets were given to the children
in their tea to drink. After their daily tea the child would sleep. Some would sleep
forever. A doctor would then come quietly, clipboard and medical chart in hand.
The cause of death was sometimes listed as pneumonia. So, Muller told me. An
injection of morphine would finish the more restless, high-strung ones. The doctors filled out forms and reports. The senior doctors administered this. Often the
younger doctors would be called. We carried out examinations. Their only purpose
was to convince us that we were involved in a medical operation.

In isolated areas were former mental hospitals, quiet confines with high
walls. Some had been castles. They were fortresses where nothing could be seen from

the outside world. There was at Nesselstedt, on the grounds of a former monastery, a wide, gray building of great stones. Here, it was said, the Reich Fuhrer physician Kurt Blome carried out experiments on human subjects. It was said that the place was an institute for cancer research. But we knew better. To test the plague vaccine, they would test it on humans. First, they would inject into them the plague. I heard Tabun and Sarin were used. We knew both were deadly. None of us protested this. We thought then it was in the name of science. It would be for the greater good.

Experiments. That is what we were told we were to be involved with. The subjects were to be of what was called an inferior class. Should they die during the experiments, it was our duty to assign the cause of death suggested by the patient's previous physical condition. One must be consistent in this. Bacterial infection. The results of sepsis. A heart ailment. Pneumonia. One must be realistic and make this believable.

I was assigned briefly, as a junior physician, to a prison camp, one near the train transport lines. It was not long before I began to suspect that something was amiss. Jews would arrive on the trains in the middle of the night. The soldiers took their names, gave them numbers, and marched them inside. They were told to shower while their clothing was being disinfected. We wore white coats and stethoscopes. How terribly efficient and official we must have appeared.

Little did I know then that the autumn of 1940 would bring a new assignment. I was called to Norway. A place of beauty- a bareness frozen in snow, where northern light strains to be seen. I lived there, working at what was known as a mother-home, many miles from the city of Trondheim. Below the hill, the train tracks led along the mountainside toward Trondheim. In winter, steam rose from locomotives, in dark clouds, disappearing above the bare trees. The trains churned toward a gray horizon, to the tunnels and walls where the city absorbed them. They came to rest in the blankness of the train yard.

There, the trains rested like dark shadows in the snowy night. In the yards, next to the trains that had concluded their journeys, there were crates. In them, we were told, there were medical supplies. The shipment was under guard. Every few minutes the guard would march north alongside the trains then turn and step back across the snow toward where we were loading the boxes. One night, my alchemy truly did come into contact with gold. It was a treasure which lay under the snow in the train yard.

We walked in darkness. Night stars sparkled above the rail yard. Under the dimmest of lights, Wilhelm Krauss and I pried a corner of one of the crates open and we saw what was inside. I reached my hand in. There was a sound of metal jingling.

"What is it?"

"Watch for the guard. Keep your voice down." He stirred inside the box with a stick. It was the sound of beads, bracelets.

"Hold it to the light."

There were snakes of gold: bracelets, gems and coins. It was a treasure.

"This is not bank gold," Will said.

"These are the spoils of war. Whose this was is not for us to say."

"Jonas, I'd say you know quite well whose gold this is. I was told that this shipment was grain taken from the north for agricultural experiments. Clearly, it is not."

"Yes, I can see that. But this..." I said, holding small fragments to the light.

"They are gold fillings scraped from someone's jaw."

"Not someone living, I imagine."

"No. These items will ride in these crates to a place where they will be smelted. They will be turned into gold bars. Then the gold will go into some bank in Frankfurt, or perhaps to Switzerland."

"But Switzerland is neutral."

"Do you think so, Jonas? Are they really?"

9.

It seemed strange to me that a man would change his name and choose to hide from the world. Jonas Albrecht von Klaus became Ezra Foote. He left secrets in his notebooks. The clues to a treasure lay hidden in their pages. We just didn't know it at that time. We were busy with other things: hopeful things like house painting and summer camps.

Laura began her first day at the Starlight Day Camp the day after the arts and crafts fair. She had a big smile on her face. Four of her paintings had sold at the arts and crafts fair. Now she was looking forward to working on art projects with the special education children at the camp.

It was also time for our new project. The house on the other side of the farm awaited a few new coats of paint. The house was bigger than the first farmhouse, the one that Therese lived in. Painting it would take at least a week, Tom estimated. He didn't seem to mind and neither did I. Even so, our painting high up on ladders had now become less certain. From beside the farmhouse windows, as I painted, I could hear Hans in the yard below slapping metal joints, tossing links into a pail. Clink, clink, clank went the metal screws and nuts into a pail. Metal links that tie together the world. These were the solid things we could work with, things we held in our hands. They were physical, tangible things. Like Tom's paint pails, or the brushes we painted the farmhouse with. I thought of Ezra. Why, I wondered, would anyone want to be an alchemist and transmute metals? Why would anyone want to take the solid things of the world and melt them and make them liquid or gas or something we cannot see, something we cannot hold in our hands?

Before I got to the farm the world was a solid and sure place. Now that had changed. I had met a man who had claimed that he was dead. A good man. But he was into some very unordinary things. Stay out of trouble, my father had said. Was that even possible at this point? After a morning of house painting, I was still thinking about it as Tom and I got into his truck. We were on our way to visit Laura in the Starlight Day Camp. Then we would all go to the diner together for lunch.

When we arrived at the Starlight Day Camp, we drove around a large building with an antenna rising above it. Beyond it we could see Laura and several of the children playing in a wide, grassy field. Laura was on one knee tying the shoelaces of a little boy. Then she stood, clapped her hands and rolled a big red ball across the lawn to about half a dozen children who scampered after it. As we drew closer, we heard their voices.

"Marie... Marie... Over here!"

"You caught it! That's very good, David. Now toss the ball back to Marie."

"David... David... "

A little girl, still powdered in multi-colors from chalk and finger paints, reached for the ball. She smiled broadly as the ball rolled across the lawn toward her.

"Catch it, Amelia!"

Amelia stretched out her arms.

"Oh, the great Amelia does it again!" Laura exclaimed. "That was good, Amelia. You caught it."

For a moment, the sunlight spilled out across the gathering on the lawn. The little boy named David pointed up at the cloudy sky.

"There's my little raindrop," Amelia said. "Rain go away."

Then she put her hands out and tried to push away the clouds. Laura also looked up at the sky. She saw us walking across the yard toward her.

"Okay, come on," she said to the children. "It's time to go inside."

The children walked in an uneven line in front of her. One by one they disappeared into the large building with the big antennae on the roof. We met Laura at the door.

"I'm going to bring them to the farm," she said excitedly. "Therese thinks it's a good idea. She thinks that maybe we can get some funding to start a special school. And once it's there, with state laws and all, that will protect the land - so nobody else can build on it.

"That sounds great," Tom said. "Hey, are you about ready to go out to lunch? How about in about five or ten minutes?"

"I have a few things to do first. I'll meet you at the diner," Laura said.

"Okay, no problem. We'll see you there."

Tom and I got back into the truck. I took one last look back at the building with the big antenna, thinking it looked a little like a UFO which had set down in a field to broadcast to some far-off planet. Then we were back out on the road.

It wasn't my idea to stop for gas at the Amoco station. The gas station was a shabby, paintless affair. A skinny teenager with a shaved head stepped out of the garage toward us. "Ten dollars regular," Tom said. The skinny kid nodded, circled the car and opened the latch for the gas tank. From the garage, two men stared out at us. I knew that I had seen them before. The unshaven, oily looking one was smoking a cigarette I thought could ignite on his greasy clothes at any moment. The short bald one, with great effort, was lifting his foot up onto a bench. They nodded to each other and then got into a dented pea-green Chevy that followed us to the diner. They entered the diner behind us and took a booth in the back at about the same time that Laura pulled up in her dad's station wagon outside. I saw them look out the window at her. Again, they nodded. I sensed trouble. A rouge faced woman was eating scrambled eggs in the booth across from me. A man sat in the next booth: his hat set down on the table beside him. He was reading a newspaper and I could not see his face.

Well, we were not about to stay in that diner with those two skinheads staring us down. So, as Laura entered, Tom and I stood up and began to walk toward the door. Behind us the swarthy one with the ugly face rose from his seat and started after us. I think I saw him crash into the B section of the newspaper. It ripped and sailed across the aisle. Then he fell and went down to the floor.

"Hey," he said, looking up angrily at the man with the newspaper. "Hey, watch your foot!"

The man with the newspaper turned toward him, his face still not visible to us.

"Excuse me. I didn't see you," the man said.

"Yeah? Well, maybe you need a new pair of glasses. Or a new face," the fat one said.

"Hey, why don't you leave the guy alone?" I said to him. "You got a problem with people having their lunch?"

"I got a problem with you," he said. "You want to have a problem?"

"Nobody had a problem here until you started one," I said.

Hearing this, a small mustached man hurried forward across the diner.

"No, no, no. There will be no hostilities in my diner. Or I will call the police," he said.

The skinheads growled.

By this time, we had met Laura at the door. We could see them glaring out the windows at us as we hurried her back to the station wagon and got into Tom's truck and drove away. But soon we saw a silver pickup truck behind us.

It remained behind us until we got to the road that led to the gate of the farm. Again, someone wanted to let us know that they had been watching.

They have been watching us ever since, across the years, across the miles. These people who watch and wait have followed me to the arctic north and back across the ocean to the wet and fertile promise of springtime in the city. Ali has always kept the doors locked. It's not like I am writing letters to newspapers about neo-Nazi groups anymore. I'm writing other things these days. I am editing the alchemist's memoirs, so people will know his story.

Yet, the watchers have a long memory. They wish to protect the brave new world of their investments. Few want associations of Nazi racial experiments hanging over their initiatives. Only the most radical among them seek to sell the idea of a master race. Yet, those who watch out for Schneider's interests remember the alchemist and the story he tried to tell. They have always looked for his notebooks and for the gold they think that he once hid with the records of the Norwegian lebensborn. They have, for the past decade, ransacked the farm where he once lived and have sought access to his bank accounts. They could follow their obsessions to our doorstep at any time.

Ali locks the door with a double lock. We lock up everything, except the cat. The alchemist's notebooks are hidden away in a secret place. Recently, Ali's father hired someone from a security firm; he keeps a detective named Brad Thorne on retainer. Best of all, our friend Ned Roland's team keeps an eye on the place. I think Schneider's people know that, so they leave us alone. But you know what they say. You can think you have it all together and all of a sudden everything can change. You just never know.

I can see Ezra still. We stand together. The clouds above us are thin and gray, like smoke. A chill wind flaps the cloak on his shoulders. He looks across the wall to the cemetery where his wife is buried, in the valley below Red Cat Farm. Something has called him back to this place, back to this farm where he has spent twenty-five years of his life. Ezra lifts his bag of groceries. He looks again at the Nazi emblem on the wall and he rises now like a ghost from beside the cemetery wall.

10.

The next day the man who had been behind the newspaper at the diner entered into our lives. I remember first hearing his voice on that cloudy October afternoon. The phone was ringing in the farmhouse, and I hurried to pick it up.

"Jake Kincaid?"

"That's me."

"This is Professor Ned Roland. I'm a fellow with the Goethe-Schiller Institute. I saw your comments in the paper."

"So?"

"We need to talk."

"What about?"

"Your German friend. I'm not sure how to say this discreetly. There is much that shouldn't be said on the phone. May I meet you?"

"I guess so. Sure."

"Shall I visit you – at the farm?"

"You want to come to the farm? Sure, that would be fine."

"We should meet as soon as possible. Is later today at four o'clock all right?"

"That would be good. What can I do for you, Professor Roland?"

"Perhaps it is something you can do for many people, Jake. And do be careful. These people are dangerous, Jake. You are, shall I say, in the midst of something. I will see you at four o'clock."

A tall, thin man, with wire rim glasses, appeared in the driveway in front of the farmhouse at four. Tom and I invited Ned Roland inside where a fire was crackling low in the fireplace. Laura set out some cheese and crackers and Tom poured some red wine for our guest.

"This Ezra you speak of is Jonas Albrecht von Klaus, a scion of German nobility with a somewhat checkered past," Ned Roland told us. "As you have said, he is a scientist. But he is one with a – shall we say, peculiar science."

"We know," Tom said. "He claims to be an alchemist."

"Yes, but that is not all," Ned Roland said, and he took a sip of red wine.

"So, Dr. Roland, I suppose you are going to let us know what is going on?"

"Well, Tom. I think you and Jake already know some of it. Don't you?"

"You're here because of Ezra."

"Yes. Jonas Albrecht von Klaus. Ezra, as you call him. Clearly, he is not so dead as he has claimed to be. But there is more. I read your letter in the newspaper, Jake. It was quite interesting."

"It was what I think."

"What you think may have been made a little too public. You speak of a neo-Nazi organization here in this region. Are you aware that they have been following you?"

"I've been followed. Yes."

"How did you know of this organization? Did Jonas… your friend, Ezra, tell you of it?"

"No. He didn't say anything about it. They followed us, so we followed them."

"You followed them?" Professor Roland said. His blue eyes looked intensely at me. He took another sip of wine and a bite of cheese and then brushed his lips with a napkin. "Then there is someone I must tell you about. You are both in grave danger. Has Jonas made any mention of a man named Schneider?"

There was that name again. I nodded.

"He mentioned him."

"Then you know who he is?"

"He called Schneider a devil. That's all."

"A devil. Jonas is accurate there. Personally, I'd say Schneider is the devil himself. The reason I am here, is that I work on behalf of some people who would very much like to see an end to Schneider. It is our hope that the two of you can lead us to him."

"But we don't know where he is."

"You have followed him. He has followed you. We think that that little bit of cat and mouse will continue."

"Professor Roland, what kind of professor are you anyway?" Tom asked.

"I teach history and political science at the university," he said. "My studies support the fact that Schneider and his son are a menace. They must be found and brought to justice."

"And you want us to do it?"

"I want you to lead us to them, yes. It is dangerous. But they will not suspect a couple of house painters."

"And if they do?"

"Then they might try to kill you. But we will assure your protection."

Tom and I looked at each other. I felt a shiver go up and down my spine.

"And how will you do that?" I asked.

"Trust me," he said. He removed some papers from his valise and looked at them, before continuing.

"You might as well know the facts," he said. "The authorities have been seeking Jonas. They lost track of him long ago. He hid himself quite well. Jonas arrived in this country with his wife under his alias, that is, as Ezra Foote. We have no clear record of any contrary activity here. But let's just say that he is sought. Now Schneider – that's another story. You have, I suppose heard of Schneider."

"Ezra has spoken of him."

"Schneider is notorious. For years he was able to live a relatively normal life as a professor in Germany. His son has made much political gain out of his father's recently discovered reputation. The younger Schneider, Gerhard, is an elected member of the Bundestag – an ultra-conservative member, an unapologetically fascist member. He speaks of a new Europe of conservatism. This he clothes in heroic names like Frederick the Great and Bismark. But it is Hitler he emulates. It is the same old monster in a new century's clothes."

"Professor Roland, are you telling us that we are dealing here with Nazis?"

There was intensity in Roland's eyes as they met mine. He nodded.

"Let's say it is a part of a legacy: an underground strain of Naziism that has not quite faded," he said. "Apparently some correspondence has developed between the neo-Nazi movement and what we might call the old guard. Gerhard Schneider has been raised from birth by his father for a cause dreamed up a half a century ago. He holds out the fantasy of a golden age. It is a warped dream of a new Aryan state. He has followers. Some of them, we think, are here nearby. They have started a number of cells in the United States. What their purpose is here we cannot be sure. But we believe that their vision is one of global proportions."

"But why would they come here to some little farm?" Laura asked.

"They are here because of Jonas. In Europe, Schneider is the political far right wing's great young hope. What is he doing here? Why is he concerned with you? It has to do with your new friend. Jonas was once an associate of his father."

"Do you mean…? Is Jonas a Nazi?" I asked.

"It appears that Jonas may have been a resister. Our concern, however, is primarily with Schneider. He has a dream, Hans Schneider. It is, unfortunately, a dream that he shares with others. It is a dream of genetically rebuilding the master race, a pure race, from what they call the List. The future they propose would be built out of the bones and the matter of the dead - if they could do it."

"But that's unbelievable!"

"Fanciful it may be. But myths have power, Jake. Now, most of this is pure speculation and sheer rumor. But we believe that Schneider is up to something. It has something to do with biological experiments and genetic charts and test tubes."

Roland took a long sip of wine. His eyes scanned the room again and, for a moment, he seemed lost in thought.

"We think that Gerhard Schneider is attempting to set up financing for a rather large business enterprise," he said. "He is luring some investors with this myth. He would have his supporters believe that these test tubes might hold the semen of selected Wehrmacht and SS officers. You see, it is a bit like the dream the Nazis once had. They dreamed that they would live again in the children born in the cold northern winters of Scandinavia."

"That's so unbelievable. Is it possible?"

"There once was such a project: the lebensborn. It involved the mating of Nazi officers and women who were believed to have Nordic traits. The Schneiders foster a myth which is a variation on the lebensborn."

"What does that mean? Lebensborn?" Laura asked.

"It means new life. Look here," he said, tapping the newspaper opened on the table. "You have seen the recent news accounts on television and in the newspaper. Several members of the Aryan League in America, we think, are right here nearby. They have started a number of cells in the United States. The recent anti-Semitic activity in this area – the defamation of the cemetery, for example – leads us to believe that they are here. What their purpose is here we cannot be certain. I have arranged for a guest lecture at the local college, as an excuse to, shall we say, drop by. Schneider, I believe, will be at my lecture tonight. So will you, I hope."

"Professor Roland, why are you telling us this?"

"It is because we have a proposal for you. We want you to lead us to Schneider. In return, we will promise your safety. And we will promise your friend Jonas amnesty. Tonight, I will be lecturing at the college on the reception of Nietzsche in the former East Germany. It seems like a harmless academic topic. But, as I've said, we expect Gerhard Schneider to be there. I'd like you to wait outside the lecture hall and get a photograph of him as he is leaving."

"I could do that," I said.

"Good," he said, as he rose to his feet. "And don't let him see you, Jake. I'd like to meet with both of you again tomorrow. I will see you then."

He picked up his hat and left us bewildered. Like bugs in a spider web, we were caught. We had stepped into a nightmare.

11.

I became his friend, going to visit him at his house, a mile up the road from the farm. His rooms were furnished simply and seemed to be filled with the past. In each room were grainy photographs of a blond-haired woman with a beautiful face and soft, deep-set eyes. Her picture reminded me of the woman in the painting I'd seen at the Red Cat Farm.

In his basement laboratory, the alchemist leaned forward over a blue flame. In front of him stood a silver chalice and a vase, the aludel in which the work was completed. It was of thick Lorraine glass, oval in shape, and it held about four ounces of distilled water. Its neck rose up some eight inches and the boiler beneath it was his furnace. On his table were talismans: rings, jewels, engraved stones, images of gardens, gems, and crystals. On the shelf beside him stood the sigillate earthenware used in medicine. There were little tablets of earthenware impressed with silver and golden seals.

"What is all of this?" I asked him.

"These are the tools of the alchemist," he said. "These are the materials for the great work in which we participate. Look here."

He lifted the cover of an old book. The binding cracked as he opened it.

"These are formulas that will show us how to proceed," he said. "You see here the four elements: earth, air, fire, and water. Each of them is designated by a triangle."

He took one of his notebooks from the shelf and began to draw an illustration on one of its pages.

"We draw a triangle upright and place a line here for air. We invert it and place a line here for earth. The triangle is fire. Water is represented by an inverted triangle."

"They look like pyramids," I said.

"Yes. These are ancient symbols."

The diagrams looked strange to me. There were charts and columns of numbers. His memories seemed to be of another world, one of magic in far off places and times. Quicksilver, his cat, bounded down the stairs, circled his feet, and then sat looking up at us.

"So, this place is like a laboratory?" I asked.

"Yes," he said. "These shelves of glass and these instruments have been my companions from the time when I was young. Look closely and you will see the possibilities of combining the elements into new properties."

He stirred the solution in the glass. It frothed up, like when you shake up soda too much.

"This alchemy interested me a great deal when I was young," he said. "You will go to the university," my father told me. I remember the sweet smell of his pipe filling the air. "Your teachers say you will go far," he would say. His voice comes back to me. I see his round, cheeky face, the smoke clouding his glasses. He was an officer in the First World War. Yet, my memories of him dissolve like this tablet in this solution. He fades into a blur amid so many memories."

Ezra dropped the tablet into the dish in front of him. It fizzled like a bit of Alka-Seltzer and then was gone.

"I will tell you how I was led to alchemy, Jacob. It was during the summer of my first year at the university that I first heard the name of Paracelsus."

"Who was that?"

"Professor Gruden at the university described him as a Swiss scientist, a brilliant man. He told me that Paracelsus was looking for the deepest secret of the universe, the one substance of which the whole world is made. It was called the philosopher's stone."

"A stone? Is it like a jewel or something?" I asked. "Is it magical?"

"Paracelsus was a curious fellow," he said. "He worked as a chemist in the mining districts of the Tyrol and in Sweden. Then he wandered across Europe in search of the mysteries of the science of healing. He served as a surgeon in the armies of great kings. He mingled with gypsies and conjurers, astrologers and grave robbers and alchemists."

"He was an alchemist?"

"Yes. Indeed, he was. Alchemists like Paracelsus lived in a time before modern chemistry. They had the peculiar dream of finding out the secret of life and turning common metals into gold!"

"A magician," I said.

"Yes, he was magical in a way, Jacob. Like a curious scientist."

"It doesn't sound a lot like science."

"Paracelsus was a strange combination of modern researcher and ancient seer. He prepared salts from metals. He made medicines. Paracelsus sought chemical compounds to strengthen the body's vital forces to combat parasitic germs. And this was 350 years before our germ theory of disease!"

Quicksilver purred. He leaped to the window ledge and huddled there, watching us.

"Paracelsus, to me, was the model scientist," Ezra said. "I was not yet twenty when Hitler marched across the German border and claimed Austria for Germany. You have heard of that time, Jacob?"

"We read about it in history class in high school."

"It was the strange time of my youth. The army marched into Poland with tanks. The students cheered wildly. I watched as our teacher, Mr. Gruden, paced up and down nervously, a pipe jammed between his teeth. He said that a new era had broken upon the world."

"A war broke upon the world," I said.

"Yes. It was a war that no one could hide from. I was immediately drawn into it."

He paused for a moment, as if something had triggered a memory for him.

"You may think it strange, Jacob, but many years ago I discovered alchemy," he said. "Today our dream is to create gold quickly. But that was never alchemy's sole purpose."

"But I thought alchemy was a search for a way to make gold," I said.

"Oh, no, no," he shook his head. "Not merely to make it. The means to analyze ore for gold was discovered long ago in ancient Mesopotamia and Egypt. Can you imagine how ancient alchemy is?"

"You mean, it goes back to when they built the pyramids?"

He nodded.

"It does. To change matter was the aim of Alexandrian alchemy. But it was not real gold that those alchemists were talking about. They wished to shape the material world to change themselves. Let me show you."

He blew a few rings of smoke from his pipe toward the ceiling. Then he leaned forward, turning the glass objects on his desk with his fingers. He dropped another tablet into the jar. Another Alka-Seltzer- it fizzled and dissolved, turning blue.

"We often treat the world as so many objects," he said. "We measure and we analyze as if all things exist for our manipulation and our use. Yet, what matters is our relationship with them."

"So how did you become an alchemist?" I asked him.

"It is strange to recall," he said. "As a young man I was concerned with healing. I wished to be a doctor and a natural healer as well. When I was young, more than half the people in Germany followed some idea of natural medicine. I sought to include this training in my medical education."

"You were a doctor?"

"Yes," he said. "I was trained as a physician and as a research scientist. Yet, Jacob, I had long been interested in other things. And so, with my father's permission, I visited the Hess Hospital in Dresden and then the Bosch Homeopathic Hospital near Stuttgart. The New German Science of Healing had opened some new centers for this training. Of course, father insisted upon the more traditional role of a doctor. "You must stay at the university!" he said."

"That sounds like my father," I said. "He says, 'Why are you painting houses, Jake? You're going to school to make movies? Jake, how about doing something practical?'"

"Yes, when we are young, we have many dreams. That seems so long ago."

He held the vase, gazing into it as if it was a crystal ball.

"When I was young, Jacob, the figure of Paracelsus began to appear again in medical texts," he said. "His name meant 'like Celsus,' the Roman doctor. I remember that I wished to be like Paracelsus. Paracelsus, everyone said, was natural, earthbound, close to the people. To me, he sounded heroic. Paracelsus did not focus only on the organs of the body; he believed in the whole person. People were beginning to say that Paracelsus von Hohenheim was the true embodiment of German science."

"It sounds like you read a lot about him."

"Oh, I read about him enthusiastically. I hung on every word. I wished to be like Paracelsus and practice natural medicine. I would find a way to heal people."

"Of course," I said. "You were a doctor."

"Yes. And like the great Paracelsus, I believed in the mysteries that lay in the human heart. Yes, I too would be an alchemist."

"But you did become an alchemist."

"Yes. That is the wonder of it, Jacob. To be an alchemist is to have dreams. Often, they are frightening dreams. But they are dreams which come true. To be an alchemist is to know the reality of coincidences and to be able to sense things. Like Elise. I know she is here with me, Jacob. There are days when I can sense her presence here."

"I feel like she is here," I said. "Her picture is everywhere."

"She is everywhere in my heart and in my memories," he said. "Yet, there is more here than her picture. Her spirit is here too."

"That all sounds mysterious," I said.

"It does" he said. "Such things are not easy to speak of. But I do know this. Only love sustains us, Jacob. When we are old men, our lives wind down. With age, all things wind down. But love is timeless."

I was not always sure what he meant when he spoke like this. He seemed to drift away like the smoke from his pipe, into reveries.

"The philosopher's stone cures every all malady," he said. "In the Middle Ages, they claimed that in one day it could cure an illness that would otherwise last a month! That is the healing I sought, Jacob. Elise and I were so happy when we were young. I wished our youth to come back."

I could see his meaning then. As he looked at me across the work of many years, we were a reminder of that youth: Laura, Tom, and I.

"Once Germany was gone, once our youth was gone, I submerged in the depths of my laboratory," he said.

"Ezra, I'm not sure I understand," I said.

"Time is always upon us, Jacob, the ravages of Time. How desperately I wished for a cure for Elise, my wife. How I sought a remedy for the ailments of our age: a fountain of eternal youth! But an elixir was not to be found. I could not save her, Jacob. I could not save her."

He stared ahead into space and silence hung between us.

"But you will remember her always," I said, finally.

He nodded.

"All these years I have remained an alchemist," he said. "Perhaps, I am the last of them."

"Ezra, what does an alchemist do?"

"An alchemist wishes to understand life, Jacob," he said, looking up into the glass in his hand. "Alchemy is a child of the Middle Ages. It is an ancient practice which arose long before science and chemistry."

"So, it goes back a long time. Is it still practiced today?"

"It is seldom practiced today," he said. "To practice alchemy today seems thoroughly strange to the modern mind. The alchemist seeks what is called the opus, the primal material of life. It is the fundamental substance which lies beneath all things."

As he moved his hands, he looked like a gray-haired wizard tossing silver dust into the air.

"Ah," he said. "What is this? Is it gold or blood? Or is it quicksilver?"

The cat stirred. His ears perked up at the sound of his name.

"The alchemist seeks through the minerals of the earth," Ezra said. "He seeks through the fire for a treasure that is hard to attain. The ancient writings say that the alchemist must suffer. He is like the metal which is scorched and shaped in the furnace. He is the master of fire. But he wishes not to find gold so much as to become it. You see, Jacob, he must enter the struggle. It is like a mirror, like a reflection: the experiment reflects the one who experiments. The alchemist takes up the material world and attempts to perfect the work of nature."

He handed me the glass. I took it in my hands and held it up to the light. It sparkled like a gem. I set it down beside the strange book on the table. Its pages were open. There was on the page a crescent half moon for silver, a circle with a dot in its center for gold. Z with another sharp set of lines through it represented lead.

"What does it mean?" I asked.

"These are the symbols of alchemy," Ezra said. "I have kept these notebooks for some time."

The book, which he now placed in my hands, was illuminated with strange figures. There were odd drawings of animals. I saw swirling clouds of lights and men with wings. Looking up, I saw rows of beakers, shelves heavy with books and scientific instruments. The dusty old book he had chosen from his shelf and set before me was one on alchemy. I turned the pages of the old book, looking at its strange figures. I must admit, I didn't understand any of it.

"Leaving the home of my youth, a nation torn by war, I came to live on the Red Cat Farm," Ezra said. "I like to think that was Quicksilver's ancestor- the red cat. When I came to the farm, it was to put my past behind me. I went underground into my laboratory, immersed in my work, like the primordial maker with my minerals and metals and tools."

"But Ezra, you can't have just vanished from the world. No one can do that."

"No. Not until one dies," he said. He turned to lift the picture of his wife and looked for a long while at it. "We were happy, Jacob. That you must know. Elise was ill. The dream was to make an elixir that would prolong life."

He smiled forlornly and set the picture down.

"To do this work alchemists throughout the ages have searched for the vital force behind life itself," he said. "We have sought perfection. We have believed all of matter to be alive. For the alchemist believes that all things have within them the divine spark."

He lit the burner before him and it sparked brightly, as if suddenly coming alive.

"Look at the flame, Jacob," he said. "And Jacob, remember this. The work must be guided by wisdom. Humans are just the conscious tip of the process. We ourselves are the flame. If we could isolate it, if we could purify it, if we could change it, we could speed up the process. We could bring about a change, a transformation."

"Science can change things."

"Science is a magnificent thing," he said. "It is about discovery. The fire chilled to air. The air becoming a great wine. It is like love, Jacob. It is like being hypnotized."

He told me more about Elise. They had met in winter at the hospital in Norway. They had escaped to America to the farm. He needed someone who would listen- and so I did. What I heard was a story as puzzling and troubling as any alchemy.

"I could not save her," he said. "All I could do was to wish her that last farewell. And so then I decided I must hide. I must hide in a new place, not far from the farm. By a will I left with my lawyer, the farm passed to the charity of the sisters."

"But why have you come back to the farm now?"

"I have heard that a man has come to claim my farm, to steal it and sell it to the developers. He will not. The farm must continue in its charitable purposes! That would be Elise's wish. That is why I need you, my friends, to help us to keep the farm."

He reached down to pet Quicksilver's and stroked the cat's back. When he turned back to me, his face was deeply serious.

"You must watch out for Schneider, Jacob," he said. "Hans Schneider again is up to no good. He knows that I am here and now he has come. He has seen that Jonas von Klaus is indeed not dead and buried in the cemetery below the Red Cat Farm. But now he will see something else. He will see me rising like a ghost from this farm. He will see us telling the world of his mad and vain dream that he has passed along to his son and we shall put an end to it."

I was startled by this. Who was this man Schneider? Who was his son? Ezra would tell me no more. Beware of him, was all he would say. Beware of Schneider.

When I left him, sometime later, he seemed lost in his recollections. Back to the farm I went. Back to Tom and Laura and to the farmhouse, where I soon would learn about this man named Schneider and the strange legacy he had bequeathed to his son.

12.

THE ALCHEMIST'S NOTEBOOK

At the end of the year 1940, I arrived in occupied Norway. Early that year, plans had been made to attack Norway and Denmark. The mission was called Weserubung. Norway was a strategic northern position from which Britain could plan a strike on Berlin. Germany, in turn, could, from Norway, initiate an attack by the Kriegsmarine, its navy, and the Luftwaffe, its air force, in a siege of Great Britain. Plans were made to secure Norway for Germany because iron ore could not be transported by sea across the winter ice. Modern warfare is made with steel and about half of Germany's iron ore supply came from Sweden, in the Gulf of Bothnia. However, Lulea, the region of iron ore, froze over in the winter. So, the ore had to be transported via Norway, to Narvik in the north and down the western coast of Norway. German ships regularly sailed this sea corridor between the offshore islands and the West coast. It became necessary to include Norway in Germany's military strategy.

Weserubung, we knew, would launch a formidable arctic war. We believed that this military operation could not be concealed. The British fleet was lodged in the North Sea near Narvik. It was believed that the British intended to mine the leads nearby which gave access to the sea. Our military was determined to counter any British intervention. And so our strike on Norway was well-prepared. The presence of soldiers on board freighters docked in Norway's harbors was concealed. The Abwehr, our spy organization, sent one of our experts on Russia to evaluate Norway's military fortifications. A journalist, Hans Wilhelm Scheart, a correspondent for the Volkischer Beobachter, provided information of attack targets. The army readied itself to try out the new paratroops and the airborne division.

I have heard that a British agent once called Norway "a playground for deception." It is a place of beauty and isolation, a land of mountains and narrow valleys along the fjords. For a soldier it is a place of deprivation, with acres of snow and glowing sunshine. One could stare at the land for many minutes and see only barrenness. In this place, communications were often poor and deception was perpetrated by radio operators sending false communications. Soldiers in uniforms of white blended in with the snow.

The peril in Norway began on April 9. From the north our army came like a furious wind. From the south they came also and the elements themselves entered the whirlwind: earth, water, air and land. Norway became fire and ice, the primal elements of the world. Swiftly, the German army secured Oslo and landed at Kristiansund, Trondheim, and Bergen.

After the invasion of Norway, I lived near Trondheim, a city which was once called Nidaros in the Middle Ages. It is a port on the western coast. When the German army descended upon Norway, Trondheim was the key to taking Norway's coastline. Its forts were occupied quickly. The German infantry came ashore protected by the powerful guns of the warship Admiral Hipper. They set their boots on the wet cobbles of the harbor walkways. The Norwegian ship the Glowworm was sunk at sea. Trondheim surrendered without fighting and Colonel Weiss secured the city.

Trondheim is the city of St. Olav, Norway's patron saint. Historically, it has been the site of many pilgrimages. Indeed, while I was there, even then I was much like a pilgrim in exile from my country. I first lived in a small house on the wharf of the Nidelva River which, much frozen in winter, runs through Trondheim. My work brought me later to a medical facility near the railway that crosses the south of the city. It was from this hospital that I later commuted up the mountain to the mother home.

The hospital in Trondheim where I worked was no luxury hotel, but there I met the most precious of luxuries. Elise Hoffmann's smile came my way as we passed in the hallway. It was not long after the emergency surgery that removed my appendix. On the first day after the operation, I walked to the hallway and paused in the evening light that shined through the windows. It was the week I had lost something unnecessary and gained someone who would be necessary for the rest of my life.

"Hello," she said, and our eyes met again. Hers were soft green eyes that I never wished to leave. Did I know her from somewhere? It was as if I had always known her.

"I am Elise Hoffmann," she said. "You knew my brother Friedrich."

"Friedrich." The name did not register in my mind at first. "Friedrich, and how is he?"

It was the wrong question to ask. Friedrich Hoffmann had died in battle the year before. There were no tears from her. She said it with a matter-of-fact tone: "He was killed in the war."

"I am sorry," I said. "It is a brutal war. We have lost many good men." I recall that I rubbed my side, as if I were nursing a shrapnel wound. "It would be good to get away from this stifling place," I said.

"I do think you must stay here, Jonas," she said. "But I will be coming to visit you. I am your nurse."

I took my hand from my side. She knew about the appendix, of course.

"I am a prisoner of war then and you are one of my captors. Take me to my room."

I still recall the touch of her hand, the light perfume on her skin, as she led me down the hallway back to my room. There love began, amid the medicine and needles. Those who had been wounded far away sometimes arrived. We wanted desperately to go out, to leave this place of antiseptic and medicinal rooms. I wished to laugh again, to take her into my arms, to go away with her, far away from stark rooms and this place that smelled of war. We yearned for space for our love. I wanted to sweep her off her feet, away from this place of blood and the sick and the wounded. One grows uneasy with kissing in hospital corridors, fumbling in prep rooms and wards. We wanted to be alone together, somewhere apart from this.

It was Elise who made the great change in my life. As soon as we could escape the confining hallways, we would be together in the city. There was floodlight on the bridge. There were shadows on the river. Those were romantic days. Elise would laugh her long, whispery laugh into the quiet of the upstairs room. Together we would laugh and love. The shadows from the branches of an elm tree spread across the drapes and the shutters tapped softly in the wind.

Elise was sent to work in the newly occupied city of Trondheim in the Summer of 1940. Her mother, Ingrid, once dreamed of being an actress. Ingrid was a tall, thin woman, with enchanting green eyes. People said that Elise looked like her mother. Ingrid was a domestic worker who dreamed of romance. She knew she would not be glamorous; she knew she had been a clumsy, awkward girl exercising her small possibilities. Yet, her good looks might carry her. The new century brought her to the city of Berlin. A homesick chorus girl in Berlin for a time, she was determined to find her way, to stay on a daily schedule as a typist, ever dreaming she might be an actress. She had absorbed a glamorous ideal from magazines and films. It was, of course, a kind of pose- the lipstick, the eyeshadow, the high, nervous laughter- presenting herself as more sophisticated and glamorous than she, in fact, was. Her language betrayed her. She was wordy and pretentious; she misused words, thinking they sounded sophisticated. Then Georg came visiting the cabaret one night. He was one of the dashing young men who were wearing their uniforms, and soon life was motherhood and Ingrid lived in fear of disappointing him. It was a great responsibility, a destiny to be a mother. Ingrid became his private sanctuary. The glittering leaves and music became hushed. Motherhood now was her stage, and she was Eve and Aphrodite, the strength and guardian of child and home.

Elise's father was a deeply injured casualty of the first war. Georg had been a corporal in a unit of field engineers. He was now partially deaf, his eardrums shattered in an explosion in a small village in the Alsace-Lorraine. Elise, as a child, would reach for him and he would lift her up high in his arms against his rough shirt. His clothing smelled of cigar smoke and Gabriele, Elise's sister, would pinch her nose and wiggle in her dance in the room where he sat reading the newspaper. He would watch Gabriele and Elise dance, but he could not hear the music.

The girls, like their mother, early showed signs of a gift for dance. Like their mother, they daydreamed of romance and they liked to dress up and play princess. They were proud of their father. Yet, Georg grew sullen, more distant with the years, fading into the clouds of his memories and resentments. When he complained about his job, about the dinner, or about the Nazis, Ingrid endured. When he drifted, liquor ridden, into his solemn solitudes, she found within herself a reserve of hope. She became a figure of security and love. For the home had filled with the sounds of little girl laughter. Elise and her sister Gabriele were like small roses blooming and it was their grace to have a mother of such strength and beauty.

A young, unmarried German woman did not have many options for employment. She could become an office worker, or a field hand, or, when war broke, she could be a signal operator. To become a nurse was perhaps the most glamorous option. Elise was a member of the Red Cross: the Frontsosters of the Deutsches Rots Kreuz (DRK). Such nurses, helferin, were required to remain fifteen kilometers behind any battle lines. Yet, they were not ever safe. Many of those who served in Norway were sent to the Eastern front of the war. They had no politics. They only sought to heal the sick. Operation Barbarossa in 1941 brought the wounded across the border into Norway. It also brought the nurses to Finland. Elise was called one day on a relief mission to the Finnish border. To see her go saddened me but what I soon learned upset me more.

I stared out the window across the snow. The reports from the Finnish frontier were not good. There had been an ambush, an act of the underground. On a mountain pass they'd intercepted a transport convoy. Nearly a dozen Red Cross nurses were caught in the crossfire. For all that afternoon I waited for answers.

My boots deep in the snow, I walked to the shed where I kept the radio. The sunlight made a harsh mirror of the snow. I unlocked the shed and thrust the door open. I noticed that my hands were trembling as I attached the wires. "Tell me, tell me," I was saying. Nothing in the cold air answered me.

The nurses had been on a mission of mercy to bring food and medical supplies to a village on the edge of Finland. For safety, they had been joined to the military transport. But the enemy believed that the shipment contained armaments and it had become a target. A voice speaking through the crackling of the radio brought the news. The resisters had surprised the transport, but the mission was not thwarted. The nurses were not injured. Terrified, perhaps, but not injured.

Two weeks later, a truck rolled into the city carrying three of the nurses. One of them, Elise, standing in the lobby of the hospital, was like a vision to me. We looked at each other for a moment. Then we hurried to each other. Suddenly, she was there before me. I took her into my arms.

"Elise, you've come back. I was worried that I would never see you again."

"I'm not going again to Finland, or home to Germany," she said. "I have been reassigned."

She looked for a long time at me. Her eyes began to fill with tears.

"Jonas, I didn't want to lose you. They were going to send me on. I thought I'd be in Germany again, that I'd be home. What is home any more, Jonas? You're my home."

"And you are mine," I said.

"I knew I would be coming back," she said. "It was already decided. But I had to go to Finland first. The people needed us."

"But you've been able to come back."

"Three of us have. We are needed here."

"Well, you are needed here – by me."

A long, searching look came to her eyes. Then she nodded. She hugged me again, then she stepped back, holding my hands.

"I've made a deal, Jonas."

"A deal?"

"With the devil," she said.

"I don't understand."

"I did it for you," she said. "I've joined the nursing corps of the Waffen SS. I am to be nurse and midwife to the lebensborn."

I gazed at her for a moment, taking that news in.

"Then I will join you," I said.

Elise became a Waffen SS nurse. On the left arm of her uniform was an eagle above the flag of Norway. She remained a Waffen SS nurse, although she could never accept SS policies of euthanasia. She became a nurse with the lebensborn program. Already assigned to obstetrics, I often joined her in delivering the lebensborn children. They were the children of German officers of the SS, the SA, and the Wehrmacht, who were introduced to Norwegian women.

The children were born in a chateau on the hill above the forest: the mother home. Its windows reflected the sun like open eyes. Beyond its antiseptic lobby, its walls were green, and the rooms were filled with old clocks and well-made beds.

There was a large upstairs room where I looked out on a bay window open on the tranquil landscape. Uniformed Wehrmacht officers sat at a table on the lawn. Beyond them, under the hills, were severe structures. The room I was in had a red, white and black swastika flag on the wall. A photograph of Hitler was on a table. A clock ticked loudly from the wall.

This is where the women and the officers would meet. It was where they would entertain. The couples circled the room to the music of Strauss. A romance might begin at a dance in the community room before a broad, sparkling fireplace. One officer was mixing the drinks: a tall man who looked gray with fatigue. He was drinking with a blonde-haired man. I was introduced to him and learned he was Rolf Heimerling, an associate of Hans Schneider. He had recently been named administrator of the mother house. Upon the mention of my name, he merely nodded. He pointed a bony finger, his face in a cloud, brow contracted into a fierce grimace. He and the blond man had toured the factories. The blond man had ice-blue eyes, a downturned mouth. There was a puffy glare to his eyes. He wore a long coat of gray.

I would come to know Rolf Heimerling across the next year. He was highly organized and seemed to be a born administrator. He told me that he had toured the shipyards and the factories. He inspected them meticulously, holding a clipboard as he went. He would have lunch with the managers and the yard supervisors. Industry merited his study for civil defense, he said. Once, Krupp had offered him a town car. I thought he spent his evenings in hotels with his mistress. When I mentioned it, he cast a hideous look my way. He had a responsibility to be a husband with resources, he said. This he would obtain from the industrialists, or from health care and the lebensborn initiative. That was his version of civil defense. He was simply doing his job.

Rolf Heimerling once said that to him the invasion of Poland looked like the Goth sack of Rome. He was mostly bluster and whiskey-laughter, but he was a hard man to fool. Rolf liked monuments; he liked Bach, and women with fine figures. Architecture, he called it. He was addicted to pageants and to concentrations of force. But one day, I recall, he was in a fog. He had received a startling call. The vice-commander from air operations was coming to visit. Himmler himself was coming to visit.

I recall that on the day of inspection, the officers drove up in a two black Mercedes past rows of red SS flags. Their black boots passed down the long hallways. Then Himmler stepped forward: a short man with thinning hair and a wispy moustache. What one noticed first were the round glasses and the look of the man, as if he were stunned, wide-eyed with surprise in an ever- fixed gaze.

They did not stay long. There were some formalities: a salute, a presentation of the nurses, the shaking of hands. The cribs of newborn children were observed. The officers were shown the plush quarters, the tidy rooms for meeting and for espousal. Then Himmler and the SS departed. Upon their leaving, I relayed a message to my Abwehr contacts in Geneva and Berlin, informing them of every officer present that day. Elise and I shared what we knew of their plans. Officers of the SS would be among the first to be mated with Norwegian women. The goal was to produce children that the high command regarded as "racially pure": an Aryan race that would one day become the leaders of the Volk in the future.

So, it was in Norway that I came to assist the lebensborn. It was an experiment begun in Germany in 1935, before the war. In 1940, we developed the project in Norway. Doctors are needed everywhere, and our allegiances are not often suspect. It was an excellent cover for counterespionage. At this time, I was drawn into Ahnenerbe, which means ancestral heritage. It was known as a research society concerned with holism and Aryan history. The Ahnenerbe studied the archaeology and anthropology of Nordic lands in a search for Germanic origins. This association had led me to be posted in Norway, a land where Himmler believed people were descended from the Vikings.

However, even as I was assigned to medical matters in Trondheim, I was soon recruited by the Abwehr, General Canaris's spy organization. I had trained as an obstetrician. In that role, as an agent of the Abwehr, my duty was to observe, to track the coming and going of the officers of the SS. In the lebensborn program, our officers were mated – genetically, that is - with the native women. This would create fine Nordic children: a future master race, it was believed. Admiral Canaris and General Oster of the Abwehr wished to know of the proceedings. They always had their attention trained on the SS and SDA. I was their eyes. I saw who arrived and who went, how they met the women, how the adoptions were planned. Some of the children were later sent to Germany. Some today are known and some today do not know of their heritage. The Norwegian Registry is well hidden. You see, I myself hid it.

Like all of Europe at war, Norway knew great pain. When the invasion of Norway turned inland, the German lines of march went to Namsos, eighty miles north of Trondheim, and south to Andalsnes, 100 miles southwest of Trondheim, off the Romsdal Fjord. Andalses was a small fishing port with a single-track railway that connected it to the inland village of Dombas. There the main railroad came north from Oslo to Trondheim. That is the direction some of our army moved in, seeking to secure the railway line. Beyond this is the Lagen River, another strategic thoroughfare which runs south to the town of Trettin. The valley at Trettin becomes narrow. This is an area the British forces held in the first weeks of battle. The Luftwaffe bombed every village along the railroad. They would fly above the road that led to Andalsnes, bombing everything in sight. People ran for the shelter of walls, drainpipes, and trees to avoid the bullets that sprayed down from above them.

The battle for Narvik went on for some time after that. The British concentrated their efforts in the north. They entered West Fjord with their destroyers: the Hardy, the Hotspur, and the Hostile. The Norge and Eidwold fought at sea with two German destroyers. From the coast, our German army moved inland: a wave of gray helmets and long coats. We sought control of the roads and the railroads. We came through towns in lines on horseback. Norwegians attempted to block the roads with boulders. Snipers set up on the mountainside. But the Resistance could not hold out for long and Norway soon fell. German garrisons were established in Norway's cities.

The Norwegians did not readily believe that German military superiority had caused their defeat. A Norwegian's character is often as strong as the rich and sturdy timber of the northern countryside. Many in Norway were convinced that there had to be some Third Column of sabotage, a conspiracy of spies or traitors that had caused their defeat. Some insisted that German agents had traveled for years through Norway, taking photographs of military installations and the nation's defenses. The reality is that espionage efforts were not quite as extensive as this. There was some surveillance through a few agents immediately before Weserubung, but our sense of the country and its proud and resilient people overall was inadequate.

Scandinavia had been pulled into the war because of Germany's strategic and material needs. We heavily garrisoned Norway, with as many as nine to twelve divisions or more of its army and navy. Yet, Germany was never able to absorb this stubborn, supposedly 'kindred' people. The Norwegians resisted all attempts to Nazify their society. Germany set up in Norway a puppet leader named Quisling. Before long, Quisling's "New Order" failed. The teachers resisted. The clergy resigned. Quisling, the traitor, was embarrassed by storms of protest. You can see him in photographs: a puppet in a jacket and necktie, broad chin, thin hair parted on the right.

The German military campaign in Norway did not go smoothly. The Norwegians are a strong and sturdy people and many fighters continued to resist. The Milorg was the official resistance. It was controlled by the military, commanded by General Ruge, who remained responsible to the king and his ministers in exile in London. I know this because I was assigned to watch the Milorg carefully, as well as to observe the activities of our own SS and SD. The tactics of the Special Operations Executive included sabotage, assassination, and strikes. The Milorg was not always in agreement with SOE on acts of sabotage. Direct attacks meant reprisals and counterattacks on innocent people. So, the Milorg was cautious. They were likewise cautious with me.

I settled into a cabin with Elise during the first snowfalls of winter 1942. Still assigned to the hospital and to the mother home, I remained on call for any necessary mission. It was while shoveling the snow in front of the cabin that the idea came to me. A thick snow had fallen, and it lay heavily across the ground and on the rooftops. It clung to the trees and the hedges as it had on that week-long retreat in the woodlands long ago. As I shoveled, the sun broke free from the clouds and cast its beams on the hill before me. There I looked up to see two thin lines in the snow. Close together they curved down the slope- thin blades on the ice, the imprints of a sleigh. It was a child's sleigh. The lines were so close together in the impression they made upon the snow. It gave me my idea. I had a pair of skis and could ski down the slope with the lebensborn records concealed in my jacket. Purely recreational is how it would appear. Then I would bury the documents under the rocks at the foot of the hill.

By day Elise and I waited at the window to watch for the children. Soon we saw them at play, their merry faces hidden by scarves and caps. There were two boys and a girl. We looked into their faces, as the scarves came down. Then I saw something was wrong. The youngest of them could hardly stand. The girl and the boy lifted the youngest boy onto the sled. Down they went, merrily down the hill.

I went out on my skis to meet them. The little boy was laughing. He turned his face toward me. Then I saw his features. He spoke to me, burbled something I did not understand, and then he laughed again. I waved to them and continued down the hill. Poor child. Had he been born in the Nazi state, he would no longer be. I would not see him on a snow-covered hill. No more would he sled down the slope with his brother and sister laughing. No. To an asylum he would go, to take the medicine. Then would he slip under the snow. Then would he drift helplessly down that hill forever.

Yet, it was he who gave me the idea, the little imperfect child and his brother and sister in the snow. It was as if some grace had come to tap me upon the shoulder. So I left them there, the secrets, records of experiments perhaps no one would ever see again. I left them there like a bomb unexploded deep beneath the earth, deep beneath the snow.

Schneider, I heard, knew what I had done. I was a dead man if he found me. And I was a war criminal, perhaps, if the Allied Forces found me. All I could do was to hide. Today it is the son of Schneider, Gerhard, who carries on this legacy. No doubt he has been deluded in the belief that he is the complete Aryan, a child of destiny. He will stop at nothing to retrieve these papers, to suppress information on the lebesnborn project. Perhaps he seeks genetic samples that he mistakenly believes are still in existence. I know of no such samples. It is a mad myth to believe that Hitler and his circle left behind children, or that they left behind their sperm, the very stuff of life, to posterity. Cells and chromosomes cryogenically frozen could not last. I do not think they could live for these fifty or more years. If they exist at all. What does exist are the children of Nazi SS and wealthy industrialists: the lebensborn. They are the remnants from the eugenics program in which thousands of SS officers and "Aryan" women were carefully selected for their superior genes. They were mated under the auspices of the state. Their offspring would be donated to posterity, to the future of a superior race that would rule the world in the next millennium.

13.

The first of the alchemist's notebooks ended there. It had let me know much about him: probably more than I wanted to know. It told me about the Thule, a secret society of the Nazi elite and their mad dream of perpetuating a thousand-year Reich. The neo-Nazis had seized upon that mythology and had formed their own dangerous secret cell. To confront them was like mixing combustible elements. It was like Newton's physics: for every action there is a reaction. To expose them would bring trouble. But we had to stop them. There was no other choice.

When Ezra returned to live on the farm, I did not know that he had begun writing another volume. I had no idea then that he would leave a notebook filled with more secrets and with hidden clues to a fortune. All I knew was that Ezra Foote had at last come home to the farm. Therese had set a room for him on the second floor of the farmhouse. In the mornings the sidewalks were cold, the farm full of light, and the train snapped along the rails in the bright glare of the day. Ezra said that coming back to the farm would give him time to concentrate on ways to preserve it. But I think it also gave him company. He especially liked the special education children who had started to visit the farm. In the mornings, he would wait for them. As he stepped to the front window, he would see the children- a row of rag dolls swinging alongside their teacher on the path from the house. Their scarves, loosened by the wind, blew in the air as they turned into the passageway to the farmhouse. They rubbed their hands together to warm them.

He grew a bushy, gray mustache. He wore corduroy pants and shirts from L.L. Bean. When the children came to visit, he would sometimes put a fur cap on his head. Then he would break out his German and Swiss folk songs, singing them in a lilting voice that filled the downstairs rooms. He looked to me like an old Swiss mountain climber out of a scene from the *Sound of Music*. His voice was low, and the songs were full of sweetness, like cider and strudel, and we expected to hear a verse of *Eidelweiss* any minute. All that was missing was an accordion and Julie Andrews.

The children were spellbound. Delight shined in Marie's eyes. Shelley would look off from her private world while her hands and feet moved to the music. His voice and his song seemed to touch some secret place inside them- a gold deep in the rich veins of childhood. He did not smoke his pipe among the children, but smoke stayed on his clothes, and they learned to associate the scent with him.

He always looked for them later in the day when they would return. So, in the afternoons, after most of the painting was done, we walked with Ezra back to the farmhouse. Often, Ezra looked tired. He stepped mechanically into the house, his coat smelling of sweet tobacco from his pipe. Then he stood at the window waiting for the children to pass by.

"It is a cloudy day," he said.

He lifted his teacup. Then he put it down without taking a sip.

"I went to Elise's grave today," he said. "It was among those that were desecrated."

"Yes, I know that," I said. "The headstones are being cleaned up today."

The Greenlawn Cemetery was beyond the woods, set apart from the bicycle path that wound around Veteran's Park. As I had jogged by that morning, police cars were still patrolling by, investigating the incident. Ezra looked out in that direction and I thought I heard him sigh.

"Will Laura and the children be coming this way soon?"

"Any moment now," I said.

"That is good," he said. "They are sunlight, you know. A garden needs sunlight."

Ezra stepped to the front door and opened it to watch the children pass by. Laura had brought them to look at the farm animals - including that stubborn cow. Ezra watched from the porch and waved to them as they passed the apple orchard. Then Laura brought the little girl Amelia indoors and introduced her to Ezra.

"Hello, Mr. Foote. That is his name, Amelia. Like your foot down there. Can you say that? Hello, Mr. Foote."

"Hello, foot," Amelia giggled.

"How pretty you look today, Amelia," Ezra said.

"La, la, la," Amelia said. "La, la, la."

Then he smiled at the girl. They sat down together. She had a cookie and a cup of milk and he drank a cup of tea.

"You are a beautiful little girl," Ezra said. "Are you happy, little one?"

And Amelia would nod her head and she would smile.

Ezra liked to walk on the farm. He liked to go down the hill to the park. Whenever Ezra went out, we were never sure if he would be followed back to the farm. But we were prepared for that. Laura knew the risk. She had conducted several "fire drills" with the children.

"I will not let them threaten these children," she said.

Therese agreed. She made sure that a police patrol drove into the farm regularly. I think that Professor Roland also arranged for the farm to be carefully watched. After all, he had promised our safety as part of the bargain. Now with the alchemist staying at the farm, he wanted to ensure his safety too. Or maybe he just wanted to keep an eye on him.

Ezra's past vanished like a whisper among the autumn leaves. He wondered about the future and he pondered heredity and chromosomes. Forever, he spoke about balancing what he called the Western medical model with a holistic model of health. He speculated about mercury in inoculations, lead, and other metals in the body. He sought ways of removing toxins from the body so that the mind and body might range more freely. He was still a doctor and he cared for the children in their small ailments- their cuts from falls, their sneezes from colds. The children had their own doctors, but Ezra was always available.

The alchemist was ever more a part of our lives. We could easily close our eyes and feel that we had been given a kindly grandfather. Yet, I had begun to feel as if we were now walking through a minefield. Each place we went we knew that someone might be watching. As I jogged in the park, now nothing seemed certain. We had entered a dangerous world.

Laura felt it too. She felt uneasy and she stayed alert as she worked each day at the Starlight Day Camp. The children would sing with her: "Twinkle, twinkle little star." Listening to their little song, it would come back to me throughout the day as I was painting the house, or as I walked outside in the evening. I wondered at the stars that shone over the farm at night. In all that peacefulness, in all that space, there was violence that lay not far away.

Each day at three o'clock Laura would bring the children back to the farmhouse from the school she had started on the farm. We were protective, always on the lookout for anyone who would be following the children. For Ezra, it was also a time of caution. Now his shawl had been drawn up higher to his collar as he walked. On clear days he hid himself from view with a well- curved umbrella, so he might not be photographed. We were conscious of every visitor who came through the farm.

Several times a week I walked across the farm to the older farmhouse to visit Ezra. There he had set up his alchemical laboratory and he would lead me down the steps to it. I sat there among the picture books filled with strange symbols.

"Here, look at this spoon," he once said to me. "You put it in your tea, to stir in some sugar. If you leave the spoon in the cup, the temperature at this end, by the handle, will rise. Molecules at the hot end are exchanging energy with parts of the spoon. This is the process of conduction."

From a nearby shelf, he took something that look like a rock: one clear and sparkling in the light.

"This is a crystal," he said. "Do you know the heat capacity of a crystal? What if I were to put it above that flame?"

He dipped his pen into the inkwell and wrote.

$$C : 3R$$

$$\overline{M}$$

"The C here is measured in what we call joules per Kelvin per kilogram. R is the gas that is constant."

"I thought a jewel was something you wear."

"In chemistry, a joule is a unit of heat energy," he said. "It is named after a scientist who studied heating. Now let's see how this crystal does in heat."

He held the crystal above the leaping flame. I thought I saw it begin to change color. Then he set it down. He took a strip of aluminum and put it over the flame.

"Metals are good at conducting heat," he said. "Silver, copper, and gold are strong conductors. Glass and water are weak. Diamond is a unique thermal conductor. Do you know why?"

"Diamonds are very hard," I said.

"Yes. They are the hardest element in the world," he said. "A diamond is hard because the chemical bonds between its carbon atoms are strong. The atoms create a rigid structure, since each atom connects with four others."

He turned down the Bunsen burner and the flame extinguished.

"Everything changes," he said. "Simply put, Jacob, a candle burns down. The Victorians in Britain came up with a frightening concept: the heat death of the universe."

"That sounds awful," I said.

"Yes. In Germany, in 1850, Rudolf Clausius discovered the law of thermodynamics. It shocked the world. Entropy is disorder. Lord Kelvin gave us the word thermodynamics. Clausius added the word entropy. Did you know that the moon has a crater on it named Clausius?"

He held up a glass to the light.

"Imagine a rainbow, Jacob. A rainbow is lovely," he said. "We see an arc of colors. A rainbow is a circle of light that is centered on a point that is opposite from the sun from the person who views it. Raindrops make rainbows by refracting the light. The colors of light are different wave lengths. So, they refract in different ways as they pass through all of that water."

"Laura paints rainbows and science measures them," I said. "Is there is a difference?"

"There is a difference in how we see," he said. "Science seeks principles: the laws of the universe. When I think of principles, I think of Isaac Newton. Like Newton, I deal in the ancient art of alchemy."

"Isaac Newton knew alchemy?'

"Oh, yes. Isaac Newton was an alchemist. He gave us the laws of motion and gravity. But he was very interested in alchemy too."

Ezra set the glass aside. He peered over his glasses at me.

"When Isaac Newton's body was exhumed, it contained large amounts of mercury. This was probably from his experiments in alchemy."

"But wasn't Isaac Newton a physicist?"

"Newton was a founder of what we know as physics. He pointed to the forces of attraction and repulsion between bodies in the solar system. But he thought of this because of alchemy. John Maynard Keynes, the economist, once called Newton the last of the magicians. He was quite serious. Newton had about 170 books on alchemy in his library."

"What about all of these numbers?" I asked him.

"Well, those are quite important," he said, looking down at the book in front of us. "You see, all of the elements have an atomic number. One way of designating the elements came from a British scientist, Henry Mosely, who studied x-rays. He measured the wave lengths to see how the x-ray spectrum was related to an element's atomic number. This helped chemistry to assign atomic numbers to new elements."

He looked pensively toward the window for a moment, looking out at the moon and the stars.

"He was shot by a sniper in the First World War," he said, shaking his head. "It seems that humanity always loses something to war."

That was something I had learned about the alchemist. He could go into dark thoughts very quickly. Suddenly, his mood would change. It was like the world had been covered by a cloud.

That November was like that: bright one day, blustery the next. I remember writing a letter to Ali. I must have written it over and over. It went something like:

> Hi Ali,
>
> I'm sure you've heard from Laura all about the Starlight Day Camp. She has brought the children here to the Red Cat Farm recently. Our friend Ezra Foote- the man I told you about, the alchemist- has been talking about starting a special school for them and for other kids like them here at the farm. They seem so happy. They have simple lives and they are affectionate. Yesterday, I mentioned to Laura that maybe we could have a party when you get back. We could do a little fashion show with the children, she said.
>
> How have things been at college for you? I enjoyed our time out at the movie, even if there were some strange things going on. Maybe we can do that again sometime. It would be nice to see you again.

One evening, toward sunset, Ezra Foote set aside his book with the strange images. His hair wild in the flame's light, he resembled a magical sorcerer as he turned to listen to the sounds beyond his window. It was as if he had been transported back to that time long ago, to the time a man and a dog could be heard coming across the new fallen snow. It was as if sixty years had collapsed, like space into the black hole left by a fallen star. Now it was leaves, not snow, falling in whispers beyond the window. Within the swirl of those leaves were voices. Through the window, I could hear them also.

Ezra took his cane from the hook on the ledge in the kitchen and walked out the back door. It was an evening of dark clouds moving across the sky. There was a sun of fire on the horizon and a moon that would soon follow it into the night. As he looked down the hillside toward the farm, he saw two dark figures approaching. In the distance they were shadows against the orange peel of sunset. One pushed the other in a wheelchair. The seated man, a shrunken indentation in a leather and metal pit, was a site of devastation. His hat was low on his skull-like face. Solitary, the two men stood against the sinking sun. From the shattered face the pursed mouth began to speak.

"Jonas, you remember me then," he said.

"Like one remembers a sickness, the puss of a wound, or its sting," Ezra said. Yes, he remembered. This memory hung like a disease upon the air.

"So, we meet again, Jonas. Ah, Jonas, I thought you had died. It would be better for you that you had."

A laugh then went out of him like the exhaust from a broken vacuum, as if it were the breath squeezed out of a corpse.

From the window I could see them. The lean, bald-headed man was standing behind the wheelchair in which sat the shriveled old man. The young man leaned over the shadow of the old crone, rolling him forward like a machine caught in wires, rolling across the space of a bare path. He had a hard and handsome face that matched the ghastly grimace upon the broken face of the old man.

"I know of your secret, Jonas" said the old one. "You are not with us? That is a mistake, you know. We must now deal with you, Jonas."

They were about to 'deal' with him when I pulled the net of cans from the roof. The sound shattered the silence and made them look up. Then sounds from behind them broke through: Tom's truck passing on the road, entering the driveway. Our shadows crossed the yard. Hearing it coming, the young man rolled the wheelchair away. Down the slope of the hill they went, disappearing across the farm.

We brought Ezra inside the house and he sat motionless, staring into space. "I knew they would come here," he said. In his chair he sat in stunned silence, a man out of time, his thoughts distant, dangling across a century like some ripe fruit about to be plucked from a tree. He was caught on an edge and about to fall.

* *

14.

Those people in that abandoned building were dangerous. That much was certain. What magic was there to draw them out? The horizon looked uncertain, ambiguous. Like a painter's swirl of ash-gray clouds cast across an autumn sky. In that unsteady oscillation between summer and fall when the light drains away, we watched the leaves turn dark and fall in a mixture of colors into a cauldron stirred by the wind. That is when we wished for change, for some alchemy to transform our troubled space in time. If only there were some magic to make these people and their dark witchcraft disappear.

It came to me that day what our alchemy would be. Stirring paint in a can in swirls, a phrase came to me: 'Mix hope with every darkness.' I pictured Ezra's basement laboratory, and I began to think of how photographs have typically been developed in the dark. Back before digital cameras, photographers would go to the darkroom with negatives in hand and from them the world would reappear reflected back in images. Underground, like the buds of spring waiting to open, are things unseen to the naked eye.

Pictures. That was it. Pictures would make them visible. Roland liked the idea. Pictures from the ground, pictures from the air: it was the way much espionage was accomplished in the Second World War, he said. Develop a photographic record. It meant that we would have to spy on them - and we would have to get close. This would have to be a quiet magic. Our alchemy.

With our cameras, Tom and I stole out from the farmhouse into the night. We were prepared this time to see just what was down in that old, abandoned dairy. So, we waited along the hill overlooking the place where that abandoned factory loomed like some great animal's shadow.

Camera on my belt, rope and smoke bombs from the high school theater in my jacket pocket, I felt ready to work some "magic." The building rose before us, shades drawn on the dirty windows like lids over blank eyes. Beyond the chain link fence, a tractor, like an ancient dinosaur, sat immobile in a half square mile of dirt. The fence was bent at one corner and that is where we went through.

Tom was the first to enter the building. I followed. Our feet touched concrete. It was dark, dense, cool. It struck me as sinister. I turned around, feeling that something was definitely wrong. For a moment, we stood listening. The cave around us was silent. Then I felt a slight vibration. There was a humming that grew louder. A distant machine began to thump, like a chaotic heartbeat, steady as a muffled scream.

From the edge of the cave, we could hear a scratching sound, the static of radios. Inching further, we could see two silhouettes against the wall in front of us. At fifty yards they were a blur. At twenty we could see more clearly. They were guards in gray paramilitary uniforms. One stood by a wall that was equally gray and made of steel. The other was leaning against the opposite wall sucking on a cigarette. I took a picture. I heard him say something to the other one and they slipped into the recess of a doorway.

Our muscles tensed. We pressed against the ledge. Ahead of us a voice barked, "Who is there?"

We crouched down as a beam of light swept over our heads. Down on the concrete we began to crawl, under the spill of light. Beyond the guard was a room. We could look into it past him and saw that it was clean and bare and clinical. On the far side of it a bare table butted against the wall. On it was a high intensity lamp and three microscopes.

"Why microscopes?" Tom whispered to me. I snapped a photo of the room.

A guard saw us. His mouth opened in surprise. The man turned and raced out. Then came a jarring sound. His head spun back, his neck snapped, blood spurted down. We looked behind us. There a rider on horseback had come into the cave: the hunter after his enemy. The man lay sprawled in front of us across the entrance to the room, blood trickling from his mouth. We were in between him and the man on the horse. The body was motionless, slipping into a soft dead weight and we passed over him, blood trickling from the swollen mouth, bulging eyes staring at us as we went by.

"*Ein Volk. Ein Reich*," said the man on the horse.

Then we saw him, the man in the wheelchair, rolling toward us. He looked as if a demon had come forth from the grave. The man had a face wrecked beyond repair. In that craggy face, evil, self-satisfied eyes flicked like flames from putrid yellow pits. I recoiled from that face. The man spat an unpleasant laugh. The sunken, yellow eyes bore into me.

"Child, Child," he said. "It is the final bloody end. The end of everything!"

He laughed again, like a coarse thing summoned up from the pit of hell. It was horror that rose from that throat, echoes from a soul eaten away by maggots, soaked in gin and fire. The horse reared up. The rider on it moved forward, ready to charge. I raised the camera.

"There's no time, Jake," Tom said. "We've got to hurry."

Then a burst of smoke rose in the cavern. Tom had tossed one of the smoke bombs. I threw another. Shots rang out and the wall behind us splintered. We ran to the end of the concrete structure. Cold air burning our lungs, we ran, looking out on pastures. In the distance were the stalls, the stables, the fields rising up a slope into a dark night sky. We ran out to the wire fence, the earth hard and rock covered. Racing toward the ridge, we threw ourselves down into the grass. For the moment we were safe.

Then we heard a rustling in the woods behind us. A figure was running toward us. Laura. She had discovered our plans for going to the cave. She insisted on seeing what was in there.

"Laura, it's dangerous," Tom said.

"No. I'm going," Laura replied. "I'm with you in this."

"It isn't safe, Laura."

"You're not going to leave me out of this. You want to collect evidence? I have to collect evidence. I'll go there on my own if I have to. Like it or not!"

"Laura, it's not safe. They know we're here."

Not hearing us, Laura rushed on. Her hair flew back as she ran. We ran after her.

We donned black hoods and became masked figures running under the quarter moon following Laura as she raced toward the warehouse. Crossing the edge of the swamp she came to the fence that loops around the factory. She found the crack in it and went through. We saw her ahead of us as we went into the building. She hurried along the corridor. Behind her we hurried, trying to catch her. But she was still way ahead of us, making her way down the steps to the tunnel.

Then we saw Schneider. He wore a hat and an overcoat over his pinstripe suit. He had piercing blue eyes, dark eyebrows that scowled as he went into the building, turning a combination lock on his briefcase, snapping it open. From it came a gun. I tried to remain calm. Tom's hand went to my shoulder. "Shhh…" We slid down behind a large crate. Schneider's eyes were focused on Laura. She heard him and turned. It was like she'd been slapped in the face.

"Do you know who I am, my dear?"

"You are Gerhard Schneider. I'm not afraid of you."

"Afraid? Should you be? What is it you would be fearful of, I wonder?" He lit a cigarette with the flicker of a metal lighter. Laura tried to steady herself.

"And why are you here, young lady? Have your friends sent you? They will find nothing here. This is just a simple property. It is an investment, shall we say."

"Like your plans to invest in the farm," Laura said.

"What do you know, young lady? What are you doing here? I suppose you are simply passing through, on my property."

He tugged at her arm and pulled her toward him. Clutching her hair with his other hand he pulled it tight. Laura squirmed, thrashing her arms out, stepping back.

"Don't touch me! she said.

"This is no place for you."

Her fingers went to his jaw, nails ready to claw and gouge his eyes and he pulled away. She slumped back, her body going limp.

I froze. Not this. Not Laura.

"Don't touch me," she said again.

Tom looked ready to spring out at them. Then we heard Schneider. His voice echoed off the walls of the cavernous space.

"My young friends, you should all return to your farm and to your business. Your concern is not here. You are not welcome here."

His hand came up with the gun in it.

"You will leave now and so will the girl. Take off your coats and lay those things on the ground. No more tricks, my friends. Leave them. Do as I say. Now go!"

He released Laura. She stumbled toward us. Tom and I pulled her down toward us and shielded her in our arms.

"Go," I heard him say again. "Do not return to this place!"

Outside we went, past the iron fences, past the darkness in the trees, the limbs of trees playing tricks of shadows around us. We began to run, stumbling along the hill, away from that place.

How had we gotten away? Had Schneider been merciful - or cautious? Did he have other plans for us? It was obvious that he did not want us there. Now that his secret place had been found it was also not likely that he would stay there very long. We had to hurry and tell Roland.

15.

A crowd had gathered at the college for the widely publicized lecture by Professor Ned Roland. There was no chance to talk with him yet. I stood outside the doors of the auditorium at the university center. There was a buzz of voices, the mingling of people in the lobby. I kept my camera in a case beneath my jacket. I had some change in my pocket and five quarters. I put it into the soda machine and a Pepsi rolled to the bottom. I finished most of it before stepping through the doors. From the back of the auditorium, I could see him- the man called Schneider. He wore a dark green trench coat, the color of pine. A rolled newspaper lay on the seat next to him, as he listened to Roland speaking of modern Germany. It was as if nothing had just happened in that wretched building. He appeared calm and collected and the lecture went on for nearly an hour.

"You have been a most interesting audience," Roland said. He spoke while never looking up at the handsome, head-shaven man who was listening curiously from the auditorium's back row. After Ned Roland had finished speaking, the moderator, a short and stocky man with thinning hair approached the microphone and looked out across the audience for questions. There was a pause and then the questions came swiftly, like the rain teeming against the windows outside.

"Professor Roland, your lecture tonight on the German philosopher Friedrich Nietzsche has been most illuminating. It is also rather timely for this particular region, considering the recent acts of vandalism perpetrated on Veteran's Park and the Greenlawn Cemetery. Do you see any connection between what you have spoken on tonight about a German philosopher's thoughts from more than 100 years ago and our present situation?"

"Actually, yes, I do," Roland said.

That brought a murmur from the audience.

"Nietzsche's thought is quite important to post-modern thinking. Unfortunately, with this has come those who would distort his thought to suit their own ends. I refer to extremists, to fascists, to anarchists of that persuasion."

"In other words, Professor Roland, you are talking about what we would call neo-Nazis. Is that not so?" said a man, who was obviously a reporter.

"Well, if you are looking to put a label on this, you might use that term."

"Is there a link between these neo-Nazis and the Nazis of the 1930s and 40s?" a woman with wiry, permed hair asked. She wore a tan pantsuit and silver bracelets. Her hair had that finger in a light socket look.

"I didn't realize when I began this lecture that we were going to have a press conference on this subject," Roland said. "But yes, I see a connection."

"And just what is that connection, professor?" the woman asked.

Roland paused, looking past his questioner. I think I saw him glance for a moment at Schneider. He cleared his throat, took a sip of water from a glass on his podium, and he continued.

"This is one of the great legal challenges of our time," Roland said. "It's a detective story, really. There are no fingerprints. There is no murder weapon. We don't even have the body. The witnesses are difficult to find. And the criminals are in hiding. You are right to say that there are former Nazis among us. By that I mean not ordinary soldiers but the members of the SS who carried out pernicious crimes against humanity. It is said that we now have only a few years left to find these people and to bring them to trial."

"But Professor Roland, the question is: are they here?"

"Yes, since the 1950s there has been some likelihood of that. Hundreds of Nazis are now, in the 1980s, living out their last days hidden in small communities like this one. Most of those who remain alive are now in their late seventies, in their eighties, or beyond. The question is whether they should be allowed to live reasonably normal lives after what they have done."

"Professor Roland," said the woman with the wiry hair. "Do you think that any of them live around here? Is that why we are seeing racist markings all over the place?"

"Are they right here in town you mean? That I cannot really comment on."

The moderator seemed shaken. He came forward again, a pudgy, tired looking man looking over the audience of students and faculty and visitors, many of whom were clearly members of the press. It was obvious that he wanted to stop the question-and-answer period, or to turn the discussion back to German philosophers. "I believe that this was a lecture on the post-reception of the philosopher Nietzsche," he said. But he was forced to acknowledge other raised hands.

"There are other questions from the floor?"

Reporters leaning on pads, recorders in their hands, raised their hands. Another woman's voice came first.

"Dr. Roland, you have said that thousands who served in the German army came here legally after the war. How are we to determine their level of involvement? Weren't they all Nazis at one time?"

"We must make distinctions," Roland said. "Soldiers fight for their nation. Then there are those who belonged to the party. There are those who belonged to the special units, like the secret police, the SS. They are at the top of the list."

"But how did they get here?"

"Some lied about their war record. Others posed as refugees in Eastern Europe and slipped through the immigration process. There were times when a refugee from Eastern Europe was protected by the United States government for information he could provide about the Communist states during the Cold War. I believe that the United States Justice Department Office of Special Investigations is working diligently to resolve matters which have been left unfinished."

That last line sounded to me like a canned and prepared response. It was something out of a service manual at the Office of Special Investigations. So maybe that was who Roland worked for; because if he was simply a professor at a college in the South, he had certainly done his research. He took another long sip of water and scanned the room to see if Schneider was still in attendance. He was- and he seemed amused by the discussion.

"There is ample documentation to demonstrate the involvement of certain persons in genocide," Roland said. "The Nazi bureaucracy was meticulous in recording the methods and facts of thousands of victims in the camps. The official word was that the deaths were due to sicknesses, constitutional weaknesses in a presumably unfit race. That was very wrong and very biased. Nazi doctors would find an ailment the prisoner had and they would then exaggerate it. But there are clues regarding the true nature of those deaths."

The true nature of genocide is what he meant. Roland was talking now about what is called the Holocaust, although he did not use the word. Schneider, only fifty feet away from where I was sitting, barely shifted his weight. He was listening intently.

"There are detailed descriptions of the experiments," Roland said. "All of the concentration camps maintained these listings. As I have said, the Nazis kept very careful records. In fact, those books of death bear a striking resemblance to accounting books. Personally, I find that rather chilling. It is the extreme reduction of human beings to numbers on a ledger. The Nazis were cold and efficient.

What we can't allow is for this to pass. It cannot recede into some misty yesterday. It is, I think, a moral lesson for us all about the pain that human beings can cause to each other."

The moderator now rose again. He looked disturbed and he looked at his watch and stuttered, "Well, thank you very much Professor Roland for your fine talk on reader response in the former East Germany. We will be having refreshments…"

Roland kept on.

"Yes, I know, Mr. Walters. Our audience must be asking, what has all of this to do with Friedrich Nietzsche? Actually, very little, I'm afraid. Just for the record, Nietzsche himself was greatly opposed to glorifying the state. His phrase "the will to power" and the idea of "the superman," the Ubermensch, was sadly taken to have a biological meaning which was never intended by the philosopher."

Ned Roland loosened his necktie and took another long drink, finishing his glass of water.

"So, to conclude," he said, "the reception of Nietzsche was slow in coming after the war. This was mostly due to associations that had been made between his idea of a will to power and the Nazis. I do not have any clear evidence of the appropriation of Nietzsche in the new Germany. Yet, I have heard of it. And I will say this: I did see some graffiti on a wall while I was in East Berlin that gave me a chill. On the end of the wall someone had scribbled: "Go Right, not Left." Those were not traffic directions. In the past several years, more than sixty percent of young voters in Germany have cast votes for parties on the right. Whether the racist elements of the past are present still is debatable. But there have been suggestions of a new nationalism in the eastern part of Europe for some time now."

Schneider had heard it all. As he got up to leave, I pulled up the hood of my jacket and walked to the end of the hall. I took two photos of him – no flash- as he went by. Then I followed him out into the rain. I stayed behind him at a distance for several blocks as he walked to the train station.

On the platform he stood, the rain slanting down around him in the lamplight. His face was tense, a solemn moon, his eyes piercing. The spread of his raincoat cast a shadow on the wall. He stepped from the dim lamplight halo and looked across the track with a steady gaze. The train's lights appeared as it turned a corner in the distance.

Moving toward the end of the platform, I kept my eyes on him. I dialed a pay phone.

"I see him," I whispered into the phone.

Tom's voice answered.

"You followed him?"

Schneider, across the track, rose up tall, casting a long shadow. Lean, head shaven, he stepped vigorously across the platform like an animal stalking its prey.

"I'm at the station. The train is coming in. I'm going to get on it and see where he goes."

"Jake, that's crazy."

"Magic, Tom. Remember. This is for Ezra."

"Jake!"

Tom's voice echoed in the phone. I hung up and hurried through the tunnel, under the tracks, the damp concrete echoing the sound of my running feet. The train approached, its brakes hissed, and it came to a stop. I saw the conductor step down, encircled in a haze of rain. Schneider stepped up. He nodded to the conductor and disappeared inside the train. Racing up to the train doors, I pulled myself into the last car. As the train began to pull away from the station, I slipped quietly into the last seat.

I saw Schneider smile and lift a cell phone from his briefcase. He dialed it and spoke something in German. I was surprised: cell phones were uncommon at that time and I'd never seen one, except in the movie *Wall Street*. Then Schneider ended his call. He gazed out the dark window into the rain. He opened his briefcase again and looked through some papers. Then he took out a paperback: Nietzsche's *Beyond Good and Evil*, in English. Dark night went by the window, streaks of rain, streams of cloud-dimmed light from the buildings.

The train rocked forward and rose above the park, past the cemetery. For an hour it went on through the dark. Beyond a passageway of tunnels was the city. Schneider got out at Penn Station terminal and walked swiftly down the platform and up an escalator. Under the beaming lights, I followed. Hands in his long coat, he paused by a magazine rack. From behind it stepped a mustached man with glasses under short, cropped hair. Schneider nodded to him - a nod of recognition. He handed the man something from his briefcase.

Seeing them, I slipped behind the news stand. I grabbed a train schedule, looking like the image of a lost tourist. The men moved toward the stairs. Up they went to rain-soaked streets and lights dimmed by rain. Up the damp steps I followed them, edging along the wall. A woman and a man jostled me as they came down. The shadows atop the stairs moved away. Then came the light from the street, the cool air, a sense of space breaking through. I looked up and down the wet mirror of the street. Schneider and the man with him were gone.

16.

THE ALCHEMIST'S NOTEBOOK

My life has become an endless war of memories. I remember how Dr. Brunner approached me one afternoon, when I was all of twenty. He had a forceful and engaging smile, a graying mustache, and a monocle in one eye. "We wish for you to specialize in obstetrics," he told me. I was obliging. I thought it a privilege to bring life into the world. Some months later, when I heard that I would be stationed in the north, I assumed that meant the clinic at Wernigrode near the Harz Mountains. The children would be born in clinics, I was told. The program was called "the spring of life." It sounded innocuous and hopeful to my ears.

In the spring of our lives, my brother Franz and I inherited the family business. Franz was given charge of industrial responsibility. I was recruited for something rather unique. To be a doctor was an honor, I had been told. Yet, what came next- an invitation to join the Abwehr intelligence service - was something greater. The Abwehr was involved with counter espionage. It also acted as cover for conspiracy. Abwehr agents could travel and move abroad fairly freely. State secrets were exempt from the Gestapo. So, there was some jealously and conflict with the SS/SD. Sprange Abwehr it was called: "to ward off." Agents would dress in enemy uniforms. These spies were recruited from officers, lawyers, and in my case, from doctors.

"No one can know this," Franz told me. "No one, Jonas."

"I could not keep it from Elise."

"Does she know of the plan?"

"No."

"Keep it that way"

What fate or fortune kept Hitler alive through those years? Admiral Canaris and General Oster of the Abwehr surely wanted him dead. They were fatalists, men schooled on Spengler's Decline and Fall of the West. They had seen the broken remnants of the Great War. They were men who expected the worst from Hitler, men who wished to delay the war Hitler clearly wanted. The generals wanted to preserve Germany, to keep the nation from being embroiled in an escalating conflict with the West. Once lebensraum was obtained in the German speaking territories, that was enough for them. Full-scale conflict with the West was suicidal madness. Hitler, of course, had other things in mind.

The planning of the generals to eliminate Hitler began before the war. It went on into the final year of the war. That was one of the things that my brother Franz insisted must remain a secret. It has long been thought that the clockmaker who tried to assassinate Hitler with a bomb secreted into a column of the Burgerbrau beer hall was acting alone. Yet, others, following the Oster plan, acted in concert. Most well-known was the general's plot in which a bomb was exploded in a meeting room and Hitler was saved by the leg of a table. But these efforts had a long history and the Abwehr knew of them. Indeed, the Abwehr, with the guidance of General Oster, participated in several plots to assassinate the Fuhrer. Sadly, each attempt failed.

Franz prominently displayed a photograph of Hitler in his office. Privately, he told me he believed that Hitler was a menace to Germany. Franz had read each bewildering page of Mein Kampf and he told me repeatedly that Hitler planned nothing less than a broad conquest of Europe. He would involve Germany in war with Russia and with the West.

"Does he believe that Germany can win such a war?" I asked him.

"It will exact a price greater than the one in the last war," he said. "And what will Germany gain by it? You know, Jonas, I am involved in high-level industrial business meetings. Among industrialists, the support for Hitler's policies remains strong. But these men only have their own interests in mind. Not those of Germany."

So, Franz was not surprised to learn that the military's concern about Hitler began soon after the Nuremberg rally of September 12, 1938. Franz had attended the event in the grand outdoor stadium. We wondered then: would Hitler make a declaration against the Czechs? Would he insist that they give up the Sudetenland? The torch lights began the march into the stadium. The bright searchlights were turned up, piercing the grounds with blue and white light. Hitler rose to the podium, to cheers, but there was no assertion of war. There was his familiar bluster but no focused provocation. Most thought that a move on the Sudentenland would be the end of peace, the lightning rod that would spark disaster. We feared that the British and then the French would respond to any military action against Czechoslovakia, or Poland. The Abwehr braced itself for action to prevent Hitler from making an aggressive move. Yet, it seemed that the British were not opposed to a plebiscite that would cede lands and leave things to a vote in Austria.

"War may bring a measure of prosperity, Jonas," Franz said to me one day. "Our business is well positioned. We can start business in Prague, just as we

expanded operations in Vienna. But in the long run, it will mean compromise with the Nazi Party. Every step of the way, it will mean compromising ourselves and our business." He then set up business in Prague and in Vienna, of course. That was Franz's first deal with the devil.

Only rarely could I share classified information with Franz, or with Elise. Mostly I kept it to myself. I had heard that inside the Abwehr offices at the Tirpitzufer, the activity around Admiral Canaris shifted its emphasis. Neville Chamberlain was coming from Britain. He made his first flight on an airplane and landed in Germany to make a deal. It averted war for the moment. But it also averted the Oster plan from going into action. Hitler's life was spared. The Wehrmacht moved peacefully over the Czech frontier and occupied the Sudentenland. The Czechs had capitulated. The takeover plan was foiled. The von Klaus family business immediately established offices in Prague. Anticipating controls by the Reichsbank, Franz created dozens of connections with financiers in Switzerland.

I could have told Franz that the Abwehr's disaffection with Adolph Hitler was based in questions about his capacity to lead. It echoed a deep concern about the direction in which the Nazis had taken the nation. It was the opinion of several of these men that these aggressions might be catastrophic for Germany. General Canaris was the Master spy. How much did he know? Perhaps everything. He certainly knew of General Oster's dissatisfaction. He knew about General Halder and General Beck. All of these men in the Abwehr developed plots to assassinate Hitler and establish a military coup before we occupied Norway. The eyes of the Gestapo were watching. But a good spy could hide behind the privilege of the Abwehr and its distinction to engage in counterintelligence. You may call them traitors, but I believe they were patriots. They developed plans to stop Hitler before he could lead Germany into a world war.

The plan was to seize Hitler, to assassinate him if necessary. This plan was later named after the Abwehr chief of staff, General Oster, who hated the Nazi regime and believed its goals spelled the ruin of Germany. Hitler was to be seized and declared insane, unable to lead. From the medical files they dug out Hitler's record from the Great War. He was a corporal hospitalized after a gas attack, who was bitter over the German defeat. Would the winter of 1939-40 be the time for the overthrow of Hitler? I have heard that General Halder bribed Hitler's astrologer. He gathered up a million marks to persuade the astrologer to tell the Fuhrer that his plans were fatal and that victory was not in the stars. It didn't work.

Hitler was charmed. Each plot went awry. Hitler moved from place to place. His schedule was erratic. He was an ever-moving target. He went with thirty SS bodyguards. His armor-plated Mercedes 770-K was equipped with bulletproof glass, on all sides. A theological student, Maurice Barvaud, pursued his own plan, carrying a pistol through Munich, waiting amid the ranks of the SA brown shirts. Hitler crossed on the opposite side of the street. Barvaud walked the Munich streets in search of his quarry while Hitler was safely 80 miles away. A pistol tucked in an overcoat was no way to kill the heavily protected Fuhrer. Nor was the bomb of Johann Georg Elser, the watchmaker. He carefully constructed a device and concealed his bomb in a pillar in the Burgerbrau where Hitler would be speaking. The timed device blew the room to shreds- twenty minutes after Hitler had left the room.

Hitler stayed alive to carry on his reckless campaign. Preparations for attacking Russia were begun in 1940. This would soon deeply involve Finland and Norway in the war. Official directives came that December. Admiral Canaris opposed the extermination policies in Poland. Herr Himmler's SS persisted in them. After the French saboteur Henri Girard escaped from prison, assisted by the French underground, Canaris did not act. He said that General Heydrich had given the orders. Of course, General Heydrich was now dead, so it was safe to say that he would never talk. The word came down that the Abwehr wished to be left out of the murder business.

It was a turbulent time and the plot to kill Hitler was short-lived. The victory in Norway led to the end of the Oster plan. Paratroopers surprised the Norwegians from the sky. Lightning attacks pounded the coast as far north as Narvik. The British Expeditionary force did not reach the Norway coast until April 12. The fighting proved fierce in central and northern Norway. But the battle was lost. The Wehrmacht had won. It was with this victory that, in Berlin, the planned coup against Hitler was withdrawn, at least temporarily.

And so I went to work in Norway. I was assigned through the Office of Das Ahnenerbe. This was under Heinrich Himmler, a man concerned with what he believed was a threat to the Nordic race. Himmler's interest in medical questions was, I think, related to his unusual interest in occult medicine and natural healing. I also had this interest. Himmler would have disagreed with Schneider, for he believed that we humans cannot improve upon nature. I found him strangely intriguing, but ruthless and contradictory. One moment he would speak of preserving the natural world and the next he would be killing and destroying life. He was a divided man. We all were divided men.

Not the least of the divided souls in my life was my brother, Franz von Klaus. Franz could be called a monk-like man. A quiet man, the clerks called him the hermit. He looked as plaster does: pasty white. His face was ever tense, his eyes alert *and suspect. His hair was thin, a hazy brown, and across the years his eyebrows grew grayer; they were the only thing in his world that seemed less well-managed with time. His poor eyesight – and our family wealth- kept him from the war. Franz wore spectacles from childhood- yet, he saw the world clearly, and he lived with a pragmatic self-assurance.*

He moved between offices in Berlin and Zurich. In his Berlin office were the well-worn portraits of the Fuhrer. Each item was carefully placed, even to the evenly stacked paper: a firm easel, corkboards for messages. Yet, as it was his habit to smoke like Dresden's chimneys, his rooms were also much like used ashtrays. The family business – in minerals, industrial supplies, aeronautics- extended from the spires of Prague, its stone steps, its twisting streets and their gas lights, to the Scandinavian north, a land of thick forests, rivers, and falling snow. Franz was a steady person, but he was sometimes brooding, and darkly so. He was more that way after Astrid died. Then he was merely a man listening to the noise of the wind, one staring at the jar on the long kitchen table. The flame of a candle extinguished. She had been a vision once- a happy face that the traces of age had stolen upon. And when she was gone, it told him of the passage of time. Once she had been reflected in his eyes and his eyes had told her that she was ever beautiful to him.

When she died, Franz threw himself into his work and the business prospered. He was widely known as an exacting manager. From the day Astrid died, he lived in the harsh light of day. Threats to the welfare of the business must be answered with the neatest compromise. If iron ore was to be transported for the German military, he would oblige. Deals were made. They were bargains that ensured the survival of the family business.

While the war was still at its height, I met with my brother in Oslo. "I had heard you were reassigned," said my brother. He had flown to Oslo for a meeting with investors about iron transport. We met for lunch. He looked weathered and noticeably pale.

"It's the work," he said. "It is this deal with Krupp. Balancing these demands from the Fuhrer."

"Retire then. You can well afford to," I said.

"Yes, but who would I entrust the business to, Jonas?" He sighed and then I heard him coughing.

"Franz, you must see a doctor here," I said.

"That is why I wanted to meet with you," he said. "My physician in Berlin recommended a specialist. You have heard of Sigurd Johannsen?"

I stared at him for a moment. It was then as I'd suspected.

"He is an oncologist."

"Yes."

"How bad is it?"

"Bad enough to seek a second opinion," he said. "I am to meet him at three o'clock."

Franz von Klaus, my brother, carried a gold pocket watch with him always. It had once belonged to our father. When father had given it to Franz on his thirtieth birthday, he could hardly know how little time Franz had left. Yet, it was the gesture of a millionaire to his son- the son who would, for a time, run his far-flung business through the entangling knots of war.

To say that we were well-off would be to put it simply, unaffectedly. Father owned an expansive enterprise. His companies made millions. Some wondered how the devil he had done it. He sought by deal and compromise to preserve all of it in the 1930s. My brother Franz, ever childless in his marriage to Astrid, took the reins of the enterprise when father died. I held, with him, controlling shares, but my focus was on my medical education and then on my military assignments. Franz had run the daily business of the firm, until now.

"Jonas," he said. "I assume that you know that you were recruited because of the importance of our family's business."

"I have often thought so," I said.

"You also know that Schneider is one of their lead men here in Norway," he said. "I have had to make a deal with him."

"You have made a deal with Schneider? With the SS?"

"It is temporary," he said. "Yet, each time I seek protection for shipments, their net gets tighter. Their goal is to steal everything from under us. I have no doubt of that."

"But you have been successful so far."

"The Eastern front has made us indispensible. But transport requires military security. We are under greater scrutiny and control. They seek a bigger piece of the profits. Soon they will try to absorb us, Jonas."

"What are we to do?"

"I have a plan," he said.

The plan he outlined was a courageous move to keep the Reich satisfied with one hand, while hiding funds in foreign accounts across the Swiss border with the other. I was taken by its craftiness.

As he walked that evening from the clinic to the waiting taxi, he knew the disease was fatal. The taxi light fell upon the snow, shining under a dark sky. Dusk *had come at four, when he left Dr. Sigurd Johannsen. It had been a raw afternoon of gray frost and fog. Gleams of light shone from windows above the frozen panes of the shops. Franz knew he had not long for this world.*

I met him on the sidewalk, beside a bronze statue of a warrior flailing desperately at the sky. The air was heavy with the damp of evening. There was the churning of a motor down the block and people were laughing. When we met, Franz's eyes were solemn. It took only a glance into them to know. It was a death sentence that the doctor had given him.

"So, it is then?'

He nodded.

"I had suspected so. What are we to do?"

"You know very well," he said. "We will dissolve the business.'

"But the Party has expectations."

"I know that. We will keep the line through Finland and Sweden in operation. We will maintain a shadow office in Berlin."

"You look pale, Franz. He says that you have how long?"

"Sigurd says I have less than a year."

"I'm sorry."

"We must move assets from the Reichsbank," he said.

"How? You know how closely that is watched."

"I will find a way. We must sell off the company assets. We will hide everything possible. I have been in contact with our bankers in Switzerland."

"And when that is done? And when you are gone? What am I to do?"

His eyes were piercing, meeting mine in a level gaze.

"Run, Jonas," he said.

17.

Laura, still shaky from her encounter with Schneider in the abandoned building, greeted Ned Roland at the door to the farmhouse the next morning. Roland stood in the living room with his papers spread on the table before him. He turned toward me. His eyes were wide.

"You went after him?"

"I got on the train," I said. "He rode it into Penn Station and met someone there. It was a dark-haired guy with a moustache. It looked like Schneider passed some tapes to him."

"Jake, I said watch him. Photograph him. I didn't say follow him. You can't take it upon yourself to follow this man. It's too dangerous."

"He's after Ezra, isn't he? I wanted to find out why."

"You should have asked me."

"And you were going to tell us?"

"It looks like I'm going to have to now. He is bold to show himself in public so soon after these events in the cemetery."

Roland shook his head. He appeared frustrated with us.

"We have been following Gerhard Schneider for years," he said. "He is a very powerful and dangerous man, Jake. Tell me, did you get a good look at the other man, the one he left the station with?"

"Better than that. I took a picture," I said. I reached into my knapsack and pulled out my developed photos and handed them to him. For a moment, Roland studied them intently.

"Ritschl," he said. "This is Andreas Ritschl."

"Who is that?"

"He's someone who definitely doesn't want you taking pictures of him. You say he handed Gerhard Schneider some tapes?"

"Schneider had the tapes with him on the train."

Roland pondered for a moment, taking in that information.

"I suspect that Schneider will be coming back to the farm again," he said. "He has some business with Jonas, the man you call Ezra. And with all of us, I think. I'm sorry about this. But I fear I've put you all into great danger."

"We're all in this, Professor Roland. There's no turning back now," Tom said.

"Tom!" Laura said. "We shouldn't be involved with this."

"It's okay," Tom said, putting his arm around her. "It's going to be okay."

"Are they after Ezra?" I asked. "Are they out to kill him?"

"He is not cooperating with their plans. So yes, it may come to that," Roland said.

"But why?" Laura asked. "Why would anyone want to harm Ezra?"

"That is what I have to tell you," Roland said. He leaned back in his chair, folding his hands. Then he leaned forward again, meeting our eyes in a level gaze. "It is time you knew what you are getting into. I have told you some of it."

"And it's all so unbelievable," I said. "Like, what is Schneider up to in that abandoned building?"

"Abandoned building?"

"There's an abandoned building on some property about a mile or two down the road from the farm."

"You've seen this?"

"We've been in it. We have pictures. There were guys dressed up in uniforms down there."

"Paramilitaries. Schneider would have recruited them."

"There are some weird things down in that cave. A guy on a horse. And a horrible old geezer in a wheelchair."

"That is Hans Schneider. It is from an industrial accident they say. It is more likely someone tried to kill him and didn't finish the job."

"Who would try to kill him?" Laura asked.

"Many people would," Roland answered. "The old man is a Nazi war criminal. He has led a perfectly normal life for years as a classics' professor in Germany after the war. Not that Schneider was ever normal. His son has been trained from birth to be a ruthless killer, as well as a virile politician. They are the ones who foster this myth: The Generation Project."

"Which has to do with the List?"

"That's right. Hans Ernst Schneider and Jonas von Klaus met sometime during the experiments. Historians will tell you that Germany annexed Norway for its strategic goal of attacking the west and then plundered its natural resources. However, one of the secret goals of the Norwegian campaign for Germany was to create a gene pool from its officers. They mated officers with Nordic women. It is not impossible that scientists would store and possibly freeze sperm and egg for a future generation."

"They could do that?"

"If they thought of it, they could do it. Of course, who would have thought of this in 1940? That is why we believe it to be largely mythical."

These days I would be streaming video off my computer. Back then, before digital, I had set a television and VCR video player nearby, at the professor's request. Roland now turned toward the screen, where images had begun appearing. One showed Gerhard Schneider with an older man: the rickety old man we'd seen in the cave. Then there was an image of that same man- Hans Ernst Schneider - as a younger man. His face was hard, scarred on one cheek. His eyes were focused on the camera. His mouth was closed. Thin downward lines accented the downward curve of his jaw. He wore a dark Nazi SS uniform.

The video returned to an image of Gerhard Schneider. The young Schneider was a striking image on the screen. He exuded ambition and pride. Skillful and suave, Schneider the politician had been primed from his youth for public office. Sharply conservative in his pronouncements on policy, he was a man who had rehearsed his moves. He had a lusty youthfulness about him, a sure and cunning smile.

"His life has been formed in violence," Roland said, as we watched the screen. "All kinds of disaffected people cling to his every word. He is a master of populist rhetoric, an exponent of racial hygiene, a nationalist calling for racial purity."

Faced by cameras, Gerhard Schneider chatted into microphones. His coolness was only betrayed by his habit of chain-smoking cigarettes. His words were carefully scripted, like hair spray that fits everything smoothly into place. Unless one looked closely, one could not see the streak of ruthlessness that lay behind the polished surface. Instead, one saw a successful man.

"He is a mannequin," Roland said. "Look. He doesn't even perspire. He is a statue- all swastikas and marble."

The next frames showed Schneider visiting a war cemetery. He faced a row of crosses.

"Watch him," Roland said. "Next he will inspect the grave, as if honoring the war dead. He promises the ones who are buried there that, with a new generation, things will be different. The young Schneider is everything the old man is not."

The blonde man gazed confidently from behind the microphone. He spoke in English.

"My friends, it is time for housekeeping. All around us there is chaos. All around us we see degradation. All around us this world is falling to pieces. What is needed is order: a new order. And where is this new order to come from? It is to come from the will of an orderly people. It is to come from orderly business. I am here to provide you with that new order."

The image was magnetic, the voice filled with resolve.

"You and I are tired of bloated government budgets and ineffective policies. We are tired of crime in the streets, aliens in our backyards, this indecent problem of guest workers who never leave. Let us be rid of the immigrant aliens. Let us clean up this society and rescue it from the gutters!"

Again, we heard him deny the holocaust. He did it so smoothly, so effortlessly. No, these camps were for political purposes, he said. "It is a lie. Today if business interests were to agree to set up a dance club on the site of a factory at Auschwitz, I would not complain. We have had enough of solemnity."

Dance he did – from place to place. It appeared that Gerhard Schneider, like a fiery planet, was always in motion. Roland told us that Schneider would arrive at a political rally, then rush off to another fundraising dinner. A man of evident charisma, he would stroll into a room and heads would turn. A bodyguard would taste his food and then Schneider would eat. At some functions he was called upon to speak- in German, in French, in Spanish, or in English; he was fluent in all of them. Then, on camera, one could observe the signal to a waiter. One heard the soft click of a lighter. The cup set down on the table with a click. Then away he would go in a gray Mercedes to some other event.

After his congratulatory address, with a pose of triumph, Gerhard Schneider bowed. When Gerta Kohlenberg poured the coffee, he gave her a passing nod; it was a mutually understood gesture.

Roland said, "Watch here."

The buxom forty-year-old woman wore a dress that revealed much. She fawned over him. Yet, nothing of their romantic love could one now detect; all was a pose. Roland suggested that Schneider's wife Gretchen was naïve to this. She was an uncomplicated sort of woman, who knew that she was the figure-piece of a politician. Obviously, he could not appear to have lusted after another man's wife. He never showed it in public. The young Schneider was a man of tricks and he had an image to protect. So, he never let on about Gerta, or any of the others. But it was recognized that Schneider had a mistress.

"His bodyguards know," Roland said. "Yet, he plays with them. Gerhard Schneider likes spontaneity. For them, that means increasing security measures. He plays with his security team: 'well, let's see if you can catch me.' He will take to one of his sports cars and drive up the side of the mountain. He races his motorcycle into the night. They will try to follow him, but Schneider is elusive. It is a game with him. He is an expert driver, taking off into uncharted regions of the mountains, placed where crowds – and not even his own security- can follow him."

On the screen, we could see him, cool as a cigarette ash, returning to his manorial estate, his place of retreat. Then, side by side with his father, such a contrast there now seemed between the two of them. The old man was cold as soot, like a darkened moon to his son's bright and smooth veneer.

"Some of Germany's leaders dreamed of a thousand-year Reich," Roland said. "So, it may be possible that next they might have dreamed of something which might endure longer: the infinite future of a proud master race."

"But how would they do that?" I asked. "They lost the war."

"That's true. And such an enterprise would have to be fostered across many years. They would need scientists who would be faithful to the project. I have a hunch that they tried to recruit Jonas. After many years, Schneider has at last found him."

"Why can't he just leave him alone?" Laura asked.

"He has come either for some information, or to settle accounts with him. But I also think it is insane to think there is any such thing as genetic materials preserved from the 1940s. Back in the 1940's, who could have thought of this? It would not have been plausible at the time. Now - yes. With the human genome project, a great deal is possible. But that is responsible science. This is sheer fantasy."

"Do you think they might be trying, Professor Roland?" Laura asked. "What if they were looking for some isolated places in some secluded area? Like maybe right here."

"Yes. It's a thought. They might make use of farmland in a rural area. Although a desert island would be more likely. That building you mentioned brings something else to mind. You have heard the stories of Hitler escaping death in the bunker in Berlin? There are stories that he was spirited away, that Hitler somehow escaped to South America, like Borman and Eichmann did. There are also stories that his remains are preserved. There is rumor about this but no evidence. The rumor asks, what if Hitler's genetics had been studied and set aside? Might he too rise in the form of an ancestor, one posing as a savior to the race? That would be his legacy."

"That's Frankenstein," Tom said. "That's complete insanity."

"Exactly," Professor Roland said. "And wouldn't a new Goebbels, the propaganda chief, use something like this? With all the craft and power of modern public relations at his disposal, it could be manipulative to an extreme degree. Imagine a new Hitler, one emerging from a biological myth that somehow Nazi scientists had saved a remnant of the Fuhrer's genetic materials. From those genes he would rise again. And a new thousand-year Reich would come upon the earth: Hitler's children."

"How awful!" Laura said. "That's possible?"

"It is a fanciful thought. The problem is that Schneider is a fanciful man. The son, Gerhard, may not believe all of this but he knows the strength of mythical belief and he believes in something equally frightening: he believes in power."

Professor Roland paused, looking over the edge of his eyeglasses.

"Some believe that Schneider is using the myth to lure investors to finance a project. Yet, no one is quite sure what Schneider is up to. We believe that he is seeking the records of the lebensborn project. The Nazis were meticulous in their record keeping. One would think that a project so secret as this would leave no paper trail. To the contrary, if there is anything at all, you can expect it to be documented in every detail."

Roland took the tape back out and set it back on the table. He picked up some papers, but barely looked at them. His eyes were on us.

"I think that your friend Ezra may know something he isn't telling," he said. "If he knows something, we need you to get him to speak about it. The Human Genome project, however one feels about it, may be credited for its openness, for its search for answers. This project, however, if it exists, is conducted in secret. They are playing with genetic secrets. And frankly, with our information technologies, little is secret anymore. If a thoroughly unscrupulous group were to get hold of that privileged information… where are the ethics or the laws to stop them? It becomes totally unpredictable."

"So, you do want us to … help out?" I said.

Ned Roland nodded.

"I'd like you to encourage Jonas von Klaus to speak about whatever he knows. It's important. We need to be watchful of these new groups of neo-Nazis. For years, observers have dismissed the threat, saying that these groups are too splintered. But now it appears that they have found a central organizer. This is a crisis of new proportions. You have a relationship with this man, Jonas, a relationship that apparently no one else has had in years."

"If you're saying that you want us to get him to confess to something, we're not going to do that, Professor Roland," I said.

"No. Not a confession. We've agreed to grant him amnesty."

"We? Who is we?"

"That I am not at liberty to say. You'll have to trust that I am working in an official capacity."

"As a professor," Tom said.

Roland smiled.

"What we need is information. Simply, I want you three to talk with him. A lot is at stake here. More than you know."

18.

It seemed so incredible, so impossible. Had the Nazi scientists explored such mad dreams? I knew of Josef Mengele's horrors. Nazi science crossed paths with esoteric research. Edmund Kiss explored a cosmic ice theory. There were rumors that Himmler kept the death ring of the occultist Karl Maria Wiligut, the man he called Welsthor. There were Teutonic cult meetings amid yule light candles.

I got on the phone and began to call American scientists. Five of them talked with me and most agreed with each other. If semen were put in deep freeze it could last for many years, they said, possibly for lifetimes. Yet, such things were virtually unheard of until the 1960s and DNA research hadn't begun in earnest until the 1970s. I began taking notes on little pieces of paper, file cards, napkins, and I stuffed these into my pockets.

The most intriguing comments were those of Dr. John Ambrose, a noted African American geneticist. He said that the Nazis could have thought of freezing the body, which is known as cryogenics. The Nazis conducted many freezing experiments to see if their pilots would survive the frozen waters of the North Atlantic. This may have given someone the idea: someone in the icy regions of Norway where SS men were being mated with Nordic women. Dr. Ambrose was a noted expert on the Tuskegee experiments: the misuses of science against unsuspecting blacks who volunteered for syphilis studies. They never received treatment and his papers on these ethical abuses were almost legendary. His studies of the Nazi experiments led me to some wilder speculations. What if Hitler himself had genetic materials flown into a secret place? Would he? It would mean a future race of "Hitler's children." The children of the SS. Had a group of neo-Nazis enlisted that outrageous myth?

Tom and I brought out painting supplies for a day of work. Our job was to paint the interior of the farmhouse. We rolled out the drop cloths. We lined up the cans. We set the rollers next to the pans in which we'd pour the paint.

"It sounds crazy. Jake. It's a rumor. There's nothing to prove it," Tom said. "Besides, who would have thought of it in the 1940s?"

"Why not? Da Vinci dreamed of flying machines. Jules Verne wrote about machines leagues below the sea. Who knows what is possible? Those Nazi doctors were as warped as that board up there."

"They were insane," Tom said.

"But what an idea! And these scientists say: yes, it is possible." I took one of my notes from my jacket pocket and read it. "Look at this one. Dr. Barton at Columbia."

Tom leaned over my shoulder to look.

"If human semen were placed in deep freeze, it's conceivable that it could last for many years – a few lifetimes maybe. The problem is – well, this would have to be the work of a scientist of great foresight. Such things were virtually unheard of until the 1960s. We didn't begin serious DNA research until the 1970s."

"So that means probably not," Tom said.

"Yeah, but cryogenics, the freezing of a body. Couldn't they have thought of that? What if Hitler had biological materials flown into a secret place, like in Oslo?"

"What you're saying is pretty incredible, Jake. You know that."

"Think of it, Tom," I said. "A future race of Hitler's children. The children of the SS. They tried to do that with that lebensborn project. It sounds crazy, I know. But a lot of the things they did were crazy. Just imagine it: Hitler's biological inheritance frozen in ice, deep under the snow. Beautiful women. The Nordic race. It makes sense."

"No, it doesn't."

Tom stepped up on the ladder. We had completed the ceiling and he was working on the trim. I was working around the windows. The incidents around the Red Cat Farm had tossed us into a perilous situation. Ezra was in trouble. That much we could tell. So were we. If Professor Roland was right, that trouble might spread to include a lot of innocent people. That thought preoccupied us in our every waking moment – and in our dreams. The seriousness of our situation was now beginning to dawn on us. We wondered just who Roland was. From the images in the cemetery and on the wall in the park, to suggestions of a cell of neo-Nazis, the professor looked as if he was as haunted as any of us. The worst of it, he said, was that he had been followed too.

"So, Roland wants us to keep an eye on Schneider," Tom said. "And we're supposed to help Roland and whoever he's working for to compile a convincing portrait of this group."

"So, they can shut them down. That's right. We'll do it with our own alchemy, Tom. He wants us to develop a visual description of that building, or whatever it is under the old, abandoned warehouse."

"I suppose they expect this guy Schneider to still be there."

"The old, emaciated man we saw. Hans Schneider. He's the link with the old Nazis and these new right-wing groups. They want us to publicly identify them."

"So, what about painting a big swastika on the doors of their truck? That would do the trick. Or maybe we could paint a design down there in that building. Like a big cow."

"I'd be glad to donate the cow to the cause."

"Sure. We could add a quotation of wisdom in German. How about we paint it on a rock somewhere? Hey, you know, Jake, maybe you've got a future in rock painting."

"The main thing is getting some photos of the place. Some incriminating evidence. That's what Roland wants."

"What Roland wants. And who is Roland?"

"I checked. He's a visiting professor."

"And my grandmother is the president's press secretary. He's visiting from where? The FBI? The CIA?"

"He's on the faculty of a college in the south, in Virginia. But he's been on leave doing research in Germany."

"Research on what? For whom?"

"Okay, so maybe he is with the CIA. Maybe it's some Nazi hunting organization, like the Office of Special Investigations. What's the difference? If he's good on his word to protect Ezra…"

"While he puts all of our lives in danger."

"We're already in danger, Tom. We were from the first day I talked with Ezra in the park."

"So, what are we going to do about protecting Ezra?"

"Therese said we should invite him to stay at the farm. That way we can all keep a watch. We'll help him move his things so he can set up his laboratory in the basement."

"But I thought Laura was bringing the children from the camp to visit. You're going to have Ezra here too? When you think that somebody is out to get to him? Isn't that a little dangerous?"

"They wouldn't think of attacking him while there are children here, would they?"

"They might. Don't be so sure, Jake. Don't be so sure."

"Okay, listen, I've got an idea. You know those extra paint cans, the empties we never threw out?"

"Yeah. What about them?"

"We can use them. We'll create an early warning system. We put them up on the roof above Ezra's window. Anybody pulls on the window they all come down on his head."

"Jake, you are bizarre," Tom said. "Where do you get these ideas? Paint cans above the window?"

Tom reached up to paint under the upstairs window. The sun seemed to cast a halo around him.

"So, Jake, if Ezra was a Nazi, what makes you think that Ezra ought to be protected?"

"Tom, he's our friend."

"And I suppose you talked with him about these rumors about schemes to create a master race."

"He's pretty quiet about it."

"So, he doesn't talk about why their SS officers went to Norway."

"No. But he knows about it, Tom. He knows they were mated with the native women. Blonde hair, blue eyes. It goes back to the Norse legends, the god Thor and all of that. They took over the country and its women too."

"And the women just submitted to that?"

"I think they were forced to in many cases. But there might have been a few love stories there too."

"It sounds like a movie."

"It would be a good movie. An innocent Norwegian beauty falls for a handsome German officer. It could have happened too. It probably did happen."

"Didn't the Nazis expect that these children might have minds of their own?"

"They must have believed in their indoctrination plan. Their *Gleischaltung*."

"Their *what*?"

"It's a German word. It means to bring everything together."

"But didn't they realize that many of those children might grow up and reject their parents' past?"

"Most of them never even knew their parents, Tom."

"Paint in the wind," Tom hummed. "All we are is paint in the wind."

He had finished the corner of the ceiling and came down to move the ladder.

"So, okay. So, there are records of this. Do you think there really are records that say they also thought of freezing genetic materials for some future century?"

"I don't know. But the idea alone - that would interest a man like Schneider. Imagine it- the genetic materials of a new what?"

"A new Frankenstein, if you ask me. Isn't that what all of this is? We don't know if this stuff even exists."

"That's not the point. Don't you see? Schneider wants to believe it exists."

"So, we make it up? We tell him that Ezra knew something? Like where these materials might be?"

"Exactly. It already exists in his mind. So, we suggest that the records of the experiments really might be hidden here on the farm. Let's say they've been here all these years."

"He'll kill for that. You know that, Jake."

"It looks to me like he already has that in mind. It would be exactly what would draw him out into the open."

"That's a very dangerous game, Jake. A very dangerous game!"

* *

The shock, I think, was too much for him. It sent his heart racing. For all we knew, his visitors may have injected him with something. They had put a terrible fright into him. The next morning Ezra walked slowly to breakfast. His breath seemed heavy and labored. He sat down uneasily. I could see a shadow come to his face. There was a wince of pain in his eyes. When Laura came to his side, he waved her off.

"Ezra, are you okay? Where does it hurt?" she asked him. "Ezra? Ezra, can you hear me?"

He nodded but no words came. Then his eyes were wide. His face, at first flushing red, became pale.

"He's having a heart attack," Laura said. "Jake, call for an ambulance!"

"Let me be," Ezra said.

"Lay back, Ezra," Tom said.

Back on the chair he laid, his legs stretched out in front of him. His eyes looked up, as if to the stars, to some place far away. Within ten minutes the ambulance arrived, red lights turning. The EMT's began their work. "It's his heart," one of them said. They placed him on a stretcher and rolled him out.

We climbed into Tom's truck. Out from the farm we sped after the ambulance. It raced down narrow roads past the farms and out to the highway. We followed its red light spinning through the farmland.

Any angel gazing from the overpass above could see him looking up, a monitor taped to his chest at the heart. That angel could see the vehicle hurrying, its lights turning against the shadows, until it reached the brick hospital.

Tom pulled his truck into a narrow space. We saw the stretcher touching down, rolling quickly toward the doors. CPR. Thrusts to the chest trying to bring him back. We rushed out, following the stretcher. Beyond the sliding glass doors was a nurse, arms crossed, watching us rushing in.

"Ezra Foote. We're here with Ezra Foote."

She looked for the name on her clipboard and frowned.

"There's no one here by that name."

"That's him. In just now. Jonas von Klaus. We're here to see Jonas von Klaus."

"And which is it then?"

"He goes by both names."

"And you are?"

"His grandchildren," I said.

How could she be so calm? In one room a baby was crying, kicking up its legs. In another a girl, in pain, her face a reddened mess, rolled to one side looking at us as we went by. In the emergency room I felt I'd discovered a new house of horror. Ezra was lying a short distance away from us.

"Stay back, folks. Stay back!"

Thrusts to the chest tried bringing him back… from wherever it was he had slipped away to. Bringing him back. His face, suddenly awakened, appeared pinched, as if he felt a sharp stabbing pain. He drew a breath. He opened his eyes to a sea of faces. For a moment, I thought he looked at me. Then came darkness, merciful darkness. He was gone.

Laura began to cry. I placed my cap down at the foot of the bed.

"Goodnight, Ezra," I said. And we stepped away.

We went down the elevator to the first floor. We walked down the hallway aimlessly. A woman lying on stretcher gazed at us. I felt dizzy. "Sir, you will have to stay in the waiting area." a plump nurse in green scrubs said. I sat down numbly in the Radiology Waiting Area. Bodies on stretchers rolled by- on their way to anesthesia and surgery. The world went by on wheels. A custodian pushed a cart past us. A dark-skinned man with a pen clipped to his shirt pocket whistled. His cart was loaded with cleaning supplies. We heard plastic bags opening and the smell of disinfectant filled the air. There was a fish tank in the corner with a large orange fish floating there. The world seemed surreal.

When the news of Jonas Albrecht von Klaus reached the media, there were several different versions of who he had been. We buried him as Jonas Klaus and as Ezra Foote at the Greenlawn Cemetery, in a grave next to his wife Elise. There were few mourners: just Tom and Laura and I, Therese, her friend, and Ida and Hans. A woman had also come, one who stood apart and left as silently as she had arrived. She wore a dark hat, a black lace veil, and a black coat, its darkness broken by a single silver broche pin. She remained at a distance.

We placed on the earth the flowers dear to Elise, the star of the alchemist, and the inscription of a red cat. Dr. Roland, the so-called professor, had plain clothes agents staked out across the hills. He knew that Schneider and his people were probably watching from a distance.

* *

The farm seemed unusually quiet that evening. The moon rose high over the trees. White electric candle lights glowed from the windows of the farmhouse. In the barn, little bats hid under the eaves, like the alchemist had once hidden away with his secrets. As Tom and I walked past the barn and up the path to the farmhouse, we talked about him. He had changed our lives and we owed him a debt we could hardly ever repay. By now we understood. He had not sought to transform metal to gold. Rather, he sought to transform himself. His life was like the band of a rainbow over the dark clouds. It was the long burn of the fading sun over the edge of a dark ocean.

Once inside the farmhouse, Tom held out a book to me. It was a notebook he had found among Ezra's belongings.

"I think this was left behind for you," he said. "What do you think this is?"

"It looks like a chemistry text," I said. Opening it, I saw H2O. That one I understood. Water. Below 32 degrees Fahrenheit water becomes ice. Above 80 degrees we begin to get vapor. I opened the book and read:

The primary goal of chemical experimentation is to decompose natural bodies, to better examine the substances that make up their composition. When we have heated a substance and have caused its particles to separate, if we cool the substance again its particles will approach each other in the same proportion in which they were separated by the increased temperature. It may recover the same dimensions which it formerly occupied. Lavoisier. Elements of Chemistry.

"He left the book behind for you, Jake. With his notes in the margins."

"Well, I'm not sure why he would leave a chemistry book for me, but I'll keep it."

Laura, hearing us, came down the stairs.

"What are the two of you up to?" she asked, as she walked up to us.

"We're talking about Ezra" I said. "Personally, I'm wondering why he died."

"It was a stroke, Jake."

"Sure, it was. But we think it was brought on by stress. And what if there was an injection, one that didn't show up on the autopsy? What if Schneider made it look as if he died by natural causes?"

"It was a heart attack," Laura said. "It was brought on by the stress."

"No. He was murdered," I said. "We're not going to just let this go, Laura."

"What's that?" Laura asked, pointing at the book.

I leaned over the notebook. On the page were symbols. The moon was high in the darkness beyond the window.

"It looks to me like a pretty straightforward book on chemistry. He copied out sections from Antoine Lavoisier."

"Lavoisier?"

"Lavoisier was one of his heroes," I said. "He was a famous chemist who lived in France at around the time of the French Revolution. Ezra told me that the government gave Lavoisier a laboratory because they were interested in having him work on gunpowder. Unfortunately, he got guillotined."

"Ouch," Tom said.

"The interesting thing is that Lavoisier and his wife started a model farm to show the advantages of scientific agriculture. I think our friend wants to say something to us with this book."

"Jake," Laura asked. "Who was that woman? The one who was at the funeral. Have you ever seen her before?"

I said no, I had never seen her. But I suspected she was someone close to our friend. How close she was I hardly knew until I saw her again. The quiet woman fading back among the trees to her car was Elke, the daughter of Elise and Jonas. She had come to say goodbye.

It was shortly after Ezra died that I had the dream. In the dream I had found Nazi gold, mingled with bracelets and rings. In my dream I was returning the gold to Jewish survivors of the Shoah and their families. I carried them to a mostly Jewish neighborhood. At the door of one house, an old man eyed me suspiciously. He simply said, "I'm sorry. But they are gone." The hallway grew dark, his eyes hollow. He turned away. I started to speak but stopped. How was I to explain? Never could anyone make up for the past.

I said, "Don't you see? The Swiss banks may be returning this gold out of guilt or because of political pressure. They want to clear the record and do business as usual. For them, it could all be public relations. But this is a private gesture. I think it means something."

The man shook his head. He did not understand.

"Each cufflink is a memory," I said. "Each pin or watchband is a memory. It was theirs. Take it. Take it." I pleaded with him to take the objects in my hands.

The man turned away, his face blending with the shadows. I held those objects that were worn with the years. Then, from the haze around us came the symbols from the alchemist's book: the queen, the magician, the fierce dragon. Like cards from the tarot, they shuffled. Among them I saw a watch that still told the time. Then I saw Schneider. With every visit to a kind Jewish home, I was telegraphing to him where they were, the aging survivors, the ones who already had suffered so much. The dragon seemed to leer down from the cloud. But then the magician turned. I saw Ezra, dropping a coin into the pond at the park. As the coin hit the water it fizzled, sending beams of light up into the cloud. The dragon dwindled and disappeared. The cloud opened and I saw the sunlight and Ezra disappeared across the bright hills of the farm.

I told Tom about my dream.

"You are haunted by this," Tom said.

"Ezra used to say his dreams came true."

"And you think this one will?"

"When Schneider came to the farm, the shock of it killed Ezra. You know that, Tom," I said. "Either that, or they injected him with something that killed him."

"You don't have any evidence of that," Tom said.

"Evidence is exactly what we are going to get," I said. "Roland wants pictures and recordings so he can bring the Schneiders to trial. I say we go back to the complex."

"We'll do it then," Tom said. "But they'll be watching for us, Jake. You know as well as I do that Schneider suspects something. If we go back into that cave, it's going to be as dangerous as a trip into hell."

"Then you'd better get ready for hell," I said. "We're going down into Inferno."

And so, as Dante says in his famous poem, we began our descent on the road, further into that dark, infernal region.

19

THE ALCHEMIST'S NOTEBOOK

The dream strangely lives on. For now, the time has come, the younger Schneider believes. It is time for the genetic engineering of people, with the ideal Aryan genes. If only there still existed the genes of those who believed themselves to be a master race. Where could they be? Do they survive at all? And the records, had I kept them, if I had told anyone where they lie, what would they contribute to this mad affair? They tell the names of those who contributed to the lebensborn project. We did not fully know the procedures for biological engineering then. That has changed. The procedures are known now. That is why Schneider and the others are so desperate to get the records. They will point to the genetic lines. But Schneider will never find them. No one ever will. For I know where they are, but where they are I will not tell. Even should I go to my death, there they will remain, where that little child brought his sleigh down a hill. For his sake, for the children, I will never tell.

Children must be shielded from the horrors of war and its violence. You see, children are gold and childhood is one of life's most precious times. Like the elements, the gold and silver in children lie as possibilities in the rare good earth. The disabled, the challenged, the needy children are a treasure to remind us of our own weaknesses and faults. They call for love and humility and kindness. They ask of us that we protect them. You do not toss the sweetness at the center of the fruit away. You press it to your lips in gratitude.

Elise and I decided that the challenged ones must be spared. The escape route for the children was across the sea. The underground could move the children in the same way that they moved refugees. They would cross Norway into Sweden and then by boat they could be sent on to the Shetland Islands. It was an arduous trip for the disabled child but a necessary one. A British RAF flyer named Saunders gave me the idea for the escape route. He was a proud, jaunty pilot who flew a failed mission and crashed in the Norwegian hills. He became one of the refugees who needed to be evacuated from Norway. His plane had gone down in a failed operation to destroy an industrial plant where heavy water was being made. The heavy water was to be used in Germany's atomic bomb program.

We were alerted to the fate of this downed pilot by telephone. We knew that our telephones might be tapped, so the message was delivered as a coded message to us. "The night is cold. Wrap your children well," the message said. The "children" included Saunders, the air force pilot. Milorg agents found him miraculously when he reached a farmhouse in the countryside. They sent him through its circuit of safe houses, toward the Swedish border. He traveled with a female agent to limit suspicions of possible local informers. Apparently, he liked the female agent a good deal. Saunders arrived with her – a thin, athletic woman with long hair and dazzling eyes. She called herself Gilda, although I doubt that was her name. He explained that traveling with her made it easier to get through the lines. But it seemed that what he meant is that it made the nights less lonely.

The people who had sent Saunders knew that heavy water was being manufactured in Norway. The Milorg resistance had made it a priority to destroy the heavy metal operations. So too had the British Secret Service and the OSS. The goal was to delay the German atomic bomb program. Toward this goal, they began recruiting agents. Fearing the worst for Germany and for the world, I had stepped over the line and I had joined them.

The story of the effort to stop heavy water production in Norway can be told briefly. In 1942, some Norwegians were trying to escape the country. The British seized their ship, the Galtesund. One of the men was a hydroelectric technician. He was a tough, outdoor sort. He could ski expertly. He liked tinkering with radios, so they taught him communications. He would attempt to infiltrate the Vermork plant. The British parachuted him back into Norway less than two weeks later. He told his family he had been on a ski holiday. Soon he was able to get work on a construction team inside the plant. He talked with Norwegian sympathizers who were on the inside. This confirmed the Nazis' goals. The heavy water was intended for the atomic program.

This British Secret Service and the OSS began their work to destroy the German efforts in Norway to make heavy water. England next sent men on an expedition into Norway but they were caught. Fugitives from Europe and downed airmen were often rescued via the O'Leary line and the Comet line. They were the lucky ones whose escape was successful. The Comet line went from Brussels to Dartmouth and south across France and Spain. The O'Leary went across the Swiss frontier to the edge of the Italian border to the sea. The downed airmen wore civilian clothes and carried counterfeit papers. A guide would bring him to a public place, like a church. There were many safe houses like this along these routes. Airmen like Saunders were often accompanied by young women, like Gilda. It was made to look as if they were couples. There were prearranged signals: a geranium pot in a store window meant that it was safe to pick up the fugitive. Go to a safe house to a couple with no children, normal lives, with at least two exits from their house. We fit that profile precisely. And no one suspected that we had become resisters.

Saunders told me that a four-man advance party was sent to prepare a landing area for an assault force near the Vermork plant. This was Code named Swallow. The Norwegian resisters of Company Linge would assist in the operation. I was familiar with them. They knew sabotage. They could fight in hand-to-hand combat. They knew how to kill silently. Four men were chosen: three from Rjukan and one from Oslo. They had spent their lives skiing, camping outdoors, and they each knew wilderness survival skills. They parachuted in many miles away from their scheduled drop point. They had to walk many miles across the rocky mountain terrain in the chilled air.

I remained quiet about what I knew. Such things are an absolute necessity for double agents. I knew that the guard had increased at the hydroelectric plant. Even so, the British assault team was prepared for action. Lieutenant Saunders was part of that team. He was separated from the team when his glider was lost in heavy fog. The telephone links did not work correctly. Aircrews were unable to talk to each other. They tried to come in under a cloud cover. His plane crashed on a mountainside. Saunders, somehow, survived the crash. About fourteen men did, but all of the others were captured and executed. You see, the shattered glider was found the next day. Oddly, no German officer interrogated them about their mission before placing them in front of a firing squad. But one could easily tell it had to be a sabotage mission.

The OSS had, by this time, developed an escape route. But Saunders had to survive on his own until the resistance underground located him. We were to provide a safe house and map out the route of escape for the pilot. In a coded communication the pilot was called "the children." That gave us the thought of saving the children by this route. This is the route that we would take with the lebensborn children.

Soon war surrounded us like the snow. Lonely nights led to brutal days. Norway's underground sabotaged chemical factories, foundries, and German boats in Oslo harbor. The destruction of the factories for the manufacturing of heavy water was a central Norway sabotage effort. It was for them a victory in the race to produce the atomic bomb. Saunders was among the SOS parachutists who dropped in October 1942. This eventually led to the destruction of the Vermonk factory, which was located in the depths of a mountain valley. After Germans repaired this *factory, the Allies then bombed it from the air. The central circuit within the factory was reinforced concrete and was not destroyed. The hydroelectric plant was.*

A raid on the Norska Hydro came later, in Winter 1943. Nine men from the underground were successful in damaging the plant and dealing a blow to the Nazis. The news excited everyone, although very few knew the implications of heavy water. The Special Operations Executive called their operation Gunnerside. They are certain that it stalled the building of an atomic bomb. The story is this: In February 1943 these nine resisters blew up the Nordska Hydra heavy water plant. In November 1943 there was an Allied bombing of factories at Vermork and Rjukan that produced heavy water. Later, in January 1944, in a bold move, the resistance sank the ferry used for moving heavy water out of Norway.

And so, we knew of many secrets- and I quietly played my role on both sides of them. Of course, Elise and I knew that we could not be effective in our secretive work for long. I had access to records of the lebensborn experiments in Oslo. I was unsure whether these records of our genetics experiments should be hidden or destroyed. The Abwehr suggested that if the facilities were overrun by the British and Americans, I was to bring them west so they would not fall into the hands of the invading Soviets. It was believed that the western powers would be more lenient. I was certain that they too wanted the insights of German science for themselves. That, I believed, would lead to mischief too. Even if we in Germany had been cut off from the international community for years, there was still much brilliance and there had been many experiments. The English, the French and the American military would want that data. I was not about to let them have it. Nor would Schneider have this information for his mad scheme. So, I would vanish from Norway and hide the records. I thought of destroying them but in the interest of science I could not. I went West with them. Further West than anyone had instructed me to. I crossed the border of Norway into Sweden with Elise and we escaped across the North Sea.

For us, our escape route was to the Shetland Islands. This was why we later had a Shetland pony on the farm: as a reminder of those perilous days. A felucca was a Norwegian sardine boat, a fishing boat. It went between the fjords and the Shetland Islands. In winter, under the subarctic night, the trip could take as much as three weeks. These boats brought agents, explosives, and communications equipment. Sweden was nominally neutral, so to get to Sweden first would have been ideal. This would be an escape line. I have heard that from Norway some 50,000 people reached Sweden. The trip from Sweden was difficult. It came to be called the 'Shetland bus.' In our escape, we transferred to a villa. Then a truck carrying potatoes brought us across the Swedish frontier. Fugitives were concealed by tarpaulins and the children were given sleeping pills. Upon awakening, they had to walk the final distance in an area impassible to trucks in low temperatures to the edge of the sea. The escape that many made was filled with fear and with anxiety.

We left for London, at our first opportunity. Soon we booked at Liverpool for an ocean passage across U-boat patrolled waters. When we went to America, I carried in my bag only one book: an illustrated text of Joahnnes Trithemius. This 15th century Benedictine monk was a recluse, a collector of manuscripts, who practiced magic and alchemy. The book was the Steganographia. The name means 'hidden writing' in Greek. Although the book was written in Latin, from it I learned the art of cryptography. With Trithemius as my model, I built my library in America like the Benedictine once had in the abbey at Sponheim. It became my own scriptorium. Cloistered there, on my wall I placed a Latin inscription in calligraphy:

"Quod propter impressuram a scrimbendis volumcinibus non sit desistendum."

"That monks should not stop copying because of the invention of printing."

And so, I copied images and memories into these notebooks. I vowed that one thing I would not ever copy – would not ever repeat- was the work of my family business. I left that behind after the war. My family legacy was kept in numbered accounts in a Swiss bank. With a portion of these funds, I purchased the farm and the horses in America. Elise and I settled inconspicuously into the rural community. My laboratory was set in a concrete room in the basement. My library in the farmhouse was a fortress of arcane books that lined the walls of an upstairs room. There I began these memoirs, which you are reading now.

> Mutanter omnia nos et mutamur in illis
> All things change and we change with them.

-E O ? (? = Yield) ^ (Fire)

I dedicate this to Elise, who has taught me to remember. I write this to her memory – to my recollection of that first moment when our eyes met. Was it love at first sight? Is there such a thing as a sudden spark of love?

It was Elise, with all her resolute will and quiet charm, who inherited the strength and beauty of her ancestors. Those nights with her helped to push the war away. They muted the sound of the bombs which still burst through my sleep. In winter, the bare branches beyond the window and the cold earth below reminded me of the yards where I'd been assigned for several months. They were months I spent looking into solemn eyes. It was those faces that came to me again- the faces of the Jews, questioning, accusing. I have never spoken of them to anyone. I repeatedly asked to be transferred to another medical assignment and this was granted when I was sent to Norway. Yet, for a brief time it was more than laboratories that I saw, and these things have ever haunted me. And so, they would come to mind, at times, when I was with Elise. As the moon arched over the farm and the tree limb tapped on the window, I would wonder. I would see the faces that haunted me.

"Heinrich, what are you doing?"

"I am correcting this man."

"What has he done?"

"He has stolen food."

"He is hungry."

"He is a Jew. It is a crime to steal food."

The man was thin and scared. Heinrich slapped him, knocking him backward.

"He will no longer have to be hungry," he said. He lifted the butt of his gun. It swung back quickly and came down crashing on the man's head. I watched and did nothing. The fear left the man's eyes and he fell. Heinrich raised his gun. He pointed it at the man.

"No!" I yelled.

I felt my hands tremble as I pushed Heinrich away. A mighty anger came to his face, a hardness filled his eyes as they met mine.

"He is a man, Heinrich."

The soldier took three steps forward and kicked the fallen man.

"He is a dead man."

The man's body hung limply across the steps. The face was a blanket of horror. The eyes were open and staring at the sun. Heinrich walked away, leaving me gazing at the man on the ground. A moment before the man had been alive, begging for food. I leaned against the fence and gagged.

That is how I remember it – as if I am there again. Now the branch of the elm tree taps against the windowpane. Elise is sleeping. Her long blonde hair spreads across the pillowcase. I remember morning light, cool air coming through the window. The farm was a quiet place. It was a good place where the memories were not so haunting. In the mornings, I would awaken before dawn and begin attending to the animals. The horses were especially fine creatures with their long, sleek backs and wild manes. Elise liked to ride the one we called Frigga. Those long rides in the autumn were sheer delight. What life to prance across the farm with Elise at my side! All the pain of war, all the madness of it passed away when the leaves fell under the horses' hooves and the woodsmoke rose across the pines. Those rides were life itself. They were wonder, as was our closeness.

Each life has seasons. The freshness of youth. The surprise of love. The long days of strength and labor, necessity, and dreams. Our lives changed- just as the mineral, the chemical, the property in stone or soil changes. My dear Elise became ill. The warmth in her faded. The joy left her face. The doctors tried cures, but the sickness took her beauty and brought a severity to the sweetness I had always known in her. We became more separate: I in my science, and she in her illness. We kept no contact with her family or mine. That was impossible. For we had disappeared, they believed. Our life was quiet, hidden from the past. Elise played cards; she read books and she knitted until the pain in her hands made that impossible. Soon she was bed-ridden, or she was confined to her chair. Then I rode alone. I tended the field and I built a laboratory where I spent my days deep in study.

I remember the elm that tapped on the edge of the window. One day I saw it there as I brought things in for storage. It was a young elm, leaning its branches in the dusk, scraping along the edge of the roof, tapping and tapping like a persistent memory.

That night, in my basement laboratory, I opened the notebooks I had once kept of the experiments in Germany years before. These were books with the formulas that took away the pain temporarily- the laudanum, the opium, the mercury chloride. I studied them again for the formulas which took away the pain permanently- the zinc, the arsenic, the mercury which became a poison.

That night the moon hung in the eastern sky, as if it were watching. I passed the barn and strode up the pathway to the house. It was then I made the fateful decision. I would give Elise the laudanum, with a mixture of mercury salts and arsenic: a poison. I would hold her in my arms and wish her off to a peaceful end. Then I would hide, hide away from the world forever. Into the barn I would lift her body, with a last kiss upon her cheek. I would lay her to rest peacefully under the eaves, on a cloth on the hay. Then I would saw off that damned elm branch and toss it into the fire. I would climb the hill under the pale new moon, past the cries of the horses, and watch the farm burn, burn to the ground.

20.

The evening had about it the cool scent of late November. We had finished painting about an hour before and now Tom was nowhere to be found. I became concerned about his absence. So, I rolled up the drop cloths, gathered up the paint cans, and brought them to the garage behind the house.

On the hill I heard them. Tom and Laura were heading across the bright green slope, holding hands. I expected Laura to be traumatized by what we had encountered at the factory. Instead, she and Tom were swinging each other in a whirling dance past where the pumpkins lay upon nets of grass and hay. Laura's dress caught in the breeze and her hair was flying back toward the dark pines behind them. They stopped whirling, standing now, holding hands. I saw Laura reach out again for Tom's arms and then she kissed him and fell back laughing.

"You should have seen the look on your face!" she said.

"So, I make funny faces, huh?" Tom said. He flapped his hands behind his ears.

"Yes. You remind me of a pumpkin." She tickled him. "Pumpkin."

"You want to see faces? Here's Jake pulling the cow. Here's Mulch with a hat on his head. And here's Ida watching the video. Oh, dear, I think I've swallowed my teeth."

Laura laughed and Tom ran to the pumpkin patch. He picked up one of the pumpkins. Raising up with one hand alongside his face, he puffed out his cheeks.

"Like a Jake O'Lantern," Laura laughed. Then her laughter abruptly stopped. Tom touched her arm. He pointed down the hill toward me. I think I saw Laura blushing, her freckles hidden for a moment by the red coming to her face. By the time she and Tom came down the hill she'd turned as red as ripened apples.

"Roland got your photos. He said they're enough to incriminate this group and send them to jail. He's preparing something."

"Another lecture, I suppose."

"No, he's not a professor, Tom. Or maybe he is. But that's not his main job. He's a government agent, Tom. I think they're preparing to arrest those people."

We stood together on the hill overlooking the place where the abandoned factory loomed like some great animal's shadow. With night the air became colder and smoke scented. Stars appeared across the black sky. A mile away, in the farmhouse window, Laura had placed a Halloween pumpkin. It glowed like the watchkeeper, its broken smile and eyes gazing out over the lawn.

Less than an hour later, Tom and I were back at the factory, taking pictures. Within minutes, we were hurrying back from the factory, with several men in gray uniforms following us down the road.

"They're behind us," Tom said. "Good."

"Good?"

"We want them to follow us to the farm."

"You *want* them to follow us?"

"Roland is sending help."

"And we're what then? A diversion? A target? "

"We're leading them back to the farm. They're right behind us."

On the curve, their pickup truck appeared behind us. The engine roared to life. Tom pushed the station wagon up to eighty. They were behind us and we tore out onto the road. Tom raced the station wagon to the gate, bumping the back of the car over a pothole, reducing speed as we entered the driveway. The door flew open.

"Let's go!" he said, motioning to Laura, who was standing there. "Laura, get inside! Go warn Therese. Lock all the doors. Stay away from the windows."

"Where are you going?"

"To the barn. We'll be at the back door. Jake, are you with me?"

"Right behind you," I said, looking around. Would they be coming up the driveway or from the woods?

"Stay low. They probably have guns."

"Yeah. Thanks for reminding me."

We ran toward the barn. In seconds, we saw them: three men, at the edge of the woods. A shot flew over our heads and struck the barn. Another shattered a window.

"Hunting season," Tom said.

We dove into the barn.

A helicopter hovered overhead. We climbed up to the rafters of the barn and looked out through a crack in the hayloft. From the blue came a shadow like a lawn mower tipping at the sun. Down it came, a swirl of blue. The blades turned and under them, inside, appeared two men- caps and sunglasses, and a face we knew well. Roland was coming in for a landing. We heard sirens. The gunfire stopped. The driveway was filled with cars, lights flashing.

When it was over, we stood together on the driveway.

"They could have killed us," Laura said.

"That was clearly their intention," Roland said.

"They'll be back. Won't they?"

"Yes. And that's exactly what we want," Roland said.

"What who wants?" Laura stammered.

"To lure them," Tom said. "That's how it works."

"What am I? Laura the lure?"

"Jake, we can use some of your video footage. It will help us to secure a search warrant from the county courthouse," Roland said.

"You want us to draw them out again?"

"It's not safe," Therese said. "You just saw the results of that kind of a plan."

Therese was shaking her head. Her face was red, and her hair seemed to be taken up into graying curls by the four winds.

"The justice department has authorized an operation, Therese," Roland said. "We would like to set up a post here."

"On the farm? This farm represents peace, Professor Roland."

"In the long run, this is about peace," Roland said. "We must bring an end to their business here. Those are paramilitaries, Therese. They are involved in criminal activities that Jake here has documented. It is time to go in and make some arrests."

"Which means violence- a violence that has already come to this farm."

"One for the greater good. You must measure that with your ethics, sister."

"There are children here, Dr. Roland."

"We will move them then. Send them away for a few days"

"You would start a battle on our grounds?"

"On their grounds, Therese. On their grounds. We are going in and we are going to bring them out."

She shook her head again and turned to look out at the hills and the fields she'd entrusted to Hans the gardener and to the rain and the sun. Then she turned toward us, her face calm and resolute, but I could see that her eyes were on the edge of tears.

"Very well," she said.

It happened quickly and when it was over, only a few men were led away. Most had escaped. In the underground passage beneath the warehouse were found traces of chemicals. It suggested that the neo-Nazi group may have been developing biological weapons. Professor Roland suggested that they might have thought to test them nearby: an experiment in preparation for something of far wider proportions. The trace of chemical found in the cave clinched it, he said. This may well be a terrorist organization and would be tried as one. There was evidence enough to convict them. They had fled quickly and were unable to clean up all of it.

"We found a shattered wheelchair, a body we could not identify," Roland said. "This may be the end of Hans Schneider. But now Gerhard has escaped. He must have been alerted. He was not in the building."

"But you have shut them down," Tom said. "This is the end of it?"

"For now, it is," Professor Roland said. "For now, Schneider is gone, yes. But someday, somewhere, he will be back. Of that you can be sure."

"But you'll be watching out for him, won't you?" Laura said.

"Yes. And waiting for the day when something like this pops up in another part of the world."

"Which could be anywhere."

"Yes." Roland nodded.

"It was crazy for him to bring this here," Tom said. "Didn't he imagine that he'd be caught?"

"He came here for a reason," Roland said. "It was to seek out Jonas von Klaus. He planted his project right next door to his farm. That was done very purposefully. Schneider wanted to put it in his face. He didn't think that Jonas, himself in danger of having his war record revealed, would speak up about this. Then he tried to use the law and the real estate money to steal the farm out from under him. He did not succeed in that. We did not succeed in catching him. And so, he's gone away. But there will be another day."

"So, what do you think, Professor Roland. Will he be back?"

"It's hard to say. If he survived this, the old man will die soon. But I have a feeling, Jake, that we haven't seen the last of Gerhard Schneider."

He put on his hat and turned to leave.

"Professor Roland," I called to him. "That was some work you guys just did. Do all those guys work at your college?"

Ned Roland simply smiled. He patted me on the shoulder and then he walked away.

Law enforcement shut down the neo-Nazi cell. Four surviving neo-Nazis were charged with arson and the fire in the barn, grave robbing and desecration of the local cemetery. There were more serious Federal charges yet to come.

Gerhard Schneider had eluded us, escaping before he could be caught and questioned. Across some ocean he must have gone. By now maybe he was in Germany in a castle in the hills, or safely in some other place in Europe. Perhaps he walked on some distant plain in South America, rolling the aged man along in his machine. In some village where the sun came up on another day, Schneider and son were there scheming that the world would one day be theirs. Had they won? No. They had vanished for now into the distance. For a time, it was over. Finally, it was over.

21

A few nights before the Thanksgiving holiday arrived a bold full moon hung in the sky over the Red Cat Farm. In the visitor's quarters we slept well, and the crisp night soon gave way to dawn. It was a time to forget the horror that the farm had been subjected to, a time to be thankful for all that we had. That morning, Laura brought the children to the farm for a celebration. It was the day before the holiday and about a dozen families of the children were visiting. We prepared for a time of family and gathering.

The farmhouses were, at last, both painted. Outside their doors, we'd set baskets of apples, gourds, pomegranates, and the last of the pumpkins. Inside the houses, the rooms were furnished in a simple country style: wide plank floors, smoke from the fireplaces, Therese's favorite needle point rug. We welcomed the guests into the farmhouse, past apple stands. The children played games: Power Rangers, Teenage Mutant Ninja Turtles. They played hide and seek with us and found us easily. We set up a cart filled with hay and brought a horse to take the kids around the farm. The Shetland pony was available for the smallest of the children for pony rides. I dove into a cool tub of water to dunk for apples. I came up splashing with one in my mouth. Then it was time for pin the tail on the donkey. I barely escaped being the donkey. Tom blindfolded me and, as Laura spun me around, I heard them laughing. She guided me forward, my arm outstretched, seeking the picture of a donkey on a wall. When I reached it there was a breath in my ear and a giggle. "Okay," I heard Tom say and suddenly I was turned away from the wall. Off came the blindfold and blinking into the light I saw Ali. Big smile, long braids, laughing eyes, she put her arms around me and hugged me. "Ali" is all I could say. "Ali." And then I kissed her.

A short time after the incidents on the farm, Alessandra Stanley and I were engaged. In 1989, I moved into a dorm at the college, a shoebox of a room in the city. My roommate Brian James and I moved sometime later into an apartment and began a video business. Ali transferred to the Fashion Institute and started doing designs for Spiegel's catalogues. Her parents set her up in a place near West 14th Street. Ali and I made our moves with a little help from those close to us, and we liked it. Ali's cat did too. We'd named him Quicksilver, after the alchemist's cat. Each evening Quicksilver sat on the window ledge in Ali's apartment, looking out the open blinds. Most evenings, I sat nearby at a desk, following the cat's gaze out the window to the few people who passed by outside on the sidewalk.

Ali and I weren't living together yet, but we spent a lot more time together at her place in those days than I did in the apartment with Brian. The world was changing then. The Cold War was ending, and our relationship was still just beginning. The champagne that we opened to celebrate our engagement reminded me of the bottles littering the streets of Berlin. On the television screen, it looked like a party. People were climbing the Berlin wall, some chipping at it with hammers. The wall had become a symbol of separation, power, and sorrow. Now, along the Potsdammer Platz in Berlin, people cheered, beside the remains of Hitler's bunker. *Alle menschen warden bruder.* All people were now brothers, they said. A symbol of hatred had fallen.

I hadn't thought of Europe much to that point. In fact, I'd never been out of the United States. That was soon to change. One evening in late November 1989, not long after the fall of Berlin wall, a newscast on the T.V. on in the next room caught my attention. On the screen, a Gulfstream IV prepared for takeoff. It was carrying one of the world's most notorious criminals. The jet taxied down the runway and climbed: a streak of flame disappearing, forty years of criminal anonymity vanishing in a shock of sunlight. The television news caught ten seconds of the OSI transport. Then a blurred photograph of the Dachau prison guard Rolf Grunden crossed the screen. The plane would fly him to Germany, where he would be placed in a prison, under criminal charges. The message was that the Office of Special Investigations was still hard at work. The guilty would be forever pursued and the shame and horror of what they had done would follow them like the Furies to the very gates of hell.

That was years ago. I remember that I wished then that it might be Hans Schneider that that plane carried. I wished his son Gerhard would be forever discredited. I turned off the T.V. but the image stayed on my mind. Alessandra broke my reverie.

"Jake," Ali called across the apartment. "It's ten o'clock."

I thought of the public service message on the T.V.: It's ten o'clock Do you know where your children are?

"I know, Ali," I said. "Did Brian call?"

"No. But he's probably working late, like he usually does."

"He's probably waiting for *Late Night with Letterman*," I said.

"You're writing again?" she asked. She came in wearing black spandex. With the towel wrapped into a turban on her head, she looked like a sheik. The thought struck me that whoever discovered spandex should have won a Nobel Prize.

"I'm editing the alchemist's memoirs," I told her.

"Do you need to get that done now?" she said, kissing me on the cheek. It was a kiss that I returned.

"I want to record how he saved those people. I think that he had something to do with the lebensborn."

"Those poor people. Are they still being blamed just for being born? They didn't ask to be the children of Nazi officers."

"No, they didn't ask for that, Ali. But you know I have to say something about this."

"Like you had to write that letter to the newspaper about the cemetery?"

"Exactly."

"Well, I'm calling my mother and then I'm going to bed. I guess you should be getting back home."

"Tell Laura that we should be out to the farm by about ten o'clock tomorrow morning," I said.

"You checked the bus schedule?"

"It leaves Port Authority at 8:15."

"Okay, I'll let her know."

I watched Ali trot off to her bedroom phone. Quicksilver slid down from the window ledge and followed. I stayed at the desk for a few more minutes, idly turning the pages of one of the alchemist's notebooks. Many questions continued to puzzle me: If a man has been considered dead and has willed a farm to charity, is that agreement still binding if he is discovered alive? I could hear Ali's voice as she talked on the phone with her mother about fashion. It is a world in which she is a rising star – or so we say, since most of her designs are for the Spiegel's catalogs. You can feel the intensity between them. Sharon recently retired from a thirty-year career in advertising. Her words are blurbs, captions, sixty-second infomercials. She speaks like that to Ali's father, David, a senior partner in a city law firm. It took some time for David to warm up to me, to get over the fact that his girl home from college was going out with a house painter with a video studio. Ali claims her parents like my peculiar sense of humor and that they don't mind my thinning blonde hair, old western shirts, and habit of watching classic films for hours. "Oh, Jake is just fine," I hear Ali say. I am grateful that Ali understands my work and how it sometimes takes me away from the city from time to time. What she doesn't understand is the claim of the past that has been upon me and how a documentary project took me back again to the world of the alchemist. It brought me thousands of miles to a northern land and back into the web of a nightmare.

We knew we had an early morning, so I gave Ali a hug and said goodnight and then headed out and walked the few blocks to my apartment. Brian had the lights and the TV on in his room. I went to mine.

Lying there on the bed, I heard only quiet, yet the darkness was vibrant, filled with uncertainty. My sense of being watched by someone lingered: a slow dying flame in my thoughts. I lay awake thinking of cold days and nights across the sea. I dreamed of villas to which once came men in long gray coats and blonde Norwegian girls with wonder in their eyes. I could not sleep and went to my desk. Beyond the window, the city seemed stripped bare, a darkness between walls bathed in lamplight and neon. I thought of Ali and Laura, the closest of friends from high school. In the yearbook, there's Ali, big brown eyes, long braids, and Laura is next to her: a soft, pretty face in profile, long hair down her back, looking like Marsha Brady from *The Brady Bunch*. Then I thought of girls entering places with names like Biogen or Gentec; girls whose wombs are harvested and who are paid in cold cash. Schneider sits behind a grand desk in a room with an imposing view. He is interested in the profits that come from these new technologies- and he is making a fortune. He follows me still: seeking to know the secrets of the alchemist and to forever suppress them.

Every time I read the alchemist's notebook, I am reminded of that nightmare years ago. My memories of it are vivid. I am reminded that the nightmare has begun to resurface again. I return to the memoirs, and I turn another page.

In the morning, Ali and I enclosed Quicksilver in a bedroom, shut the door on our Christmas decorations, and caught a Short Line bus from Port Authority out to the farm. Therese, who still runs the place, likes to call it the Canaan Farm, but we still think of it as the Red Cat. It still looks much like the place where we once painted, and it reminds me of experiences that still haunt me today.

When we arrived there, I found Laura sharing breakfast with Therese. The dogs were curled up on the floor. Pots and pans sputtered on the stove. Christmas garlands and candles decorated the windows. Therese wore one of the same sweatshirts I'd seen years ago. Laura's hair was longer than I remembered it from the last time I was there but the brightness in her eyes was the same. Ali and I sat at the table and I helped myself to some sausage and eggs.

"It's good to see you, Jake," Therese said. "How have you been?"

"Things have been good," I said.

"Ali, you look lovely. So how are the two of you doing with life in the big city?"

"We love it," Ali said. "Jake has started a video company."

"So, I've heard. You're still making movies, Jake?"

"We do commercials for local businesses and short industrial films mostly."

"Does Ali help you with doing that?"

"No, she's a fashion designer. She has her own projects."

"Is that right? Well, she's certainly helping you take good care of yourself. Do you still go jogging?"

"In Central Park. Whenever I can," I said. "But if Laura keeps cooking like this, I'm going to look like those little old men who play bocci ball in Veteran's Park."

Ali laughed and tapped me on the shoulder. She swallowed a bite of breakfast and her braids bounced slightly as she turned toward Therese.

"You've done a lot with the farm," she said.

"This farm is not going to be sold," Therese said. "We've decided on that. Those were Ezra's last wishes."

"That's great news," Ali said. "So, what are you going to do with the farm?"

"We've got big plans," Laura said. "Isn't that right, Therese?"

"Curt Casey has informed me that Ezra has left a great deal to us in his will," Therese said. "And no, his will has not been invalidated. Curt is working on that. It seems that Jonas Albrecht von Klaus was quite a wealthy man. He has left his alchemy lab to you, Jake."

"Well, how about that!" I said.

"But you've got to stay in college. That's part of the agreement."

"Part of it?"

"He also wants you to study film making, Jake. And he has left money to the farm and to you and Laura and to Tom, to start a special education school here. He writes about each of you. He says that you were his friends, the children he never had."

"I miss him," Laura said.

"Yes, we all miss him," Therese said. "But at the end of a long and troubled life, I think he has made some sort of a difference."

That's when Tom entered by the back door. He looked like he'd come off a construction site: short-cropped hair, work boots, jeans. His brown jacket sleeves looked like an accordion.

"Hey, Jake. There is a letter for you," he said. He grabbed my hand and pushed the envelope into it.

"Jake, your alchemist friend seems to have a special project for you," Therese said. "There is this strange stipulation. He says that he wants you to find his children."

"He had children?"

"Adopted, it seems. They were lebensborn children, Jake."

"Children who were born of Nazi officers."

"Yes. Of Nazi officers and unwed mothers: the women of the occupied countries. I've heard it became something of a scandal."

"Those people must be fifty or sixty years old by now. Where are they?"

"A man has sent this letter to you. He will contact you by phone. He has already called here at the farm."

"But who is he?"

"He says that he was a friend of Jonas Albrecht von Klaus. He wants you to go somewhere, Jake. I think he wants you to shoot a documentary."

"You're kidding. When do we start?"

"I think he said you'd be leaving as soon as next week."

"Leaving? Where am I going?"

"I think he said something about Norway."

22.

A letter prompted my journey- one in an uneven hand from a man named Eric Knudsen. It was a strange message from a man I did not know, insisting that I meet with him at the Plaza Hotel. He followed his letter with a phone call to say that he had arrived in New York on that cold January morning shortly after the holidays.

"Do I know you, Mr. Knudsen?"

"That is unimportant," said the voice. "I have a business proposition. It is a matter of some urgency."

"Is this about a documentary project?" I asked.

"It is about Jonas," he said.

His use of the alchemist's given name sent a chill through me. Back in those more innocent days when we were not so alert to terrorism in our world, I knew Jonas. I was about twenty then and the small video and film studio I run in Manhattan was then only a dream.

"There is, of course, a need to document things. If you understand my meaning," he said.

I took a subway from our film studio near West 14th up to Columbus Circle and walked east along the southern edge of Central Park. I paused to make sure I had not been followed and entered the hotel lobby. A man in a wheelchair lifted the glass in his hand and tipped it toward me in a salute.

"Eric Knudsen?"

"Yes."

He looked at me with piercing blue eyes. He was an older man, with a long, angular face. His hair was gray, tossed sideways, like a thatch across a roof. To his attire there was a certain formality: a jacket and a silk tie, a dress shirt of a European make. He was wearing cologne and holding a glass of wine.

"Have you been followed?" he asked.

"No," I said.

"They soon will be following you again," he said.

"You know of that?"

"Of course," he said.

"So, tell me… why am I here? How did you know Jonas?"

"Jonas saved my life," he said.

"I'm afraid I don't understand."

He gestured to the chair beside him, and I sat down. I was intrigued that he had known Jonas. Even so, his message could have meant anything. Jonas was a complicated man: a man haunted by his own demons, surrounded by danger. What part of Jonas's life had this man come from? Why, in all of this world, had he called me?

"I have heard that you do commercials and short documentaries," he said.

"You have traveled here to ask me to do a documentary?"

"Something like that," he said, reaching to the blanket beneath him. "I have something for you."

From under the blanket on the wheelchair he produced a brown leather volume. He lifted it carefully and handed it to me. He gestured for me to open it. I noticed the drawings and alchemical equations first. The writing was in Jonas's hand, in German.

"Guard this with your life," he said. "I believe that it holds a clue to the records of the lebensborn. I have brought a translation. I understand that you studied German in school. But this makes things easier." He held out a ring binder filled with paper.

"You know that I studied German?"

"He told me several things about you."

"And I know nothing about you."

"Surely, you have figured out something. I come from Trondheim in Norway. I am fifty-eight years old. I am living proof that racial engineering does not always produce the desired characteristics."

"You are of the lebensborn."

"I am a physically challenged member of the master race," he said with a somber smile. "I am a contradiction, of course. For years we have hidden in shame and in fear. Many of us had not known of our origins until a few years ago. Our parents are old. On their deathbeds they have told us."

I looked again at him. The small lines etched alongside his eyes lent a wizened severity to his face. He appeared like a slightly sad Van Gogh.

"You have read his journal?" he asked. "You have one that looks like this?"

I acknowledged that I had.

"There are several children whose lives he saved. Some have agreed to be interviewed."

"You still haven't answered my question. How do you know Jonas?"

He looked into the distance. He took a sip from his glass and tears seemed to come to his frost blue eyes. A slight gleam appeared in them, as he remembered.

"Jonas and I met a lifetime ago. One day I was sledding on a hill," he said. "My sister had put me on the sled. I was unable to use my legs, but she wanted me to play. Jonas saw me and took pity. He knew what my fate would be. He and his wife Elise arranged for my escape to the Shetland Islands in England. Others were not so fortunate. It has taken a long time for the world to recognize that we were entirely innocent of the circumstances of our birth. But there have been no reparations paid to the lebensborn. A documentary could help us, Jacob. And I will pay you for this. You could shed some light upon this unfortunate episode. You are familiar with it?"

"I have been studying this," I said.

"Tell me," Eric Knudsen said.

"Six to eight thousand children were born of unwed mothers and Nazi officers, during the Second World War," I said. "They called the program the 'Source of Life.'" The Germans claimed that the children of Norway had Viking blood and that they would be part of the master race of the future. Many of the children were sent to Germany to lebensborn homes."

"The homes were set up in Norway also," Eric said. "My mother was introduced to a German officer at a party. She then worked in the Reich's service in Trondheim after Norway was occupied. She had blonde hair, blue eyes. I was abandoned to an orphanage. You see, within a few years, it became clear that I was lame. Jonas and Elise treated me. He and his wife knew I was destined for a quiet end. They took me, at the risk of their lives, to the northern coast from which I was sent on to England. Elke stayed behind."

"Elke. That was the name of their daughter?"

He paused, looking at me a long time before he answered.

"Yes," he said.

"Why me? What is it you want me to do?"

"Jonas chose you for this work," he said. "He hoped that you would one day do a project on the children of the Nazi occupation in Norway."

"He told you this?"

"He wrote it in that journal you have there in your hands."

"But lebensborn children have been a scandal. Do they even wish to be known?"

"It is a secret some have wished to keep," he said. "But there are now many of us who want to speak. Some have brought claims of damages against the government of Norway. And while the government has been sympathetic, it has not come to much."

The alchemist's notebook told me that lebensborn "homes" were created at villas throughout Norway. They were set up at hotels and ski chalets, where well-placed elites from the German army would visit. Soldiers were encouraged to father children with the local women, chosen for their Nordic characteristics. Jonas, the man I call the alchemist, had been in medical training for obstetrics and had served in a clinic in Trondheim. Illegitimate babies could be delivered there. The files guarded the identity of the mothers. A high protein diet was created for the children, who were to be the Reich's claim upon the future. Lebensborn babies who were born deformed, or who were sickly, like Eric, were dispatched to euthanasia clinics to be poisoned, starved, or medically sentenced to die.

In 1945, all of Europe was in ruins. Naziism collapsed. The children were scattered, unidentified, set adrift. The secret files of the lebensborn were lost. The Allies pushed through Germany and the "homes" were shut down by the SS. In Germany, children were shipped to a villa outside Munich. Files may have been burned or dropped into the Isar River. Yet, some still survive. The files in Norway were not altogether destroyed, Eric told me. Jonas hid some of them. He urged me to look for them.

"The archives that remain will help the children to find their parents," he said. "You will travel as a documentary film maker. You will ask to interview those of the lebensborn. Some may refuse, at first. But persist until you can speak with them and listen for anything that they say that may give you a clue to where the records are hidden. Finding those records will reveal the past. It will help many others. It will force them to come to terms with the past."

"This is a good thing? Forcing people to face the past?"

His face grew serious. He put aside the drink and rolled his wheelchair a few inches closer to me. The blue of his eyes grew intense.

"It is necessary," he said. "Let me give you an example. I will tell you of Gisela. Gisela had a certificate from the SS Mother Home with only her mother's name on it. Her father was anonymous. Her father called his girl after sixty years, when he was dying from cancer. He said that he had been genuinely in love with her mother. He had gone to South America and had become an industrialist after the war. Gisela was totally innocent of her father's war crimes. She lived for sixty years, never knowing the story of how she came to be in this world. You will find people like this, Jacob," Eric said.

"In New York?"

"You realize that the search will range a good deal further than here," he said. "I have already made the arrangements. Let's just say, you will not be lacking in funds," he said, handing an envelope to me. In it were one-hundred-dollar bills, twenty of them. "That is a small advance. We have booked your airfare. Your accommodations will be taken care of."

"That is assuming that I accept your offer."

"You will accept it," he said. "But you will never be safe. Schneider will send people to watch you. It all depends how much of a threat he perceives. You will be looking into a history that will discredit him. This has to do with the reputation of a great man. Schneider's people will be watching. Of that you can be sure."

It was then that I realized that the alchemist had set an obligation upon me from beyond the grave. It would lay claim to my life, compelling me back into a dangerous world that I thought I had left far behind. Then, I saw that Eric Knudsen had another surprise waiting for me.

A woman appeared across the lobby, like an apparition in the distance, walking towards us. She was a slender woman in her sixties, dressed in a gray pantsuit and a lavender blouse. Eric looked up, his gaze riveted upon her.

"Eric," she said, smiling broadly. Her hands took his.

"Jacob, I'd like to introduce you to someone," he said. "This is Elke."

Her voice was warm, her speech accented. She took my hand.

"Thank you," she said. "My father spoke of you. He once said that he found something of his own life in you and your friends. He said that you reminded him of when he was young."

Her eyes were ice blue, like Eric's- soft, like the sky on a spring day. I recalled that she had worn black lace to the alchemist's funeral, a dark hat, and sunglasses. She stayed distant from the mourners, motionless amid the headstones. Like a tendril of smoke, she had begun to vanish as soon as the ceremony concluded. I'd followed her a few steps across the cemetery grounds. She walked away, melting back through the trees to her car. Now she was here, a few feet away, her gaze focusing upon me, her words drawing me to respond. But I had no words now. I only nodded.

"You have some important business to do for us," she said. "I suppose that Eric has told you. My father wished to tell the world secrets of the lebensborn experiment."

"He did. Yes," I said.

"We believe that he may have placed the records in a safety deposit box in a bank in Switzerland," she said. "There are other treasures there. A great sum, we think. Unfortunately, we don't have all of the numbered accounts. He was forced to destroy that information. Father told me that he had entrusted it to you."

"I don't understand."

"He said that he had taught you about alchemy."

"I don't practice alchemy, Elke. I'm a media specialist with a small studio."

"But you know the symbols and methods of alchemy. He has told you some of the history," Elke said.

"I remember a few things," I said. "But it is like an American learning a foreign language. You need to use it, or you begin to forget."

"We hope you remember enough," Eric said. "Jonas left this information for us, for you. It explains his past. It is a testament for the future. He left us his message in code, we think. Those notebooks are like a key to a vault."

"Or one to Pandora's box," I said.

"That is why he guarded his secrets," Eric said.

"And you want me to open them? You think that they are in the notebooks and that I can read them?"

"Yes. He thought that you could," Elke said.

"We need to locate the numbers of the bank accounts," Eric added. "His family's business was quite lucrative. We think that the records were hidden and sealed because they implicated his family in the war."

"And would there be others who don't wish to be implicated?" I asked.

"You mean Schneider."

"I do."

"Jonas was murdered," Elke said. "Surely, you know that."

I nodded.

"I am sure that you are aware of the dangers," Eric said. "But you would not have come to meet me here if you weren't curious, if you didn't want to help."

I had to admit that was true. Yet, a sense of danger hung in their eyes: Elke, who, like her father, had spent half her life in hiding; Eric, who, with his disability, held out his mission for me. The alchemist had left his legacy- and a code in alchemical symbols to his secrets and his fortune. It was a curious, troubling gift from his generation to mine- one of war and kindness, hazardous biochemistry, and genetic promise. I thought of the children in the special school at the farm, gathering in a circle around their teacher, Laura, and singing:

This old man, he played one

He played knick-knack on my thumb

This old man had played knick-knack with creation. I looked back into the eyes of his children: at the girl born on the edge of war through certain love; at the boy unable to walk whom he had saved from certain death, and I knew that I must clear his name. I knew I must tell his story.

That story is filled with shadows- like the dark suited man I passed by outside the front door of the hotel. He wore a long black coat. He held a cigarette in his hand and his face was shadowed by an awning. As he watched me leaving, I took the Yankees baseball cap from my bag, placed it on my head. Then I walked briskly away toward the subway at 59th Street.

He already knew where I lived: four stops away on the A-train. What he didn't know is where I kept the alchemist's notebooks: in a safe, deep in a secret drawer in a desk. Jonas had recorded his past all too well- in English, in German, in alchemical formulations and line pencil drawings. The brown leather book Eric Knudsen had given to me resembled the alchemist's notebooks that I had found some years ago. From the secret drawer of the hand carved desk, I lifted a black leather volume and opened it. The fine calligraphy of the dedication on the first of the pages caught my eye. The pages of Jonas's story, written in a careful script, were penned in his native language. On the first page were the words *"fur mein schatz."* The pages were dedicated to his wife Elise. I turned to what he had written about the first day we had met. As I did, I thought of Eric Knudsen's last words to me:

"We are in great danger, Jacob. The future cannot be left to evil. It is about transformation, Jacob. It is a matter of taking the sorrows of the past and transforming them. Jonas has initiated you into the secrets of his craft. He has given you a mission. You have been chosen to carry on the legacy of the last alchemist."

23.

I had an assignment now. It was a challenge, a request really, one that I was appointed to fulfill. I had to go to interview the people that the alchemist had saved when they were children in the war and winter snows of Norway.

Alessandra needed convincing. At first, Ali wasn't about to let me go on a dangerous journey alone. When I told her about Erik and Elke and about how they'd chosen me to go to find the alchemist's secrets, she said, "Good. When do we go?"

Ali can be a dreamy daredevil and it is hard to hold her back when she gets some idea into her head.

"*We* are not going anywhere," I said. "I'm going."

"Jake Kincaid. What if I *want* to go to Norway?"

"It's not like it's a ski weekend, Ali. And I need you here."

"Here. There. What's the difference? I want to be with you, Jake."

"I need you to stay here and crack the code," I said. "Ezra left clues in his notebooks."

"What kind of clues?"

"I don't know. That's why I need you. I can't take the notebooks with me. And can't let them fall into the wrong hands."

"What makes you think that I can figure out this code?"

"You're good at it. I need you to work on it. You're like a genius at Scrabble and crossword puzzles. Ali, you could have broken the famous Enigma Code in World War II if you'd been there."

"That's a fine excuse to have me not go with you."

"I want you to be safe, Ali."

"Is that why you sent me the flowers?"

She pointed to the corner, where she had placed some colorful flowers in a vase.

"I didn't send you flowers, Ali," I said.

Her eyes met mine and there was puzzlement in them.

"Well, somebody left them outside the door to the apartment."

"That's strange," I said, inspecting the flowers. "Orchids?"

She shrugged and began to rearrange the orchids. Then she turned and put her hands on my shoulders.

"So do you think I want you to go risking your life for some documentary?"

"It's for Ezra, Ali. It's the right thing. And it's my work. You know that."

"I do. And so does Schneider. You're a target, as soon as he finds out."

"Then let's not give him two targets to aim at," I said, holding her.

She looked at me for a long time then. There was that quizzical look she gets in her eyes.

"Jake, do you really think it's going to be any safer for me here?" she said.

Ali's father and mother invited us to dinner that day. She must have told her father, David, about the trip I was making to do the documentary because he called me later that day.

"Norway," David said to me on the phone. "You are going all the way to Norway for a documentary? So, what is it this time, Jake? Something for the History Channel? Are you doing the story of Leif Erikson, or the Vikings?"

"No," I said.

"You know, the only Vikings I pay much attention to are the ones who play football in Minnesota," David said. "Hey, I guess you could go jogging in Norway. But it must be cold there. I'll bet you'll do some skiing."

"I'll be too busy," I said. "There are a lot of interviews to do. A lot of moving around."

"Well, that's one way to stay warm. Gets pretty cold there this time of year I'll bet. Doesn't it?"

"I'll dress for it," I said into the phone. "Gloves, hats, long underwear- that sort of thing."

"Don't forget the woolen socks. Back when I was in the service in Korea, we used to double up the socks. You make coffee?"

"Sure do."

"That should keep you warm. We had a guy used to make coffee. It tasted like piss water. We'll do better than that tonight at dinner. I'll promise you that."

Ali had gotten home from work early that evening. She showered, put on jeans and a blouse, and those high, tan boots of hers, and I felt dizzied for a moment from the fragrance of her perfume. She left some food out for our cat, Quicksilver. We double-locked the door, took the stairs down, and hailed a cab on Eighth Avenue. We talked about the Norway trip as we headed uptown.

"So, Jake, did you ever think you'd be shooting documentaries in Norway?" she asked me.

"Not in my wildest dreams."

"I'll miss you. How long do you think you'll be there?"

"Not long. Ten days maybe. It will be mostly research and interviews. I'll be editing the documentary back here in New York. Or maybe out at the farm."

"You're going to edit at the farm?"

"It's probably the best place to pull together all the pieces about Jonas and Elise."

"And you think that Elke is their daughter?"

"I think so. That's what they led me to believe," I said. "You know, I was going through the notebooks yesterday and I saw her name there. There were some symbols next to her name. One was the symbol for King Hakkon VII of Norway, who was in exile in England during the war. It looks like a little like the number seven between brackets."

I drew the image for her on the back of one of the business cards in my wallet:

$$[\text{--}7\text{---}]$$

"You think it means something?"

"I think that she must have been seven years old when they left the country."

"You always amaze me, Jake."

The journals in my possession suggested that Elke had escaped Nazi occupied Norway with her parents in the late autumn of 1943. They had lived briefly in Britain and made their way to the United States after the war. Sometime later, Elke had left the Red Cat Farm, either marrying, or entering a profession and her identity was kept secret. Perhaps, like Jonas Albrecht von Klaus, she changed her name. Yet, both Ali and I doubted that she had ever returned to Europe. If anything, Jonas would want her to be safe and as far away as possible from his enemies like Schneider. Schneider's people had global reach. They were especially present throughout Europe. Elke would be safer in America. Surely, she had gone into hiding. That is why Erik had been unable to find her for many years.

It seemed to me that the alchemist left some clues about her in his notebooks. There was more to the memoirs than his life story. They also certainly held a code. They pointed to something – and I was sure that something was money. He had hidden gold and the records of the lebensborn. He had hidden this not on some lonely hillside but in numbered accounts in a bank. The figures in the notebooks suggested as much. And if there was money, it belonged to someone. We had become trustees. The farm had inherited his estate. It was our responsibility to find the funds. It had also fallen upon me to get these memoirs published and to produce a documentary, so that this story might be told.

So, I looked carefully for clues in the symbols of alchemy: the strange language he had taught me. I pored over those pages almost every night. It was a code, I was sure. I wrote down the numbers of chemical elements. There was a hidden message somewhere in these numbers. Every element has an atomic weight, a boiling point, and its freezing point. Maybe those numbers might mean something. The alchemist had talked about atomic numbers with me. Gold is **Au** and its atomic number is 79. Iron is atomic number 26. I began to look for numbers like that also.

I was especially interested in finding patterns of alchemical symbols set next to each other. I looked for everywhere the text where he had said something about gold and for any drawings or symbols that appeared on the page. Silver looked like the devil's pitchfork: three arrows pointing into the air. Copper was an **X** with three strong horizontal lines through it. Iron was an **I** with an arrow shot through it pointing east. It was also the symbol of Mars, the god of war. For years the alchemists had borrowed symbols from each other. So, there were many variations.

O

+ could mean Venus, or Copper.

[ ]

← meant Potassium.

How was he using these symbols? What had he hidden here?

That is when I saw in the notebook the image of a wizard – the skillful, confident magus with a halo above his head. I remembered this image from the 78 cards of the Tarot. It represented a doctor, an inventor, a scientist, whose words are magic. He is the one who can reveal. He is also the one who conceals. I stared down at the book. "Jonas, what are you trying to show me?"

There may be no better place for a person to hide than in a big city. I thought of that as the cab Ali and I were in rocketed past the theater district, on by Lincoln Center, and up across the west side. David and Sharon live in a spacious apartment in the West seventies, within a short walk of the Dakota and Central Park. The building is unassuming enough, unless you happen to notice, as I did, a little gargoyle face under the corner near the roof. I wondered, as I looked up, if it was truly there to ward off evil or was just an architectural embellishment with a view of Central Park.

We tipped the cab driver, a little bug-eyed Latino man with a wide smile, who obviously liked cigars and meringue music. A uniformed doorman smiled as we went in. We took an elevator up.

Sharon, Ali's mother, had prepared a spiral ham while David made one of his inimitable chef salads and selected a bottle of Pinot Noir to serve with dinner. We spoke over the clink of silverware on china and something that sounded like Beethoven quartets. The room was alive with scents and the sound of Sharon's high, reedy voice and David's low, percussive one, full of the accent of a lifetime in New York. With a clink of glasses, we responded to his toast to our journey. Or, as it turned out, it was a toast to what would be my journey to the anguished past of the people I was to interview in Norway.

"So, Ali. You've decided not to take up skiing in Norway this winter."

"I thought I'd stay in New York," Ali said.

"I thought you liked the snow, Ali," David said. "I remember how you used to almost catch frostbite playing outside every winter at the lake house."

"Jake's only going to be gone for about a week," Ali said.

"Two days in Oslo and about four in Trondheim," I said. "That's up on the coast. The cruise ships come in there."

"Well, that would be a nice way to see Norway," Sharon said. "I suppose they go up along the- what is it they're called? The fjords."

"I won't have much time for sightseeing," I said.

"This is a work week for Jake," Ali said. "He has to conduct some interviews. I can stay here. Mom and I can catch up on some things."

"Does that mean you're bringing the cat?"

"Oh, he's no trouble."

"But Schneider might be," I said.

Ali glared at me.

"Is that another cat?" Sharon asked.

"He's a politician, mom. Jake thinks there are some people who don't want this documentary to be made."

"Is that right?" David said.

I shrugged but Ali spoke more gravely.

"Do you remember when I mentioned those neo-Nazi elements that were near the farm a few years ago?"

"That again?" David shook his head. "Jake, I seem to remember that Bill didn't think it was a good idea that you were writing all those letters to the newspapers."

"Well, my father didn't exactly understand the situation back then."

"And what is the situation now?"

"I'm not entirely sure. But I think there are people who may be uncomfortable about the subject of this film."

"This is about those Nazi children?" David asked.

"They're not Nazi children," I corrected him. "They are the sons and daughters of Norwegian mothers who were matched with German soldiers during the war."

"You mean that their parents were married?" Sharon asked.

"Usually not," I said. "The children were placed in foster care and were adopted by parents chosen by the Party, who were responsible for their education."

"I take it that this was controversial," David said.

"There were thousands of these contacts in Norway during the war," I said.

"Jake's done a lot of research," Ali said. "Many of the women and children were treated badly after the war. He thinks that there may be records that have been hidden for years. But some people are concerned about exposure. Others may not even want to know."

"I imagine it must have been difficult. Not to have known your parents," Sharon said. "Or to find out you were the child of a Nazi soldier who just disappeared."

"Harrowing," David said.

"So, we think that maybe it would be better if Ali didn't make the trip," I said.

"And you think she shouldn't stay alone in her apartment either?"

Ali nodded.

"It'll give us some quality time together, mom."

"Just how serious is this?" Sharon asked. "Jake, are you saying that this is going to draw attention to us here?"

"They already know whatever it is that they know," I said. "I don't think they have any reason to spend time around here, Sharon. But they might follow us if we are in Norway together. So, I think Ali might be better off here."

"Well, we'd love to have you stay for the week, Ali," David said. "I could put Brad Thorne's team on this. He does the investigative work for our firm."

"Oh, I don't think it will come to that, dad," Ali said.

"Listen, it's a good security firm and I want my little girl safe. We use them all the time. It wouldn't be any trouble at all to have them watch the apartment or to keep an eye on you when you go to work."

"You know, David, you might do that," I said. "It's a good idea. But I have somebody else in mind."

Ali caught my look as I glanced her way.

"Ned Roland?" she asked.

I nodded.

"Of course, if any of Schneider's people start to enter into the equation, he should be the first to know about it."

"You keep mentioning this person Schneider."

"He's a politician in Europe, mom," Ali said.

"And that presents a problem?"

"He is very charismatic. His father was with the SS."

David seemed to choke on his food.

"He was a Nazi?"

"Schneider was a Nazi with Himmler's SS," I said. "We had some trouble with him at the farm a few years ago. My sense is that Gerhard Schneider, his son, the politician, wants to suppress information about the lebensborn program. He doesn't want the whole story to be told."

"And who is this Ned Roland?" Sharon asked.

"CIA," I said.

"How's that?" David's eyes widened.

"It's a long story," I said.

Ned Roland works in Virginia, I explained to them. You would not know by looking at him that he is a spy. He is a tall, thin man with the lanky build of a basketball player. He wears wire rim glasses and has the look of a professor. For years, tweed jackets and shoulder-bags stuffed with research papers and faculty meeting notes were his cover. He taught history and politics as a fully tenured scholar. Ned Roland once studied military history at Annapolis. He served as an officer in the navy and was brought to Langley soon afterward. They liked his nondescript looks and his sharp intelligence. We met Dr. Roland that autumn when trouble was flying like leaves around the farm and we soon suspected that he was something more than just a professor at the local college.

These days he has a nice house with a two-car garage. The house is a bit more expensive than most teachers can afford on a professor's salary. It has a wrap-around porch, a picket fence, and a built-in swimming pool in the yard in the shape of an oval. Working as a field agent in Europe and in the United States has its benefits. For a long time, marriage was not one of them. But now he is married and has two children. He has a desk job at Langley, with the Office of Special Investigations. You might say he is a semi-retired spy.

Ned's team at Langley has an interesting array of technological toys. When I shared my idea about Schneider's connections with the biotech industries, he told me that his team had already been long at work on the problem. Their computers held files on scientists, corporate investors, and on donors, he said. Usually these were young women, between the ages of 18 and 30, who sought money for everything from cars, apartments, and jewelry to college tuition. Most often, they were white, blonde, and blue-eyed, like their predecessors. The clinics and research centers that lured and accommodated them ranged across North America and Europe. There were also several in South America, in Argentina. These, Ned Roland's team believed, had a direct correspondence with escaped Nazi fugitives. Schneider's dream had not changed greatly over the years, he said; it had just been modified- and everything they were doing was legal. I told Ned I wanted to explore this further. As in the old days, when we had first met, Ned Roland told me to stay out of it. Instead, I went deeper.

24.

In the beginning was fire and ice. So, say the Eddas of Norse mythology. Somewhere beyond Midgard, the land of our experience, lies the storied land of the gods- of Thor, Odin, and Freyr: the mythic land of Valhalla. The Norse legends have drifted for centuries like the mist above the rugged coastlines and mountains of Norway, a land that once lay covered by a sheet of ice.

Norway is a quiet, scenic part of the world- a northern land of sturdy and resourceful people. In the Second World War, Norwegians were beset with a Nazi occupation: one which, like an earthquake, had some profound aftershocks. It has taken me years to begin to tell this story. It has taken others in Norway much longer to tell theirs. The story of the lebensborn of Norway is an unresolved tale of the consequences of war. When men and women fall in love, often children are born- and the future is born in them. The promise of childhood is nurtured by love, by parents or guardians who respond to the gift, who share their lives and secure the child's world. Yet, for the child born of war, parents are sometimes a mystery, a loss, and a story. This is how it was for the children that Elise and Jonas saved. I was curious about them and about this starkly beautiful northern land.

My deal with Erik Knudsen was sealed at the Park Hotel in New York on that cold January day. I decided that I would oblige Erik Knudsen's wish to develop a documentary that exposed the dreams and sorrows of those like him: the lebensborn. Shortly after my meeting with Erik, I packed some of my video equipment for the trip to Norway in one of the company vans. Brian James, my business partner, gathered most of the necessary equipment. I would rent the rest in Norway: lights, two cameras and lenses, and a small soundboard and mixer. Brian would keep our small studio going in New York, while I was gone. We talked about it the day before I left.

"Brian, I'll be out of the office for about ten days," I said.

"Sure, Jake. I'll take care of things."

"If Terry calls about the radio spot, I'd like you to handle that."

"Sure, Jake. Do we still have the lawyers coming in for the commercial shoot?"

"They'll be here. You'll set up the lighting?"

"Got it. Two fresnels and some back lighting for the table. Like we talked about. Two cameras. I've got it all here in the notes. By the way, you got a call from Tom Sheffield."

"Tom called the studio?"

"Yeah, it was something about some guy named Jonah. Wasn't that the guy with the whale?"

"No. This is somebody else," I said. "Hey, take care of yourself, Brian. And keep in contact."

"Will do," he said.

I never imagined that I would ever journey toward that strange greenish glow of the northern lights. Yet, the next morning, I was off on my journey. The flight from New York's Kennedy Airport to Oslo's airport takes about ten hours. There was a connecting flight to Trondheim, following a brief layover. I had arranged for a stay at the Raddison Hotel on Kjopmannsgate. Soon after arriving, I called Ali. Then I sat quietly by the window, looking out on the beginning of a snowfall. Norway that first night was a dark sky and a sheet of drifting snow. I lit a candle in remembrance of the people lost long ago in war. It reminded me of the flame in the alchemist's laboratory, a kind of eternal flame on the grave of the Unknown Soldier.

The plane I had been on had moved out across the Atlantic, a kind of migration- a passage by flight across the sea. I thought of how the lebensborn project emerged from the migration of German soldiers to Norway- like so many gray birds arching across the sea and the sky. The belief in a master race emerged from a worldview that life unfolds by the survival of the fittest: the claim of the sharpest claw, the sweep from the sky of the deadliest hawk, the stealthy uncoiling of the snake with the most venom. The Nazis survived by what they called strength: a power arrayed with tanks, with bombers and machinery. For them, strength was violence; superiority was force; it was biology, race, an inexorable will larger, greater than humanity. It was destiny. So, death they brought and sorrow: the unintended consequences of war. When a plan was made to mate Nazi officers with Norway's women, some of the women were forced – raped as surely as were Norway's hills and its ports of raw material. Some were women who loved, young girls enticed by romance and the virile embrace of strangers. They were cast off; they were called traitors- and if the mother was disgraced, so too was the child.

So, that first night, I sat uneasy by the window, watching as winter surrendered to snow. Rooftops, like Atlas, seemed to hold up the frozen world. Icicles were pulled downward by gravity. The moon seemed to be circling earth like some detached companion drifting along. And I dreamed of lives erased by time, the glow of their pleasures like streetlights distant, their names forgotten. I felt the cold on my hands, the cold on my face. I reached across space for Ali's voice on the phone and the memory of her warmed me.

Ali had gone to stay with her parents. She brought our cat, Quicksilver, a few books and movies, and more clothing than she could possibly need. David had hired the security firm to ensure her safety. We called each other twice every day, talking about simple things, like the cat, or the line of sunflower blouse designs she was developing. "How's your mom?" "Oh, good, good." "And your dad?" "Oh, he's watching his weight. He'd like to be playing golf up in Westchester but it's a little cold for that. But he's been good." Our conversation went like that and just to hear her voice was enough. I talked about the hotel and the weather in Trondheim and I never said much about the project. We could never be sure who was listening.

Then the trouble started. A frantic call came from Brian on the second day. Someone had broken into our studio in New York. The files and desk drawers had been torn open. The shelves had been ransacked. Tapes, papers, and wires were everywhere. We'd worked out a code, a kind of a media-speak, to send messages to each other. He insisted that the bad guys were on the loose.

"Did you call the police?"

"I called. They've been here twice. They think it was a robbery. But whoever broke in didn't take anything, Jake," he said.

"That's because they were looking for something and they didn't find it. Hey, Brian, you be careful," I said.

"Hey, Jake, I can put the place back together in about a week. You need me, just call. ET phone home. You know? So, how's it going there?"

"Good. No Jokers so far here. Harry meets Sally tomorrow."

"Oh, that's good. Make sure to get them on a reel."

That meant that I'd arrived safely. There were no bad guys, as far as I could tell. And I was meeting with the first of our documentary subjects, a woman, tomorrow. Brian's call put a little scare in me. It was obvious to me that Schneider and his people were looking for the alchemist's notebooks. And only Ali and I knew where they were hidden.

I imagined Ali sitting up in bed with the alchemist's notebooks, working through the code. The memory of Ali's warmth was my safety zone. The softness, the scent, and pull of her, the way she takes me in, seemed to be the only sure thing, the only guard against the uncertainty of bad dreams. I imagined her safely at home, asleep, breathing small breaths, and I lay on my side in the hotel, still thinking. The heat was on in the radiator. I imagined Ali, far away, wrapped warmly in bedcovers. Then the phone rang and broke the daydream.

"Jake Kincaid. Do I have Jake Kincaid?"

"David?"

"Jake, is that you? What's this with my daughter, Jake? What is she doing?"

"Calm down, David."

"No. No. I want to know what she's doing."

"I don't know what you're talking about."

"She's missing, Jake."

"Missing?"

"She's not in New York. She took off somewhere."

"She what?"

"She's not here. She didn't say where she was going."

"Ali's very independent, David. Are you sure she's missing?"

"She went looking for something. I don't know what it is. Our guy hasn't seen her. We can't talk on the phone, right? Wasn't that the deal? But you've got to call her, Jake. We've got to find her."

"David, I'm in Norway. How am I supposed to find her?"

"Call her. She'll take your call. Call her. Okay?"

"Okay. Okay. I'll call her."

"And call me back when you know something."

"Okay."

I felt my breath catch and felt my chest tightening. Missing? Where was she? David sounded even more nervous than me. What was she doing? I felt afraid for Ali. I feared that one of Schneider's people was chasing her. I imagined her running from him: how the woods fell behind her, how she went down for cover, sprawled in the dirt. It was one of those movies in my head. Her breathing was loud, as she stumbled forward. Her mind was racing. She crouched low by the house, alert. Then she hurried across the gravel, away from the sounds. No shots came, no splinters of gunfire. The darkness was beckoning. Into it, she ran. Branches, forest, shadows consumed her. She kept running. She ran through my daydreams. She ran into my troubled heart. The phone was ringing. Where are you, Ali?

"Hello?"

"Ali, are you okay?"

"Jake. Hi, honey. Of course, I'm all right."

"Your father just called."

"I had to get away from that detective, Jake. I don't need twenty-four-hour surveillance. I'm fine, Jake. Look, I'm finding out more about the code."

"Not on the phone."

"Well, just to let you know. I'm investigating. I've got a good sense of what our friend King Kong has been up to."

I paused. It meant that she knew something new about Schneider.

"Okay. But be careful."

"I'll do that," she said. "Talk later?"

"Yes. Sure. Of course, we will. Ali. Love you."

"Love you too, Jake."

I set down the phone and looked out on the snow-covered streets beyond the window. Trust is a funny thing. You get in your car and you expect it to go down the road. You get latex house paint and you expect it to be white. You get a job to paint a farmhouse and it turns into a strange nightmare. I was worried about Ali. Yet, I just had to trust her, and I had to trust that she would be okay.

To calm my nerves, I went for dinner. It was a traditional Norwegian meal of cod and potatoes, at a restaurant near the hotel. Trondheim is a medieval city on the western coast of Norway. It is dominated by the Nidaros Cathedral: a gray, blackened Gothic marvel with its spires pointed toward the sky. Its west end, finished in 1300, is lined with statues of Bible characters and its front had great long windows and the magnificent curve of its central window. I could see the top of the cathedral from the Raddison Blu Hotel, where my room faced the river. The crisp, cold air seemed to freeze upon the factories along the docks and on the shingles and roofs of the old churches. At night Norway sank into darkness and its stark landscape became like the melancholy ending of an Ibsen play. Lamplight fell on frozen snow, glowing on vast white spaces between brick and concrete buildings.

I am told that there is ice on the streets from late October through winter. Walking the icy sidewalks, I looked from the red Old Town Bridge across the Bakklande, which is filled with shops and cafes. In one of the shops, I bought a fur hat for Ali and the small figurine of a troll, which I kept in a paper bag.

There was a park behind Stiftsgarden, the royal residence built of wood, and I sat there for a moment thinking of the Beatles song, "Norwegian Wood." I wandered on Dronnigensgate, looking at the baroque façade of the Britannia Hotel. Then I walked into the town center to try to find the café where I would meet the woman who would be the subject of my first interview.

Her name was Freyda Tikven – or so she was called. I had found her living in a small apartment in the city. She was anxious that anyone had found her. She had chosen a small café in the heart of Trondheim for our meeting and entered it wearing a gray hat, a blue and white dress, and sunglasses. She was a woman of about sixty, a tall woman, although she seemed to slouch a bit. There was a trace of rouge on her cheeks and, as she took off the glasses, there appeared her bright blue eyes- as blue as the sky- looking apprehensively at me. I introduced myself and got to business immediately.

"I am looking for Elke von Klaus," I said.

The woman drew a quick breath. Her eyes looked apprehensive.

"Why do you come to me looking for Elke von Klaus?"

"You were at the orphanage."

There was another deep breath, a halting in her voice.

"Erik told me you would come here," she said.

She pulled the scarf more tightly around her, as if it would protect her not only from the cold but from the unknown.

"You have agreed to be interviewed."

"I have… on a few conditions," she said. She waited until the waiter had brought our coffee and pastries and then resumed speaking.

"You will disguise my voice. Erik said that you can do that."

"I can use compression and some distortion on your voice. I assure you; no one will recognize you."

"So, we are agreed upon anonymity. You will put me behind a screen."

"You will be a shadow behind what is called a scrim."

"A shadow. How appropriate," she said. "I have been a shadow my entire life, Mr. Kincaid."

"Call me Jake."

"Erik tells me that you were a friend of Jonas Albrecht."

"I was."

"He was a great man. He and Elise saved my life. The orphanage that they chose was both efficient and compassionate. It was dedicated to St. Olaf. Did you know that he is the patron saint of the city?"

"No, I didn't," I said.

She looked off wistfully. Her forefinger circled the rim of the coffee cup. "I was a child when I knew them. That was many years ago," she said. "We girls were trained at the mother house, schooled, and disciplined in our daily round of marches and studies. Jonas and Elise were on the medical team that arrived to measure our health and our stamina."

"They had you moved to the orphanage?"

"Yes. That was the first step. They continued the routines there. The schooling, the discipline. That was done so to not arouse suspicion."

"But the neighbors- they found out?"

"Oh, yes. They knew. They would spit on our mothers for having children with German soldiers."

"They wished to have you deported."

"Yes, but Jonas and Elise saved us."

"Freyda, we would like you to come to the farm that they lived on."

"To America?"

"Yes. Erik has made the travel arrangements."

"But I can't just leave."

"It will only be for awhile, Freyda. It is for a reunion of the children. Erik has a surprise."

"Jonas and Elise's children, you mean. Yes, we are something like their children. I never knew my parents."

"That is what we are going to discuss," I said. "If it is not too difficult for you."

"No. It is all right."

"This will be the preliminary interview. Erik has arranged for a studio loft in a renovated factory a few blocks from here. We will tape our next interview there tomorrow."

"So, where shall we begin today?"

"When did you first learn that you were a lebensborn child?"

"I had long suspected that," she said. "Blonde hair, blue eyes. I was always quite tall. I was told that my father was German and that he had died in the war. Of course, that information was wrong."

She stirred her coffee, adding some more cream to it. She nibbled on one of the pastries.

"A man contacted me three years ago," she said. "He told me that he was my father. He found me through the orphanage records, he said, like you and Erik have done."

More coffee was brought to us. Her voice was nearly a whisper.

"Why do you tell me this now?" I asked him. "Because I am dying," he said. "The cancer has become inoperable." He wanted to resolve the past. As if that were an easy thing to do."

She shook her head and took a sip of coffee. Her face appeared lined with a lifetime of care. I was lost in her blue eyes and Ezra's voice echoed gently in my memory: "enchanting."

"I was furious," she said. "I faced this man and there were only years of frustration. "You were alive and you let me live in an orphanage?" I said. "I could not stay here with you," he told me. Something did not fit. This was an officer who could not stay after the war. Why did he not simply live in Norway then and raise me where I was born? "No. I could not do that," he said. He could not do that because they hunt down S.S. officers."

"Did you ever meet your mother?"

"No," she said. "My mother is more of a mystery. My father did not say much about her, except that she was born here in Norway. "I loved her," is all he said. "She was a beautiful woman. She is gone," he said. Helga was my mother's name. She met him at an officer's ball during the war. The country was occupied then. He must have been a tall and handsome man. They fell in love. It did happen. Oh, perhaps it was arranged. Perhaps it was for a strange cause. But people do fall in love."

I asked her about Elke.

"She was a quiet child. Yes, I knew her when we were little children. We would play sometimes. We were friends."

She paused, looking vacantly out the window past the curtains.

"Did you know her parents?"

"I did know the doctor. Yes. But I did not know my parents. It is strange. My birth certificate was vague. It did not mention my mother's name. It only mentioned the mother home. Elke, I think, moved away to America after the war. I did not see her again for years. We met at the train station here in Trondheim when we were young women- oh, about twenty years old or so, I'd guess. She told me that she was looking for her adopted brother, a boy named Erik. I remember that because I told her it sounded like a Viking name. She said that he was disabled and that she had not seen him for a long time. She hoped that he was still alive, but she did not know if he was. Elke said that she was spending time with a fine young painter, who had a gallery in New York. He was an American, but his parents were Scandinavian. I did not see her after that. I am sorry that I cannot help you more."

"You have helped me a good deal," I said. "Your story will be helpful too."

"We have lived separate lives, quiet lives," she said. "We do not want trouble. I did not ask my father to be an officer of the S.S. or ask my mother to give birth to me. It would have been nice to have known my mother. I think of her often in my dreams. I wish things could have been different. But a cup of coffee or tea is what it is. Is it not? Life is what is given to us."

She laughed for a moment and shook her head.

"Silly of me," she said. "We think a lot, you know. It is just something that Norwegians do. A national trait maybe. To look at the stars and wonder where you come from. It must be these cold nights."

She looked around her – at the tables set for breakfast, at the couple in the corner, the waiter bringing a tray of pastries to them.

"I think I'd best go now. It has been good meeting you. I hope you find what you are looking for."

The street outside was bathed in the half-light of morning. I watched Freyda walking past the shops, in the direction of the city center. She paused, looking around her, as if to check on whether she had been followed by anyone. But her eye was not a well-trained one. She did not pay attention the man in the long black raincoat waiting at the bus stop. He struck a match and I saw it glow for a moment like a fitful bug, as he lit a cigarette. He tossed the match away and took a cell phone from his pocket and made a call.

I hid for a time in the shadows at the edge of a building. The man seemed to vanish like a shadow. I walked back to the hotel, certain that he knew precisely where I was staying. My project was now clear. The secrets of the past had to be reopened. I was thousands of miles from home, in a strange place where some continue to hold on strongly to the past and have not let go. Yesterday hung in the chill air like distant ghosts, and around each corner were watchful eyes. I had to watch my back.

The cold and remote building that had once been the mother home was about five miles from Trondheim. It was essential to include this setting in my documentary. From the city, I drove to the mountain, passing through a valley of ice and snow. The days had become short. By late afternoon there was already twilight. The river had frozen over and I could see the crack of the ice on Lake

Glimmer. Beyond the bare trees, the thin line of sunlight was making its last effort to shine on the horizon. There was new snow. The tracks of a reindeer led into the forest. There upon the hill was the shadow of the building. I walked up to that abandoned world.

I took the tripod from my backpack and set it up on the snow. For a moment, I considered the angle. The gloves on my hands came off, so I could adjust the video camera. The wind had begun its antics: cold air through the trees was kicking up the snow. I'd come all this way. I must get the shot. The camera focused on the hulking shadow of the building on the mountain. Give us magic. Snow like silver. Heavy roof and stone walls, wooden porch, and broken gables. I filmed it all.

Down the mountain I walked, hoping that I would not lose my way. I took a snow-clotted path to the road. If dusk came on, I would be lost. I moved through shredded light, passing the pines thawing in the sun. I reached the cabin just as the trees took on a pact with the sky, turning toward shades of darkness. I was cold and shivered and the stars came out clear. I soon reached my car, parked where I'd left it, along a road under the cold, open sky. I drove it to the city. I had another interview, another to survivor to meet.

25.

Jan Sorensen's tale was among the most horrific. Jan was a survivor. He had endured beatings, verbal abuse, and more than a decade in an insane asylum. It was a harsh punishment for something for which he was not responsible. His mother may have fallen in love with a Nazi soldier. He might have been sent with care to the mother home. But the war ended, and the Germans were forced from the country, and in that final disarray, he was sent to hell.

He could still hear the screams, he told me. Sometimes it seemed as if the wall would shatter. He pulled the pillow up around his ears, but it was no use. The screaming went on. A thunderous voice replied, and then came the echo of fists hitting at the wall like small explosives in the night. The scream echoed down dark corridors: narrow passages feebly lit in the light that seemed to struggle to make it into his room. He remembered fiery lights, the wings of bombers throwing shadows, long ago. No, he was not crazy. Jan Sorensen was as sane as the people on the outside, he was sure. Child of a Nazi social experiment, the lebensborn, he knew only these cold walls, this prison of humanity. Yet, he could imagine a mountain pass, a ski trail, a place where he could go to find peace. *A fa fred og ro*. In the barren north he could find peace, near Transo, in some desolate place deprived of light for half a year. There the northern lights burned and burned. There no darkness, no evil could be hidden. He might build a stone wall. He would work hard like the free men of Norway: fishing, building sturdy ships, chopping wood for pulp and paper. Once free, he would go for walks and make a solitary search for ski trails.

A ga pa tur. Orphan child. Your father is dead. Your mother has abandoned you.

There was that relentless banging, the pulse of some random revolt down the hall. It sounded as if Thor, the god of warriors, was pounding his magic hammer. It was as if Loki, the shape-shifting god, had tricked them all into this prison. He thought of Jonas, the man who might have saved him. If only Jonas was here with his strange alchemy. He could melt these prison bars.

For eighteen years he was 'not well.' Then he was free. In a city so sprawling, so pitifully cold, one needed a job. One needed a house in which to light a fire. He had no skills. He could barely write. And so, he came to work in a factory, exchanging sweat and muscle for pay. He lived in a flat that he rented on a street in Oslo. Jan Sorensen was the son of a German officer and a Norwegian mother he never knew. Nor did he know the doctor who had delivered him at birth, or the nurse, the doctor's wife, who had tried to save him. He was to have been one of the elites, the blonde and blue-eyed future of the thousand-year Reich. Now he was one of the fortunate ones: one who had lived and endured- thin, sallow faced, his hands calloused, his once blonde hair now gray at fifty. He sat over a simple meal of bread and cheese and potatoes. On his wall was a landscape of a mountain pass, painted by a local artist. The fireplace glowed like the midnight sun. The walls of the asylum were gone but yet, one could see, he lived inside them.

For years the lebensborn had hidden in shame, in fear. Hitler's children, they were called. They were the daughters and sons born of the genetic plans of the Nazi Third Reich. They had been secreted away, trained to be the Nazi-future. For years they lived submerged, as was Jan Sorenson in the tomb of that asylum. Now they had begun to speak. And nothing on earth could stop their cry for justice.

Jan Sorensen's apartment was in a concrete building in the heart of the city. He lived simply, in a three room walk up. When I arrived there, night had come but every light burned brightly in his rooms. He was neatly dressed for his interview.

"It is a privilege to meet with you, Jan," I said. "Your story should make an important contribution to our documentary."

"Oh, I am sure it will," Jan said.

He was a thin man with a graying beard. He wore a woolen shirt and jeans and a silver watch on his left wrist. There was a teaspoon in his hand, and I watched as he poured honey into a cup. He looked intently into the cup as he stirred the tea. I could see the hard lines, the ravages of time in his face. He told me that he had built the room. It was freshly painted. When I told him I once painted houses, he laughed. "You will not get many painting jobs here," he said. "The men and women of Norway are fiercely independent. We like to do our own work."

I smiled at that and took the video equipment from my bag.

"I'm going to set up this video camera here on a tripod. You don't mind, do you?"

"No," he said. "I requested this interview."

"Thanks," I said. "I think that if we move this a little over here. That's good."

"You want to talk about the asylum?" he asked.

"Tell me about your work."

"There is not much to tell. I work at a factory. It is steady work. But it is not very exciting."

He seemed to ponder my request for a moment. Then a thin smile appeared on his face.

"I am learning to be a machinist. I am Adam Vigsund's apprentice. Usually, he gets them younger. But it is the first time I have had the chance to study with someone."

"Your formal education was limited."

He nodded twice, taking a sip of tea as he did.

"Because I was sent away," he said. "We had school when I was small. Even after the war, the goal was to teach the children who went to Germany. But I was left behind. In the school the other children taunted me. They said that my mother was a traitor, my father a criminal. I argued back. I fought for my rights. The teachers said that I was a troubled child. The more I fought the more they said that. Then I was sent away."

At the asylum, there was a tree in the courtyard beyond the window, he said. There were bars on the windows, but he would sometimes look out at the moon. It seemed to move slowly, he said, like a fingernail across the darkness, shining on that tree, shining on the ground. Why he remembered the moon, I don't know.

"I feared sometimes that they would come for me," he said.

"Did they hurt you, Jan?"

"That was their way," he said. "You Nazi, they would say."

"Were you medicated?"

"Yes."

"Did they hit you?"

"They beat me sometimes with a paddle. Sometimes with a coat hanger, or with their shoes."

"This occurred in broad daylight?"

"In the night, or in the day. When they wanted to. It didn't matter."

"You never deserved that."

He nodded.

"I am not responsible for the war," he said. "Maybe they felt like the guilty ones. Nils Gundersen, the therapist who worked with me later on, thought so. He said they felt ashamed for how they had been overrun by the Germans."

"It was terrible for everyone," I said.

"Yes. So, they turned shame and hate upon us."

"But to put you in an asylum was unjust."

"The Nazis put Norway in a prison," he said. "That was unjust too."

"Do you think it was a form of revenge? They could not catch all of the S.S. but they could catch and abuse an innocent child?"

"Oh, I don't know about that. Most of the people I have met here in Norway are very fine, very good people."

"Do you think that it was human nature for the people who ran the institution to think that they were the sane ones?"

Jan shrugged. "You ask difficult questions," he said. "Some of them were the insane ones."

He finished his tea and turned the cup upside down on the table.

"They did this," he said. "They turned the world upside down."

Jan Sorensen was a brutally honest man. He had suffered and endured and had begun to learn to hope again. The images that he described were as dark as those of war. They were the emotions of a prisoner, a victim of abuse haunted by unexpected violence and indignities. His life was an ongoing testimony to the human capacity to endure.

When I left his apartment, there was no one in the courtyard outside. There was a high, twisting tree which I was sure must have reminded him of the one he had seen outside the asylum many years ago. Night had come and I stayed on the well-lit main streets, walking toward the lot where I'd left my rental car.

I knew that someone's eyes were fixed on me. It is an intense sensation that creeps up on one, like a shiver on the back of the neck. I quickened my steps and covered the distance as swiftly as I could. Someone was following me, but I had seen no one.

Suddenly, something exploded above my head and I went down. I lay on the ground, frozen for an instant, then I scrambled back toward the light. I came face to face with a black iron fence, a concrete cistern, the sarcophagi in the burial ground beside Nidaros Cathedral. Wind rushed through the fields- and something else: the sound of someone quickly approaching.

I heard the sharp fall of footsteps, saw shadows round the fence. They were after me. I dashed around the semi-lit wall of the fortress and the courtyard, seeking the central garden. There was a gaping entryway. Upon a wall above was a bronze eagle, wings spread to the sky. A tunnel went down, like a steep ramp in front of me. I'd gone the wrong way. High overhead a man stood, a hawk that had found its prey. I raced down into the tunnel.

The tunnel became darker. Down I went. My feet echoing, my heart pounding. I entered a chamber, cut by pale glimmers of light. I reached out my hand feeling along the wall. Below me the stones were spotted with trails of blood. Air- I needed air. Breathe, breathe. Blindly, I fumbled along the wall.

He was close, the one who was behind me. At a turn in the tunnel, it seemed like the wall parted. Narrow stairs led upward. I took them toward a light that beamed above, as if the wall had been cut open by a cold switchblade knife. Out I hurried, out to the night.

I ran in the direction of my rental car. The night became a swirl of lights, cold air, running feet. At the car, I fumbled with the keys. I shivered, turned on the ignition, and pressed the gas pedal. The car plunged forward into the night, rapidly accelerating. Out of the city I drove, headlights following me.

The road was dark, broken only by headlights racing. Then a car surged forward behind me, its headlights brightening like a searchlight. It hit my back bumper sharply on the turn. The back of my car swerved. Suddenly, I was skidding off the road, into the trees.

I blacked out, awakening dizzily to flashing lights. There was a voice, asking if I was all right.

"*Hvorden har du dat?*" How are you?

Faces gazed down at me. Faces in circles of light. "*Jo takk,*" I was saying. I'm fine, thank you.

"*Hva heter du?*" What is your name?

"Jacob."

"*Snakker du norsk?*" Do you speak Norwegian?

"*Ja, lit.*" I said. A little. Very little, as they quickly noticed. The voices shifted into English.

"There are many deer and elk," one said. "Young man, you must watch out here."

"It was another car," I'd said.

I was taken to the hospital. In a bland hospital room, I gazed blankly at the ceiling. I must have fallen asleep, thinking of Ali, thinking of home, and then the old man came to me in a dream. His was an ancient, lined face, filled with the care of the world. He stood in the doorway to a distant room and his heavy coat was bound with snow. He rolled up the sleeve of his coat, shaking off the snow, and I saw that his frail arm was marked with numbers. I tried to recall them. Then voices awakened me. The nurse was introducing me to a man who had entered the room. He was a solidly built man of about thirty years of age. He had no particularly distinguishing features, although I remember that his face was perspiring. Daylight crept in through a split in the blinds over his shoulder.

"Young man, I am Rolf Hansen," he said. "I am with the police. We are investigating your accident. Could you confirm your name for us?"

"Jacob Kincaid."

"You are an American?"

"That's right."

"And the purpose of your visit is?"

"I am conducting research for a documentary."

"The subject?"

"The Second World War."

"How is it that you take photographs of this subject?"

"I photograph buildings mostly."

I saw the firm mouth, the glint in his eyes.

"Is there any reason you are aware of that someone might want to get hold of those photographs?"

"Not that I know of," I said.

"I see," he said. "Well, that will be all for now. We will leave your documents here with you."

He placed my wallet and my passport on the end table near the bed.

"And somebody left this for you," he said. "The nurse gave this to me."

He placed a vase of flowers down on the end table next to the bed. Then he left the room. I sat up in the bed, looking into a colorful arrangement of orchids.

It was shortly after the man had gone that I was startled by the ringing of the phone.

Erik Knudsen was on the phone and his voice sounded frantic.

"Freyda's house was broken into, Jake."

"When?"

"Last night. Her place was turned upside down. Jacob, we must get out of here!"

My heart sank when I heard the news.

"We must get you out of the hospital and out of the country," Erik said. "I have contacted Roland."

"Does he think that it was Schneider?

"Schneider is clever. He would never want to be associated with this."

"But is he too clever to kill?"

"He is sending a message, Jacob. His people are looking for something. Tell me you have hidden the tapes and made duplicates."

"Yes. I've already done that."

"Good."

"What about Jan? Is he in danger?"

"Yes. We have made arrangements to move him. Do you think you could help us to get him to the farm?"

"The Red Cat Farm? But what if Schneider's people follow us there?"

"They may. But I want us to go there because we are in danger *here*. I've already bought the plane tickets. We can finish the project at the farm. You can edit it in your studio. You've got to get out of here, Jake!"

Minutes later a nurse appeared in the doorway.

"Two men are waiting to meet with you," the nurse said.

The news set my heart racing. Someone had tried to push me off the road. Had they now come back to finish the job? Then in the doorway I saw a familiar face: Ned Roland.

"Jake, we've arranged for your release from the hospital. We have your things in a limo outside."

A tall, distinguished looking man with gray hair had come into the room with him. The man wrapped his hand around an umbrella handle and stared down his nose at me, as if down the slope of a mountain. I had seen Solomon Levy before. Professor Roland had given me a videotape of the head of the Special Investigations Office speaking at a Senate committee press conference last month. I could see Solomon Levy in that video, standing in a room full of reporters, kind of like those you see on CNN. Now he stood in front of me, the scraggly beard and the scar on his left cheek, and again I felt entranced by those penetrating dark eyes. When Solomon Levy stares your way, he can scare you. His dark locks hang over his eyes, as if he hasn't known the services of a barber in years. But then the eyes train on you, even as they did on the cameras that day, and when the guy starts to speak it is a low but almost entrancing tone that emerges.

"Jacob Kincaid. You have certainly gotten yourself into a mess again. Haven't you?"

"Let's get him out of here, Sol."

Ned Roland had secured my release from the hospital. The agency packed my bags from the hotel room. They'd also packed an ashen-faced Erik Knudsen into the limo that was waiting outside the hospital entrance. There was a deep unsettling look of fear in his eyes.

"You're sweating, Jake," said Roland, as he escorted me to the car.

"They're after me."

"Pushed your car off the road?"

"The doctor said I have the scars to prove it."

He opened the car door.

"Get in."

"Jake, it is awful," said Erik. "I never thought it would come to this."

"It's not your fault, Erik."

He was silent then, turning his face back to the window as the car sped away.

"We're getting her out," he said, finally. "We're having Freyda and Jan both moved to a place where no one can find them."

"That's good, Erik," I said. "Good thinking. Keeping everybody safe."

I sat between Roland and Solomon Levy, our long legs stretching out in the spacious limo. Looking down at my jeans, I remembered what I had hidden away.

"Ned, I have something for you," I said, reaching down to my ankles. My hand came back up and offered him a small envelope packed with photographs. "If they were looking for these, they couldn't find them."

Ned studied the envelope and his eyes widened. He passed it to Solomon Levy.

"Well," Solomon Levy said, holding the photos up to the light. "How did you manage this?"

"Socks," I said, and I lifted my foot. "Secret pockets. They're for travelers."

"You hid this in your socks?"

"The socks have pockets in them."

"Ah- and what will they think of next?"

I handed him a photo of a long-faced man under a hat. His face was ashen, his eyes glassy. There was a scar across his chin.

Solomon Levy stared at the picture and breathed out deeply.

"Hans Schneider. Twenty years older. Yes, this is him."

"The photo is from a few years ago," Professor Roland said. "This is our link, Sol,"

Solomon Levy nodded that he understood. He turned over the papers in his hands. "If this is the man you say he is, by all rights he should have been tried and prosecuted years ago in Nuremberg. Jacob, we looked for this man for more than twenty years. Hans Schneider is dead," Solomon Levy said. "Did you know that?"

"No," I said.

"We confirmed that he has died. We used DNA samples to make certain. His son: that is another story. And this?" he said, tapping the next photo in his hands. "What have we here? Andreas Ritschl? When was this taken?"

"That one is recent," I said.

"You have seen him before."

"At the train station, a few years ago. Schneider handed something to him."

"He is a colleague of Gerhard Schneider. Andreas Ritschl. As you know, Gerhard has gone underground. But he still has quite an effective network. Wouldn't you say so, Ned?"

"Deadly," Ned agreed.

"Yes. And Andreas Ritschl is a key figure. A rather brutal one, I'm afraid. May I keep these?"

"Of course. They're yours," I said.

"All right, Jacob. Very good," he said. He slipped the envelope into his jacket pocket. "Now, tell me a little more about this Jonas. Of course, I know a great deal, but I want to hear it from you"

"Jonas was a doctor. He was an alchemist. He had to escape."

"Escape? What do you mean, son?"

"He was a medical officer," I said. "He saw some things."

"Jake, do you realize what those men did? I mean the human reality."

"It must have been horrible. Jonas knew that. He lived with that for years. I think it is why he chose a Biblical name."

"You say he was a medical officer. He was engaged in… the experiments?" His voice caught on the word.

"He only wanted to be an alchemist," I said.

"How's that?"

"An alchemist, sir. One who takes base metal and turns it into gold. He explained it to me. It's an ancient practice which came before chemistry."

"Yes. Yes. I have heard of alchemy."

"But what he explained to me about alchemy is that it is about transformation. It is about trying to change the world."

"I see," Solomon Levy said. "And so Schneider is at the old game."

"Schneider wants to change the world too, sir."

"Oh, I have no doubt. The fall of the Berlin wall was a fine excuse for Gerhard's radical party. He is global now. Influence on several continents." Solomon Levy turned toward Roland. "He knows about the biological labs?"

Roland nodded.

"Ezra suspected that Schneider was exploring biomedical technologies," I said. "He came looking for Ezra, to silence whatever he knew about his plan."

"His plan?"

They looked at me curiously, but I didn't say anything more. Roland was the first to break the silence.

"For years, Jake, we have been exploring for links between these new radical right-wing groups and the National Socialists of the 1930s and 40s. It looks like we may have found another connection here. That means continuity. You're familiar with the phrase, "history repeats itself?" In this case, it appears to us that the insanity of it all is attempting to repeat itself. This spits in the face of over fifty years of German democracy."

On our way to the airport, Solomon Levy talked about hate groups, anti-Semitic groups, local cells of militant nationalists, potential terrorists hidden in obscure corners of the United States. It was the same scary stuff Professor Roland had already told us about years before. "They pretend to believe in freedom," Solomon Levy was saying. "But arson and blowing up buildings and people, that's not my idea of freedom."

"I'm more concerned right now about them blowing up Jake Kincaid," I said.

"We can keep you safe, Jake," Roland said. "We'll get you home."

And that is how I came to be here, staring at a tallow candle flame, listening to every small sound that stirs from the snow outside this window. That is how I came to hide. But not forever. For I have things to do. Things that Solomon Levy cannot know. Things that the man named Schneider will not very much like. Dangerous things. And if I do not live, at least I will have told you about the alchemist.

26.

The flight home took a northern route, out across the strange geography of Iceland and Greenland and the North Atlantic, then down across Maine and Massachusetts. The lights of buildings and highways came into view from Albany down along the Hudson toward New York.

The panorama reminded me of a film. Back in the early days of film making, creating a movie required a special kind of alchemy. Film used chemical processes and emerged from dark rooms. Script, lighting, sound, and the actor met under hot lights and fused like chemical elements. Movies were magic. We live now in a digital age and movies can still be magical. But the special effects once achieved through stop motion film and brilliant editing are now computer generated. Ali and I watch movies on cable. We save the chemistry for the bedroom. I looked forward to getting back home.

When my plane landed at JFK, Ali was there to greet me once I got through customs. She wore a bright golden scarf and a blouse with one of her sunshine designs. There was a trace of tears in her eyes. I must have held her for close to five minutes.

"I missed you," she said.

"Missed you too."

"Jake, I was so worried about you. Did someone really push your car off the road?"

"It was deliberate, Aly. Let's not talk about that."

"Roland had to get you out of there. Did you get anything accomplished?"

"Yes, I think so. We have some interviews, some footage."

"But that poor woman. They broke into her house. She must be terrified."

"Ali, I don't want to talk about it right now," I said. "Can we just go home?"

The city at night on the road back across Queens was a marvel of lights. In the distance, the Empire State building was lit with a band of red for Valentine's Day. We added our own sparkle at home with a bottle of champagne, celebrating my return.

"You want to watch a movie?" I asked.

"You just got home, and you want to watch a movie?"

"Absolutely. Movies are the world's greatest escape."

I started reading the A's in my media cabinet. "*Aliens, Apocalypse Now, American Graffiti, A Nightmare on Elm Street*. Then the B's: *Back to the Future, Big, Body Double, Battle of Britain*. "I definitely don't want to watch a war movie," I said. "How about *Citizen Kane*?"

"Again? You've seen that movie five times."

"Six."

"It's a long movie. Isn't it?"

"Two hours. One hundred and nineteen minutes, to be exact," I said. "It's one minute short of two hours. Of course, it might be two hours if you include the credits. If you don't want that, we could watch *Working Girl* again."

"I think we should make our own movie."

"You have something in mind?"

"I think it's a love story."

"That sounds good. Tell me it's not some dark, made for TV drama."

"It's a happy movie, Jake."

I soon discovered that the movie had only one set, the living room couch where we put our arms around each other and could kiss. Ali was right: it was a happy dream.

27.

A new day brought a trip to the farm. It was familiar and seemingly unchanged when Ali and I went back there. The farm seemed like a second home to us. We knew it now was a matter of safety to bring the alchemist's "children," there. Erik and Elke, Jan and Freyda needed a safe place. I wondered if the farm could be used as place to finish the documentary. Therese agreed to the plan, but Tom was opposed.

"You can't do it, Jake," Tom said. "You shouldn't bring them here. It's too dangerous."

We had begun to walk toward the barn. The sun came slanting down through the maples and spruce and pines and memories came rushing back.

"Jake, it's good to see you," he said. "But if you're getting involved with this business again, we can't be part of it. We've just gotten over all of that."

"It's only for a little while, Tom," I said. "We need a place where we can finish the documentary."

"If Schneider and his people are watching you, they might follow you here. If you bring those people here, is anybody safe?"

We sat down near the hay door at the back end of the barn. Above me was rutted wood, shiny with age, the ceiling planes punctured by roofing nails.

"Tom, it would help to be here, in the old house, in the lab area," I said. "I can't do this in the city."

"Why not? Because they are watching you?" Tom asked. "Because you think they'll break in and steal the notebooks? Do you think they'd hurt these people?"

"Or hurt Ali," I said. "We need to have the setting of the farm in the film. This is where everything started."

"This is one of the first places they'll look, Jake. The farm is not the same. It's not like it used to be. There are responsibilities here with the children. You remember what happened last time. They're going to follow you here. And we've got this school with the children now."

"We'll only be here for a few days. I just need you to put the notebooks in safekeeping."

"But you want to come out here to study the notebooks. Those people are looking for them, Jake. And they will turn the farm upside down. Like last time. You remember the fire in the barn, the people at the abandoned dairy."

"How could I forget?"

"It's dangerous, Jake. We can't go through that again."

"I'm not asking you to, Tom."

"But you're here."

"I'm here."

"Are they? Is Schneider? He has a network. He will send his people."

"Look, Tom, Ali and I have come here for a visit. I'll stay a few days. You'll meet the alchemist's daughter and a few interesting people, and then I'll go back to the city. We have to put the documentary together."

"Jake, you're still living out Ezra's wishes. We have the school for the children here now. Some good came out of all that hell. Isn't that enough?"

"Ezra wanted to make amends."

"And you're going to do that, at the risk of your life?"

"I was asked to. Erik has had the will to live all these years. And Elke is a beautiful, gentle woman. I want to say something about how Ezra saved them."

Tom lifted himself from the ground and dusted off his pants.

"It sounds like you are chasing after the impossible," he said.

"You know that has never stopped me, Tom," I said, as I got up from the grass beside the barn. "Nothing is impossible. My sense is that all the clues are in the notebooks. I'll show you."

The barn door was open and we went inside. I took one of the books out of the case I was carrying and opened it on a bare table that served as a work area.

"Look, Tom. Na. That's sodium. It's a code."

"There is a code in his notebooks?"

"I think so. He taught me how to read it, Tom. I'm the one who has to figure it out. It's gold, Tom. Look at the symbols. This circle with the arrow coming out of it is the alchemical symbol for gold. In modern chemistry, Ag is silver and Au is gold. Look at how he writes Ag and Au here. The Nazis were not just transporting iron ore across Norway. They took gold from the central banks of the countries that they occupied. They took gold from the Jews that they sent away to die in concentration camps. They re-melted the gold, so it couldn't be identified. They put millions into numbered accounts in Swiss banks."

"But I thought you said that this was the alchemist's money."

"Yes. He had family money. They owned an industrial business. That's for sure. He and Elise had the funds to buy this farm and to live here for years. But Erik says that he once mentioned that they had Swiss bank accounts."

"So?"

"I was appointed a trustee of the estate. So were you, Tom. We have a responsibility. Look, the journals he left tell us a lot."

He leaned over my shoulder to look at the leather-bound notebook I had opened on a table in the barn.

"It was a family estate," I said. "He and his brother fought to preserve it so it would not be seized by the state. The von Klaus family was a network of industrialists involved with mining and manufacturing. Jonas and his brother inherited a small fortune."

"So, they were rich."

"They were. And the family apparently supported Hitler in the early to mid 1930's. But they had a change of heart. Jonas Albrecht von Klaus, our Ezra, chose a career in medicine. His brother chose the family business. The brother ran the firm, but he died in the Allied bombings in Germany and left no heirs. Only Jonas."

"So, what became of the business?"

"It was dissolved after the war and the assets were sold off," I said. "But they were worth millions, Tom. Millions."

Tom's eyes seemed to light up at the word.

"Back in the 1930s, they supported mineral imports from across Western Europe," I told him. "The Nazis moved iron ore across Norway from Sweden. It was necessary. Steel was at the center of their war making. The family had been involved in that trade for years. So, they could only stand to profit during the war. He's left a legacy, Tom. And he also seems to have hidden a Nazi stash of gold bullion."

"And Schneider wants it."

"Not only that. Schneider knows that the records of the lebensborn would disgrace him. I think that's why he came to the farm years ago. He was looking for this. When he couldn't find it, he went after Ezra. Then he did everything he could to discredit him."

"All that business with the neo-Nazi group. Was that a terrorist operation?"

"Ned Roland thought it was. That's why he sent his men in to arrest them. But I think that there was something else going on. And Schneider was planning to pin it all on Ezra. He wanted to discredit him and to seize the family company's assets. The easiest way to do that was to make him look like an enemy of the state. Ezra made us trustees, Tom. His family used to run a major corporation. He had money. Lots of it. We need to find account numbers."

"And if we find it, then it goes to the farm?"

"If Schneider gets it, it goes to terrorism or to politics. It goes to political campaigns and media ads, or to insane speculative biological experiments and legal fees for shadow and shell corporations. If we get it, some of it might go to the farm. But I think Ezra would have wanted some reparations for the families from any of the gold the Nazis stole."

"So, if it is Nazi gold, we give it away."

"That would only be right."

"So how do we tell which is which? Which is his family money? Which is Nazi gold?"

"I'll keep studying the notebooks," I said. "They might give us a clue. There must be business records, some legal documents."

"Meanwhile, you're planning to bring everyone here. And Laura and Therese agreed to this?"

"They think it is necessary to protect everyone's rights."

Tom thought about this for a moment and I saw him nod.

"Okay. It's a deal," he said. "But listen, Jake, no trouble this time. Okay?"

I couldn't exactly promise that there would never again be any trouble with Schneider, but I said, "okay."

"Okay. So, what did you find out about Schneider?"

"Hans Schneider is dead, Tom. But Gerhard Schneider has been working behind the scenes. No more flashy speeches in front of the cameras."

"So, what's in it for him?"

"Power. The real problem is his international influence. It used to be like he was a movie star over there."

"Well, I guess he won't mind your filming him then," Tom said.

"I'm staying away from Schneider," I said. "He won't be in the film. Not a word about him. Or any of them. It's better that way."

We paused on the path that leads to the farmhouse. It was exactly where we had stood together years ago. Tom saw me pause, looking in the distance to the field, as if listening across the years for the voices of ghosts in my memories.

"Is there something else?"

"Actually, there is. I'm thinking of safety," I said. "That's why I'd like to invite another guest."

"Another one? It sounds like this is going to be one big party. Who do you have in mind?"

"Ned Roland."

Tom must have wondered about that as I left him and walked the stone path toward the second farmhouse. Therese had informed me that my makeshift video studio could be set up there. I'd set up cameras and editing equipment in the room next to what was once the alchemist's laboratory. It would be an ideal location. That is, if I could deal with all of the sound on the floor above me. From eight to four each day the special school would be in progress, except on Saturdays and Sundays.

Outside there was the chilling cold, but, as soon as the door was opened, it was easy to hear that inside the special school the recreational schedule was underway. Laura met me at the front door and guided me in.

"Well, this is it, Jake," Laura said. "We'll have Parent Appreciation Day on Friday. The schedule will be the same, except for lunch with the families and a three-hour break in the afternoon."

Sandy Lee Perkins, the new recreational therapist, pushed a fragile looking girl in a wheelchair into the room ahead of us. The little girl, Jasmine Knox, had about her a labored beauty. She wore a pink dress and had curly dark hair. She was wearing a bead necklace around her neck. Laura explained that Jasmine had a mild form of cerebral palsy.

We continued into the next room, where Jasmine said hello to Benny, a boy by the doorway who looked like a broken branch. He was slender, with red hair that stuck out like a batch of shredded carrot sticks. You'd think that the sight of children crumpled into wheelchairs would be depressing. But the place was filled with life. The children were living with an unexplained deficit, an epileptic chemistry, a disease that froze their small limbs in place, leaving their bright minds to wonder at what could not move. But they were playful, noisy, and even delirious with joy.

"We're making progress with the school," Laura said. "Come on. I'll show you."

As we entered the recreation room, I saw small wood desks, colorful cushions, and *Sesame Street* figures. There were a dozen children playing games. I could hear Survivor's song "Eye of the Tiger" from the motion picture *Rocky*. A teacher was playing a clapping game with a small boy. John Freeley, a member of the staff, was wearing a Mets baseball cap and he tossed a ball to a child.

"Chauncey. Look here, Chauncey," said John Freeley to the little boy. He rolled the red ball toward him.

"Hi, John," Laura said. She picked up the ball and rolled it toward Chauncey.

"There you go, Chauncey. Good one!"

The boy rolled the ball back and his eyes followed as Laura passed it to John. John Freeley then rolled the ball back to Chauncey again and a kind of delight filled the boy's eyes for a moment.

"He responds to music," Laura said. "John Freeley is the perfect special education teacher because he loves all kinds of music. Show tunes. Pop songs. Rock songs. That rap music by Run DMC. We use music to teach Chauncey language skills and speech. John practices rhythm, stress, and vocal inflections."

"So, music is a good thing for autistic kids."

"Absolutely," Laura said. "John gets Chauncey to vocalize. Then he sings question and answer with him. It's a challenge to get autistic kids to interact. But sometimes music does the trick. Did you know that Chauncey has perfect pitch?"

"You're kidding."

"These kids have all kinds of hidden gifts and talents."

"I can see that."

"Can you, Jake? Actually, a lot of people can't. They just see a room full of kids with disabilities and they feel sorry for them."

"At least it's not 1930s Germany," I said.

Laura stopped and stared at me, then shook her head. "Jake, you've got to lighten up," she said.

I paused by a window, looking back across the room.

"Do they stay here all the time?" I asked.

"No. Not yet. But that's the plan. We hope to have a residential care unit built nearby. You never know, we might have another painting job for you, Jake."

"I don't do that much anymore, Laura. You know that."

"But I bet Tom would like it, if the two of you got together and did a job for old time's sake."

"Maybe when I get the documentary finished."

"Of course, it's going to take some more money. We might be able to get some state funding. Have you been making any progress on the numbers of the alchemist's bank accounts?"

"I think so."

"He really hid them well, didn't he?"

"He was a master at hiding things, Laura. You know that," I said.

28.

New York felt bare and haunted to me that winter. I was sure that I could still count on protection from Ned Roland's team. Even so, Ali's father insisted on putting extra security on the job at her apartment. Some nights we saw the man standing under an awning on the corner, drinking from a paper cup, hat slung low across his eyes. More often, he'd be sitting in a heated vehicle up the block. That man, Brad Thorne, told us that he had seen a street person looking through the garbage can outside the apartment building. A tan Buick had paused by the curb for ten minutes. We dismissed this. We wondered what Schneider, or anyone else, could have to gain by watching an apartment building. From outside one could see a pale light in the windows. We kept the shades drawn. Our shadows seldom moved behind them. We double-locked the doors. Every walk up the stairs of the building was one of caution.

Outside, snow lay piled by the curb. Snow had fallen around the fire hydrant. In the water run-off by the front steps lay broken glass, crushed cigarette butts. I was startled by the sound of footsteps behind me.

"Easy there, Jake. It's only me," a voice said.

The face of Brad Thorne appeared from the shadows.

"They shoveled the snow pretty good," he said. "You got a light?"

"I don't smoke," I said.

"That homeless guy sure did. Set the ashcan right on fire. Probably trying to keep warm at night."

"Don't you get cold standing out here?"

"I got the car. This is foot patrol time. You see anything suspicious?"

"Just you."

"Very funny. You got a real sense of humor, Jake." His gray eyes settled on me and he blew a cloud of cold mist into the air. "Look, you might want to know this. This Schneider guy, I seen him around."

"You've seen him?"

"Oh, yeah. Looked like him. He's definitely in the city. I'm just here to warn you."

"Okay. So, we've been warned."

"You want some advice, kid? I'd get out of here if I was you."

"Yeah, good advice," I said, brushing past him. "I'll take it."

"It's good advice. That's what they pay me for," the man said. I heard him cough and turn away as I went inside.

29.

Schneider's world shocked mine like an electrical current the next day when I opened the door to my apartment. I had come home for lunch. There was Schneider. He sat in an armchair, petting our cat, Quicksilver. I felt as if the room was spinning. My mind was paralyzed. He fixed his gaze upon me like a magnet on metal. He was sitting in my living room. It was improbable.

"Your eyes are not deceiving you, Jacob Kincaid" he said. "This is a fine magic trick, isn't it? Entering a locked room. It is almost as good as transforming lead into gold."

He raised his hands, palms outward: a gesture of peace.

"I come unarmed," he said.

"You think you can just walk in here?"

"Perhaps you'd like to call the police. That would not be wise," he said. He let the cat go. Then he lifted a framed photograph of Ali and held it in his hand. "Your girlfriend, I assume. Very pretty."

He slapped it face down on the end table.

"I can always get to you, Jacob Kincaid. And I can get to those you love."

"Are you threatening me? In my own home?"

"The cameras are off, Jacob. The phones are disconnected. And that detective of yours will like his date with Miss Fischer. She is a very attractive woman we've set him up with. It is now your word against mine. So then, let's just say that this little visit is payback for all of your unethical prying into our business."

"You're a fine one to talk about ethics, Schneider. Threats, trespass, harassment… That will look good for your business and on your political record."

"Our attorneys have a considerable problem with your intrusions."

"And we have a problem with your threats."

"It is a pity that you have hidden things, Jacob. We will find them, you know. Whereas your prying into our business will turn up nothing."

"It will turn up the truth."

"The truth? In the modern age the only truth is power. You are making a documentary. You are writing a biography of Jonas von Klaus. Ha! This is what you would call historical research, I assume. It is laughable." He rose and began walking across the room. "Why would anyone believe your stories? Everything you are writing is just so much fiction. Alchemy. Nazis. Quaint little farms and a local painting business. As if this has any bearing upon the modern world."

"It is all part of the world, Schneider. Love, children, people making discoveries. It's just that you've forgotten all of that."

"Power," he said. "The modern world is about power. There are no angels to save you, Jacob. There is no magical alchemy. You see, I can do the impossible, Jacob. We can build the master race. We have the means. People want master children and they will pay for them. The world is full of possibility. Isn't that what Jonas always said?"

He turned at the door, facing me with an icy stare.

"I was never here," he said, opening the door. "You were never investigating my business. Neither of us will press charges. And your commentary on the lebensborn will be thoughtful and respectful. You will watch your step, Jacob Kincaid."

With that, the door closed and he was gone.

In the afternoon, I sat up in the chair, sure that I had heard a sound. "Ali," I whispered. I stood up, crossing the room, turning to face a reflection in the mirror: my own. I stood still on the carpet. I flicked open the drapes and looked out. The sidewalk below was empty. The evening was pierced by city streetlights.

I returned to the chair, thinking of Ali, thinking of how each of our apartments had become like prisons. I sat with the light off, but the anxiety lingered: brain chemistry on a slow simmer. I dreamed of movies and that I was caught in the Matrix. I dreamed of chemical equations, the markings in the alchemist's notebooks. The symbols of metals and their atomic weights swirled up from my unconscious. Yes, that's it, I thought. Where he had written of gold and of Switzerland there was a clear sequence of numbers. They came to mind now. When he had mentioned the "children" and their escape from Norway, there was another sequence. I was sure that I had uncovered the key to the secret accounts.

I went to my desk and under it I opened the secret compartment. There they were- the alchemist's secrets- right before my eyes. Schneider had gotten into our apartment, but he hadn't found the notebook copies. I had hidden them well. I brought them up to the desk and spent the next hour matching the numbers in the book to those in my dream.

"Ali, look! It's right here!" I said excitedly when we met that evening. "Look at where he talks about his family legacy. He says there are numbered accounts in a Swiss bank. He's telling us. He points right to the memoirs."

Ali leaned over my shoulder, looking at the notebook on the desk.

My library in the farmhouse was a fortress of arcane books that lined the walls of an upstairs room. There I began these memoirs, which you are reading now.

Mutanter omnia nos et mutamur in illis.
-E O ? ^

"All things change and we change with them," she said.

"That's pretty good."

"I studied Latin in school," she said. "So, obviously, those symbols mean something."

"Yes. They do," I said. "The **E** means element. Next to it there is one of the alchemical symbols for gold: that circle with a strong dot at the center. That thing that looks a little like a question mark means yield. That's like in the yield of gold. And there, next to that, look Ali! It's the symbol for fire!"

"Fire?"

"Fire burns."

"How does that tell you where the bank account is, Jake?"

"It's a homonym. The bank account is in Bern."

"Jake, that's in Switzerland."

"I know where it is. I have to get the contents of a safety deposit box there."

"Not without me, you're not."

"Ali, it's dangerous."

"That's exactly why I'm going. No arguments, Jake."

30.

Switzerland is a neutral country with secure banks and modern cities that lie under the Alps. What could be dangerous about that? The banks of the Swiss offer financial security and privacy. Jonas had chosen a Swiss bank to avoid the risk of disclosure. We were hopeful that the symbols in his notebook would lead us to answers. Yet, the plan was like Swiss cheese: full of holes. Nothing was certain. In 1989, the Swiss state was found to have kept secret security files on some of its citizens, including former German Nazis and left-wing activists. Amid a turmoil of public protest, Schneider was hiding his plans from the secret police. He was orchestrating something dangerous. There could be no hesitation.

Things moved quickly the next morning. Ali and I met for breakfast, as we always did. We arranged to drive out to the farm. In the car, Ali sat with the alchemist's notebooks on her lap. She read aloud the passages I had marked, matching the numbers of atomic weights with the periodic table.

When we arrived at the farm, we learned that Erik and Elke had located the bank in Switzerland into which Jonas Albrecht von Klaus had deposited his secrets. Erik had given Jan Sorenson the airline ticket that would take him to the farm. He would arrive at the farm shortly. By the time we walked in, they had all finished dinner and were gathered in the farmhouse with Therese, Laura, and Tom. I told them that I believed that I had discovered the numbers for the overseas accounts.

Roland came in soon after us.

"We've identified the bank. It is on the Banhofplatz in Bern," he said. "We need to do this quickly."

"Good. I'm ready to go. The numbers seem pretty clear to me," I said.

"Jake, you're not serious," Tom said.

"If you seek out this bank, Jake, you will be followed," Therese said. "You are too obvious. You are already a target."

"We can go undercover," I said.

"You watch too many movies, Jake," Laura said.

"Well, we can't send Elke and Erik can't get around well," I told them. "Tom is here with Laura and the children need her at the school. So, I guess that leaves me."

"It isn't safe," Therese said.

"I'm going too," Ali announced. "I'll keep him out of trouble."

"Ali, you can't!" Laura said.

"I will, Laura. We'll do this together."

"You've got to be kidding," Tom said. "Schneider's people are watching your every move, Jake."

"We need someone who has the numbers in his head. We can't afford to put them on paper," Erik said. "It has to be someone who is healthy. Someone who can act as proxy for the names specified in the documents."

"We have to keep the circle small. Jake is as good a choice as any," Roland agreed. "We can protect them."

"Ned Roland, I object!" Therese said. "This is an impossible dream. Jake, you could get yourself killed."

"We can protect them, Therese, but we need to work quickly," Roland said. "We'll insert you in Geneva. Get you to Zurich or Bern. In and out, like a surgical operation. We'll fly you back on a military jet."

"Quick and safe. Right, Ned?"

"Listen, Jake," Roland said. "The OSS was not unaware of the arrangements that Muller made in the late 1930s. It knew about the lebensborn also. Our interest is not in who those people are. It is in exploring links to Nazis who escaped prosecution and to these emerging neo-Nazi groups. We want to see if there are links to Schneider and this biological research that he is involved in."

"I'll help with that, if I can," I said. "But I'm not giving up Jonas."

"We've already granted he and his heirs immunity."

"You have a deal then," I said.

"Yes. It's a deal," Ali said.

It was a lot to ask Alessandra Stanley to join me in this quest. She didn't hesitate. Ali is the one I didn't deserve: a smart, talented, attractive girl who could melt my heart, or jar my nerves. The adventure was hers now, even as it was mine. Once she made up her mind, there was no convincing her otherwise. For Ali, there was no other option than to take this to the end. I knew one thing for certain: we were in this together. And it was time to get moving.

31.

Ali and I sat in a Suisse Air jet that took us high across the Atlantic. We played poker. We drank Coca-Cola, ate peanuts, and read magazines. The in-flight brochure said that Suisse Air had recently signed an agreement with Delta and Singapore Airlines to achieve "Global Excellence." Alessandra had stitched the code to the safe deposit box into the inner sleeve of my jacket. Yet, I feared that Schneider's men might be following us: that I'd turn and suddenly there would be the man I'd seen on the train. Schneider was in the shadows, watching us.

There was no in-flight film, but a dozen movies flashed across my mind. Chase scenes. Shoot outs. I imagined that moment in the movie when the guy you're watching in the film is backed into a corner. Suddenly, Darth Vader in a black suit appears. His storm-troopers blast through a door and subdue the rebels. Ali is caught by the bad guys and it seems like everything is about to collapse. Then the dream faded, like the last reel of a film, and I thought about where we were going.

In the Swiss banks many European Jews deposited their money in the 1930s to avoid taxes, or in case they had to hurriedly escape. They put their possessions into safe deposit boxes: their coins, their jewelry, and formal papers. Some opened accounts in their own names. Others did not. In threatened places, in tight railcars and sullen prisons, they held onto secret numbers of accounts locked behind walls, beyond the reach of the Gestapo. Gold was hidden in boxes and diamonds were concealed in bags, cannisters, and lipstick cases while the Jews were deported to the East toward a terrible fate. I imagined the rooms where they had tried to hide, the cobbled paths, a cry for mercy, the closing of a cold door. They were stamped with numbers, meticulously recorded with cold indifference.

The clouds below gave way to vistas of the land below. From the air, the Alps are spectacular. Snow-capped and mighty, they go on for miles. Towns lie nestled in the valleys below them. Past the massive peak of Mont Blanc, we flew on a path into Geneva. At the airport, the officers packed us swiftly into a limo. We raced through the rain dampened streets.

Swiss banks are among the most secure in the world. The one to which we went was at the center of the city of Bern, the nation's capital. The doors were heavy, rimmed with gold. Our faces were reflected in the glass. Roland had fitted me with tinted glasses and had given me a new passport. Ali wore a blonde wig, dark glasses, a blue business suit. I wore a black suit, like the agents to either side of me.

We went in. A guard was at the door and a male receptionist was at a desk in the lobby. The receptionist passed us on to Herr Gustav Woolfson, a tall man with a craggy face who greeted us formally and brought us back to his office immediately. He wore a gray suit, wire rimmed glasses. He was joined by a security guard, who pressed a buzzer. We passed through another door.

"The account number?" Herr Woofson asked.

I recited the numbers from memory.

"Password."

"Mercury."

"The name associated with the account?"

"Jonas Albrecht von Klaus."

The banker did not move.

"You are sure?" he asked.

"Yes."

"Any other?"

"Elise Hoffmann von Klaus. Elke Albrecht von Klaus."

"Very good," he said. He took two small envelopes from his pocket and set them on the table. He looked up at the agents, stone-faced beside me. He looked at Ali, up and down. "There are two keys for the box: my key and your key. I will place the box on the table and then record this transaction in the ledger. You may then depart with the contents."

He slid the safety deposit box out and carried it to the table. Then he left the room. Inside the box, in a velour pouch, lay a box within a box. We lifted it out and set it on the table. I did not open it. The box would remain closed until we returned home.

When we reached the lobby, Ali's eyes met mine. Something was wrong. The receptionist was not at his desk. The guard had disappeared. The agents noticed it right away.

"Mr. Kincaid, keep moving," an agent said.

I stood, looking at him.

"Jake," Ali yelled. "We have to get out!"

I felt frozen in place. The glass door shattered. The floor mirrored the falling glass.

"Come on, Jake!"

"This way," the agent next to me said. "Go!"

He fell to one knee. He drew a Glock from his jacket and motioned for us to exit by another door. Quickly, he inspected that doorway for explosives. He found it clear and we followed him through it. Soon we were outside, moving toward the car. Suddenly, across the street, there was movement. I recognized the man there, pointing a gun toward us. What was Andreas Ritschl doing in Switzerland? He gave us the answer. Bullets hit the car and the wall behind us. The agents returned fire. One of them pushed me into the car and it sped away.

Ali held tightly to my hand. Every suspense movie I'd ever been terrified by flashed through my mind. Suddenly, a car would be cutting us off, a motorcyclist with dark glasses would soon be pulling alongside us with a machine gun. Ali was passionate. She urged the driver to "hurry!" And he must have heard, for the car rocketed out on the Autobahn. There were lights on the highway to the airport. The moon was high in the sky. We saw lights and a jet waiting on the tarmac. Ali held to me as we ran to the plane. I held the box in my hands and carried it aboard. I placed it under my feet, strapped myself in, and soon we were in the air. It was over. We had gotten away with a secret cache, a treasure chest, an archive marked in pain.

32.

The dark night has come and beyond the window blazes the full moon. It seems to float, like a coin, above the trees. Or perhaps it is a tablet dissolving in a tray in the alchemist's laboratory. The phases of the moon remind me that the world is full of change, ever waxing and waning. Seasons come and pass. Clouds cover the moon and then it comes free, shining its light again.

Now I gaze at the light of the movie screen, hoping to be entertained, to escape into the scenes that appear before me. I look for lightness, for laughter, but I know that my film will bring dark revelations. Early film gave us *The Birth of a Nation*, with its grisly night rides and hooded figures. The Nazis gave us Leni Reifenstahl's *Triumph of the Will*. As Heinrich Himmler sought evidence of Aryan origins, the zoologist Ernst Schafer made a film on the ancestral heritage. It was noxious propaganda. Fortunately, film can be put to better purposes. My documentary has been circulating at film festivals. People are beginning to learn of the lebensborn. Others, Schneider's people, have been watching me. The safety deposit box that we took from the bank held records of the lebensborn experiment in Norway. We found lists of names, of parents and children: the secrets that the nightmare the Second World War and dreams of human potential had wrought. We have given those records to Norway's archives in Oslo and in Trondheim, and we have contacted dozens of people who have for years been seeking clues to their past. We also found the key to the alchemist's family fortune. He had bequeathed it to his children, to Elke, and to the children that he and Elise had saved. Freyda, Erik, Elke, and Jan have relocated. They are working and living quiet lives, far from trouble.

The alchemist's will and testament specified that the remainder of his estate would be set aside for the special school on the farm. His fortune would be directed toward medical research into the causes and cure of the diseases that affected the lives of the children there. With this he left a legacy: one with the hope that healing may be found for the innocent ones, that a new alchemy might sustain life. Jonas and Elise offered an alternative for biological research: a hope that medical science may one day genetically counter disease and change the course of lives.

David and Sharon Stanley have donated some of their own money to the cause. Like my father and mother, they now have a better idea now of what their daughter and I were doing. They let go of that awful detective, Bradley Thorne, and took more of a liking to Quicksilver, our cat. They also came out to see the farm and to visit the school.

We are proud of the farm and the school. They will continue be a memorial to Jonas, the last alchemist. His story always reminds me of the weight of individual destiny. History falls heavy on those who attempt to understand. Youth is lighter, filled with ideals and dreams and a sense of possibility. History is filled with the night. It sings with the voices of those who have gone before us. It is strange that something now far in the past, like the Second World War, can have such lasting claims upon the world we live in today. It is a great shadow across many German's spirits. Even the best will feel it: that tug of history, the tide that pulls from beneath the stability of the present. It urges efforts to develop a normal and positive sense of identity with their past. Generations completely innocent of such a past feel a need for atonement and for understanding.

These days, at the Red Cat Farm, now called Canaan, Therese is developing an organic farm. It is her way of creating a better environment for the future. The children are safe on the farm, in the special school that has been designed for them. Laura runs a staff that includes Sandy Lee Perkins, a recreation therapist, and John Freeley, who continues to work with children with autism and a wide range of other challenges. The farm continues to grow organic foods and to sponsor educational programs. The most recent was a conversation on biotechnology with Dr. John Ambrose. His elegant wife Glenda introduced Dr. Ambrose, the man who had told me of H.M. Muller's work. He is a likeable African American man in his sixties, with a bushy mustache, like Einstein's, and he seems partial to cashmere jackets. He leans forward as he walks, as if he is being pressed down by a strong wind on the waves. The day he visited the farm, someone had left a bouquet for the guest speaker. I saw a surprised look come across Dr. Ambrose's face. He twirled one of the flowers in his fingers.

"Orchids," he said, looking at the flowers. "Interesting. Complex fertilization. After Charles Darwin wrote his famous book *Origin of Species*, he wrote his next book. His subject was how these flowers are fertilized. His book was on orchids."

The orchids were no gift. Schneider was sending a message.

Schneider lives more quietly these days, shaping the political world with his money. We are never sure when any of his people are watching us. However, as Ned Roland says, his operation is legal. It is well-tended by attorneys, and it prospers by the industrious work of biotechnology scientists and advertising experts. His global businesses are well-managed. His campaign contributions are clean. The science is conducted all within the legal bounds of each country in which it is practiced. He continues to encourage the neo-Nazi movement. There is no way that we can stop him- at least for now. So, we have decided upon a kind of peaceful co-existence.

The documentary will likely embarrass him a bit. But we do not make any charges against him in it. We simply show the lives of Erik, Freyda, and Jan, and others like them. We tell the story of the lebensborn and hope that people will listen. We hope that Schneider will simply leave us alone.

We know that Schneider's people may still be watching. Yet, Ali and I still often head out again to the farm. There's no sense in letting anybody stop us from living our lives – unless they decide to stop us from living. Anyway, one day, Ali insisted upon first going to Babies R Us. I think she has been trying to tell me something. There were many young couples there. I heard a mother singing to her child in the parking lot and saw her pushing her girl in a stroller into the store. There were aisles full of clothing: Carter and Gerber and cotton and colors. "Daddy's Little Girl," "Grandma's Little Girl," "Mom's Champion," and "Grandpa's Hero." Pink pajamas with booties. Boxes stacked along the sides of a large warehouse room. Strollers and nursery furniture for a future life. Ali seemed to want to look at everything. I think she has something in mind.

These days, when I visit the farm with Ali and look around, I like to remember the day that the farm was dedicated. Years ago, when those troubling incidents were over, with the coming of Spring, a new school had begun at the farm. It was the school for special education children. In the house where the alchemist once had lived with his wife there were new beginnings. The children arrived each day to study in its rooms and to play on the hills.

Soon new families came to the next season's arts and crafts fair at the farm. The land deed had preserved the farm and helped to expand it. Newness grew there. The older farmhouse was now freshly painted. We called it the Elise Hoffmann House. Home to the new school, it was Ezra's dream coming true: a farm renewing itself season by season. That was the gold he had always been seeking.

We met together there year after year, remembering him, the one who had taught us so much. I never did get into the movies. But I continued to work in my studio with Brian James and every year I made a new video of the people at the farm. The people came and attended the education programs at the farm. There they learned of the earth, and the children reminded us that it is a little diamond in a great universe and how we must learn to preserve it. And the children sang, "Twinkle, twinkle, little star..."

Ali and I were married and Tom, of course, married Laura. They got married at the farm. I was the best man and Ali was the maid of honor. Little Amelia, the smallest of the children, was the flower girl. After it was over, I hung a sign on Bessie the cow that said, "Just Married."

While I was doing that, one of the cufflinks from my tux must have come loose and fallen to the ground. Mr. And Mrs. Eisenstein, Amelia's parents, found it on the ground and brought it to me.

"We thank you," they said. "Thank you for giving this wonderful new place to Amelia."

I thanked them for Amelia. As they were walking away, I looked down at the cufflink on my wrist. It was like the one I'd seen in my dream. Cufflinks hold things together, I thought. They are like the connections between us: the solid and sure things in life – like love. We had the alchemist to thank for these things.

I took photos that day at the farm and a video that won't win any awards but is good for the memory. It shows Tom and Laura in an embrace surrounded by a lot of smiling people beside a wide, blooming dogwood tree. Behind them is a painting, a work of Laura's, set in a place of honor beside the tree. It is the final portrait of a man who was the last alchemist. In the painting he looks at us with a look of hope, as if he is looking upon his own children. There in the sunlight, as I look at it again, I think I can see a smile in his eyes.